The Night Blossoms
© 2022 by Leylah Attar

Editing by:
Erica Russikoff

Proofreading by:
Christine Estevez
Soulla Georgiou

Cover Design ©:
Hang Le

Interior Design and Formatting by:
Champagne Book Design

10 9 8 7 6 5 4 3 2 1

ISBN: 978-1-988054-06-3

THE

NIGHT

Blossoms

New York Times Bestselling Author
LEYLAH ATTAR

PITCH73 PUBLISHING

For my mother

PRESENT

One

DEATH WAS AN EASY GUEST TO HOST—NEAT, QUIET, and invisible. If Vee hadn't let her in herself, she would have missed the way the air stirred on the other side of the door as she roamed the hallway at night. After Rafael left, she was bolder, stepping out of the shadows when Vee's back was turned, standing so close that her skin prickled.

Vee wasn't afraid. Death never abandoned a single soul. Parents, friends, and lovers came and went. Vee had even succeeded in pushing Rafael away. But Death remained, unwavering and loyal, waiting to envelop Vee in her embrace. If she had come just for her, Vee might have reacted differently, tiptoeing around her edges—a little nervous, a little curious. But Death was hovering around her child, and that made Vee a formidable adversary. It turned her bones to steel. Death wanted Vee to choose—her life or her baby's. If she failed, the choice would be made for her—today, tomorrow, when her belly was heavy, and she was sweeping purple petals under the jacaranda tree.

The glass of water Rafael had brought into the sunroom remained untouched. Vee picked up the pill they'd fought over and held it in her palm. Who would have thought the end of a marriage could weigh a few milligrams?

"Why, Vee?" Rafael's words haunted her.

Sheets of water poured down the glass panes of the sunroom. How many thunderstorms had they watched there? Huddled like kids in the eye of the storm, knowing no matter what the world unleashed, they'd always have each other.

"You left me no choice."

"We ran out of choices, Vee. We went to every clinic, consulted every specialist, and they all said the same thing. No more pregnancies. We agreed to stop trying. Even if you carry the baby to term this time, the risk is too high. I can't lose you, Vee. I won't."

"And I can't end this pregnancy. I won't." The sensation of being on opposite sides was so alien that they stared at each other across the table.

"Tell me something. Was this an accident or did you come off the birth control?"

Vee's gaze averted to the window, to the random paths the rain traced over the glass.

"Look at me, Vee." Rafael reached for her hand. "It makes my blood boil that you put yourself at risk, that you have such little regard for your own well-being."

A tear rolled down Vee's cheek. She stared at their

hands. They'd held together through everything, forged
dreams out of nothing. Vee wanted one more dream
to come true. She knew Rafael wanted it just as much,
maybe even more.

"Nothing's going to happen to me."

His jaw clenched. He grabbed his phone. "Take a
good, hard look at these."

Vee glanced at the images he pulled up on the screen.

"The thought that any of these complications could
happen to you makes me sick. Your womb is scarred,
Vee. You could hemorrhage to death. The baby could suf-
focate. Do you know what it's like for me to see you go
through this again and again? To stand by helplessly and
watch you grieve? You think I don't mourn each loss just
as long, just as deeply? If we go down this road again, I
could lose both of you, and that's not a chance I'm willing
to take." He withdrew his phone and started dialing out.

"Who are you calling?"

"I'm calling Dr. Sterritt back."

"There's no need for that." Vee grabbed the phone
and ended the call. "She already knows I'm pregnant."

"You've been to see her?"

Vee nodded.

Disbelief marred Rafael's expression. "How far along,
Vee?"

"Nine weeks."

"And you're telling me now?"

A brittle silence stretched between them.

"Are you..." He softened. "Is everything okay?"

Vee stepped closer and hugged him. "I'm fine."

Relief flooded her whole being when his arms en-
circled her.

What could be worse than the things that had already
happened to her? The past had stripped her to her bones,

but it couldn't touch her spirit or the parts she had re-built with Rafael.

They rocked back and forth, not knowing who was comforting whom.

"Don't ever keep things from me, Vee. We're in this together."

"I'm sorry." She buried her face in his throat.

"So, what did Dr. Sterritt want?"

"Well, when I went to see her, she gave me this..." Vee retrieved the pill from her handbag.

"What is it?"

"It's to terminate the pregnancy. She advised me to end it. I was supposed to take it at her office. I let her think I did. She probably called to check up on me."

A flicker of pain crossed Rafael's eyes. Then his lips brushed Vee's forehead. "I'm glad you waited until I got back. There's no way I'd let you go through this on your own."

Vee shot him a puzzled look. "Go through what?"

"Ending the pregnancy."

"What?" Vee's head snapped back. "I thought we decided to keep the baby. You just said we're in this together."

"I was referring to our marriage. I haven't changed my mind about the pregnancy. You're nine weeks in, Vee. The window is closing fast. You need to take this pill right away."

Vee watched in disbelief as he filled a glass of water.

"Are you serious?"

"Are *you*?" He lashed out. "You got pregnant and kept it from me. You saw Dr. Sterritt on your own. You let her think you took the pill. If I hadn't come home early and intercepted her message, would you have even told me about the baby? You were waiting, weren't you, Vee? You were waiting until it was too late to end this pregnancy."

Vee met his eyes without flinching. She'd almost told him before his trip, but they'd been happy after so long.

Rafael's mouth twisted. He was hurt, angry, disappointed, frustrated. "Don't you see? You're jeopardizing both yourself and the baby."

"My life, my decision."

"*Our* life. *Our* decision," he shot back. "That's my child you're carrying."

"Exactly. You've always said that family is everything. You couldn't do anything to save your parents, and now you want to kill our child?"

Vee regretted the words the moment they left her mouth. It was a low blow—stupid, careless words, hurled in battle.

"Rafael..." She reached out, but he recoiled from her touch.

In that instant, their relationship stumbled. The air grew charged with jagged fragments. It stung to breathe. Vee reached for him again, but he took another step back, then another, until he was standing in the shadow of the doorway. Lightning illuminated his strong, proud face as the thunderstorm raged outside.

Then he was gone, and Vee stood staring at the silence he left behind.

She waited for his return. She'd pushed him away time and again, but he always came back. He was one of the pillars that held up her world. Vee had crossed a line this time—betrayed him, disappointed him, hurt him. But she knew they could do this. They could have the family they always wanted. She saw him with their baby, joy radiating from his core. It was such a sharp, vivid vision that she woke up every morning living it and believing it.

It was the stage upon which all her other thoughts flitted across during the day.

Vee knew this time would be different. She just had to convince him of it.

But Rafael didn't come home that night. He didn't answer her calls the next day, or the day after that. On the third day, he turned his phone off and Vee's calls went to voicemail. That night, she capped the toothpaste and broke down. It drove her mad that he squeezed the tube from the top, but the indent made her ache for his fingers, his scent, his foggy reflection in the mirror. She wanted him, and she wanted their baby. Why did it have to be one or the other?

Vee rolled the pill between her fingers. When did Death slip into their home? The moment she brought the pill home? The night she got pregnant? Years ago, in a different world, a different life? The answers didn't matter, because she was waiting in the wings for Vee's decision.

Vee walked into the sunroom. It was dark outside, but everything glistened in the rain. The jacaranda tree lit up as lightning streaked across the sky. The silhouette of a hooded figure flashed under its branches—stark and unexpected. Vee gasped and peered through the window, but saw no one outside. About to turn away, she froze when the figure reappeared, this time so close that her heart jumped in her chest. Face shadowed under the raincoat, it stood motionless and bizarre against the onslaught of the storm. In the next instant, it disappeared under the cloak of darkness.

A chill ran down Vee's spine as she retreated from the window and turned the light off. Before her eyes could adjust to the dark, something came hurtling through the pane. It shattered the glass and landed on the floor with a thud. Rain poured into the sunroom, the droplets glinting off broken shards.

Stunned, Vee stared at the rock on the floor. It was about the size of a brick—a landscaping stone from the front yard. Her eyes darted outside, but she couldn't make out anything or anyone. Vee's hand dropped instinctively to her belly.

She grabbed her phone and called for help.

Two

RAFAEL ROZA VANISHED TWO NIGHTS BEFORE THE GIRL in the raincoat smashed the window. He never made his mind up about the afterlife when he was alive. The idea of resting in eternal peace was sublimely appealing, yet terrifying. It was easier to wrap his mind around simply ceasing to exist, but he couldn't shake the feeling that reality was broader, grander, and more complex than he could comprehend. So he told himself he'd figure it out when he got there.

When Rafael's heart stopped, he experienced a flash of expansion. His senses rippled outward. He didn't know if there was more beyond that point, because he was resuscitated.

"You didn't think I'd let you go so easy, did you?" A voice floated over him. "It's not time yet."

And so, like a kite tangled in the trees, Rafael remained suspended between earth and ether, life and death. At times, he slipped beyond himself to the edges of a cosmic symphony that buzzed and crackled with a strange yet familiar energy. Other times, he contracted into his bones and burrowed deep into the void because there was far too much at stake to let go.

Rafael was to die at the hands of someone who claimed to love him. Worse, the woman he loved was next, and there was nothing he could do to stop it. Like a book with the ending ripped out, his life was coming to a senseless conclusion. And the same thing was going to happen to her.

Rafael wanted to fling the doors open and scream: *Run. Get as far away from here as you can.*

But he was voiceless and powerless. Still, he had to find a way to warn her, if it was the last thing he did.

Three

VEE DIDN'T LIKE THE POLICE, AND SHE DIDN'T LIKE them trailing through her home, so she tried to get through the process as quickly as possible.

"A broken window," the officer interviewing her noted. "No attempt to enter the premises?"

"It was dark, so I can't be sure."

"Can you think of anyone who might want to harm you or intimidate you?"

"No."

"Did you have a dispute with someone? A grudge? An argument?"

"No."

"How long have you lived here, Mrs. Roza?"

"In California?"

"In this home."

"About five years."

"Any recent break-ins, burglaries, or vandalism in the neighborhood?"

"Not that I know of."

"Do you—" He broke off as a woman entered the room. She gave the officer a nod. He relaxed and nodded back. Black tactical boots peeked from under her pajamas as she walked past them to the sunroom and greeted the officer investigating the scene.

"Sorry. Where were we?" The officer glanced at his notes. "Do you have security cameras on the property?"

"I wonder if I can trouble you for a cup of coffee." The woman re-entered the kitchen.

"And you are...?" Vee asked.

"Detective Laura Burke, Pasadena Police Department." She slid her headband off and stuffed it into her pocket. "Also an insomniac."

Vee put on a pot of coffee while Detective Burke reviewed the responding officer's notes.

"You have kids, Mrs. Roza?" She toyed with the magnetic alphabet on the fridge.

"No. My husband and I leave messages for each other."

"Pi the wise one?" She read the one Rafael had left before his trip.

"It's an anagram. I haven't solved it yet."

"Cute." Opening the fridge, she peeked inside. "Does your husband work late, Mrs. Roza? It's 2 a.m. on a weeknight."

"My husband left two nights ago. We had an argument. I'm not sure where he is. He hasn't returned my calls." Vee handed her the coffee and sat back down.

Detective Burke inhaled before taking a sip. "Ah.

Hot, dark, and bitter. Just like my ex." Pulling up a chair, she listened as the police officer took down the rest of Vee's statement.

"Why didn't you mention you had an argument with your husband when Officer Ramirez asked earlier?" she piped in.

"Sorry?"

"Right here." She reached for Officer Ramirez's notes and slid them toward Vee. "He asked if you had a dispute with someone. An old grudge. An argument. You replied 'no.'"

"I didn't think it was relevant."

"You had an argument with your husband. You haven't heard from him in two days. Someone threw a rock through your window with a note wrapped around it saying..." She scrolled through the notes. "Garden." Her eyes probed Vee's.

"Are you suggesting my husband smashed our window because we had an argument?"

"I don't know enough about you or your husband to suggest anything." She pulled up a blurb about the Rozas on her phone. "Striking couple. The tall, handsome math professor, and the stunning founder of a successful start-up. Do they have frequent arguments? Does he pull a disappearing act often? I don't know, Mrs. Roza. I'm just trying to fill in the blanks."

"Shouldn't you be gathering evidence instead of dissecting my marriage?"

Detective Burke rose and placed her empty cup in the sink. ""Why don't you show me exactly what happened. You said you turned off the light. This one here?" She walked over to the switch.

"Yes."

"So you're standing here. You turn off the light. And then what?"

"Then the rock came hurtling through the window."

"Right away? Ten seconds later? Twenty?"

"No more than five seconds later."

Detective Burke walked to where the rock landed. "This is all glass." She motioned toward the expanse of windows in the sunroom. "Whoever was out there had a clear view of you when the light was on. But the rock came through here—nowhere close to where you were standing. I think we can assume that this person had no intention of hurting you."

"You think someone was trying to scare me?"

"I'm merely making an observation."

"If we're done here, I'd like to wrap things up. It's been a long day."

"With no promise of slowing down."

"Excuse me?"

"Do you often have people dropping by in the middle of the night?" Detective Burke pointed through the window.

A figure stared back from the front yard.

"That's our neighbor, Jeanne. We must have woken her up. Excuse me." Vee left to greet her.

"Is everything all right?" Jeanne asked. A few weeks from retiring, she was like family to Vee and Rafael. "I woke up to flashing lights and saw the police car."

"Nothing to be alarmed about, Jeanne. Someone broke one of our windows."

"Heavens." She drew her robe around her. "Are you okay?"

"I'm fine. Everything is fine. Really."

She nodded but remained concerned. "I thought it had something to do with Rafael."

"I'll let you know when I hear from him. Don't worry. I'm sure he's just cooling off."

"How can I not worry? I can't remember the last time the two of you had a falling out. And now one of your windows shattered. Come stay with me until it's fixed."

"Thanks, but someone's coming by in the morning." Vee gave her a reassuring squeeze.

"Well, if you're sure." Her eyes fell on Detective Burke, watching them through the window.

Vee walked her home and waited until her porch light turned off before heading back in.

"We have everything we need." Officer Ramirez and his partner met Vee at the door. "We're taking this in for prints." He held up a bag with the rock and note.

"Of course." Vee stepped aside to let them exit.

Detective Burke followed. "You'll let me know if you remember anything else?"

"I will." Vee accepted the card she held out. She was about to lock up when Detective Burke stuck her foot in the door.

"One more thing, Mrs. Roza. Do you drive both cars in your driveway?"

"No. The silver one is my husband's."

"You said he left two nights ago. If I recall correctly, we had a thunderstorm that night."

"Yes."

"So your husband left on foot after your argument?"

"I guess. I haven't been out since." Having miscarried in public, Vee was terrified of leaving the house. "I didn't realize his car is still in the driveway."

"And he hasn't been back? Not even for his car?"

Vee tried to think of an explanation, but floundered.

Detective Burke observed the play of emotions across her face. "I'll be in touch, Mrs. Roza."

A cold knot formed in Vee's stomach as she watched her drive away.

Where the hell are you, Rafael, she thought. *And what the hell is going on?*

Four

THE GIRL IN THE BLACK RAINCOAT DUG HER NAILS INTO her palms on the bus ride home. She had done a loud thing, and it rattled her. Loud noises rattled her. Loud people rattled her. But the worst was when things got loud inside, and she ended up doing something that put her back on the radar. She had been good for a long time, but she'd slipped. She'd given in to the overwhelming urge to act out her inner world.

When she got off the bus, she kept her eyes on her feet all the way to her apartment. As she walked through the courtyard, she listened to the raindrops falling around her.

"Red."

"Purple."

"Green."

"Yellow."

Fumbling with her keys, she entered her apartment and locked the door. Her hands shook as she balled up her raincoat and stuffed it in the corner of the closet.

"Stupid." She scolded her reflection in the bathroom mirror. "Stupid, stupid, stupid."

Filling the tub with cold water, she slipped inside. Her clothes stuck to her like second skin. She took a deep breath and plunged her face under the surface. Eyes open, she stared at the ceiling through the fluid veil of water and waited.

Dunking her face in cold water triggered the mammalian diving reflex, which slowed her heart—something Rafael taught her when she needed to calm down. She lay underwater until bubbles stopped popping to the surface. Then she came up with a gasp and started shivering.

Neither she nor Rafael could have predicted that all the hours they spent together would lead to this point.

Five

IF THERE WAS ANYONE WHO COULD TRACK RAFAEL down, it was his friend, Damian. The two of them had been through hell and back together.

"Could you call him, Damian?" Vee asked when he answered his phone. "I can't shake off the feeling that something's wrong. I messaged him about last night and he didn't respond to that either."

"That's not like him. Unless he's gone off-grid."

"Maybe. But his car's still in the driveway."

"Leave it with me. Are you all right? Did you get the window replaced?"

"Yes. And I'm fine. I'll be better when I hear from Rafael."

After the call ended, Vee took her prenatal vitamins

with a quick gulp of water. She knew she should stay hydrated, but she was terrified of going to the bathroom, terrified of spotting blood again. Her anxiety escalated with each pregnancy. What should have been a joyful experience was filled with dread. The slightest twinge set her on edge. Another miscarriage would not only be devastating, but potentially fatal. Vee had to get her thoughts under control. She had to eat, sleep, rest, and do whatever she could to see this pregnancy through.

Her phone pinged with a text alert.

Are you okay? Rafael responded to her text about the broken window.

Grabbing the phone, Vee messaged back.

I'm fine. Where are you?

I'm taking some time off.

Come home, Rafael. We'll sort it out.

Vee waited for a reply, but nothing came through. Her fingers hovered over the keyboard—typing, deleting, typing, then deleting again. If Rafael needed time away, she would give it to him. Knowing he was all right made things infinitely more bearable. The dark, heavy feeling crowding around her receded to the edges.

Vee's eyes fell on the anagram on the fridge.

Pi the wise one.

Grabbing a pen and paper, she rearranged the letters.

Wipe the noise. Made no sense.

Hope nite wise. Hmm.

Rafael always followed up with his messages. Sometimes he played them out in the bedroom. Vee's senses leaped at the thought of his touch.

Glancing out of the window, she noticed Jeanne dragging her garbage bin to the curb.

"Hold on." She rushed out to help.

"Thanks." Jeanne let go with a sigh. "Rafael has

spoiled me. I can't remember the last time I took the garbage out myself."

"Well, you'll be happy to know I finally heard from him." Vee hit an uneven slab of cement and almost tipped the bin over.

"Is he okay?"

"He's fine." Stuffing back the garbage that had toppled out, Vee snapped the lid back on. "He's just taking some time off."

"Time off? From you and the baby? You must have had one hell of an argument. I hope you feel better now that you've heard from him."

"Yes, I'm glad he got in touch."

"Vee?" Jeanne paused, then shook her head. "Never mind. It's nothing."

"Tell me."

"It's just that..." She hesitated. "This is going to sound crazy, but do you think there's another woman?"

"Another woman?" Vee laughed. "That's absurd."

"It is, right?" She chuckled. "I don't know what I was thinking."

Jeanne walked away, but long-buried insecurities stirred in Vee.

"Wait," she called. "What made you say that?"

"Oh, no particular reason. Just thought of the woman he came around with when you were away last year."

"He brought someone home?"

"Yes. I was leaving some pie on your porch when they pulled into the driveway. He introduced her as his student."

"Rafael brought one of his students here?"

"He said she was on his research team. I only thought of it because there was something off about her."

"In what way?"

"Well..." Jeanne paused. "She wouldn't meet my eyes and she had a hoodie on the whole time."

"I'm sure they were just picking something up."

"Of course." Jeanne smiled, but Vee glimpsed something in her eyes. Concern? Pity? Sympathy?

Another woman. The thought plagued Vee that night. Was that why her husband was missing from her bed?

Her heart didn't believe it, but her mind stayed up playing tricks.

Was there another woman in Rafael's life?

Was she the reason he stormed out? Because she could give him kids without the agony of miscarrying, over and over again?

Was she the one who'd thrown a rock through the window?

And why the note? *Garden.* It made no sense.

Was Vee forgetting something? Someone?

No matter how many scenarios she created, it came down to one thing: her relationship with Rafael. No one could touch it if it was as solid as she believed.

So why isn't he here, Vee? Knowing you're pregnant, knowing someone vandalized your home?

A seed of doubt sprouted and took hold.

Do you ever really know someone, or do you just know the parts they want you to see?

PAST

THE FIRST TIME RAFAEL FELL IN LOVE, HE DIDN'T KNOW it was love. The realization came later, when he recalled the feeling of being with her—the rush of happiness, the ache of innocence stripped away too soon. Suspended between life and death, he experienced each moment more intensely, as though looking through a kaleidoscope of sharp-edged memories, all of them tumbling through him in an instant.

His first glimpse of Lina was the afternoon he skipped his math exam. Hiding in the tamarind tree, forty feet from the ground, he spotted Tía Maria get off a tuk-tuk with a strange girl. Strange, because she was wearing a bumblebee costume. The kids Tía Maria fostered were victims of drug war, orphans, or children abandoned by their parents. Store-bought costumes were a luxury that put her in a category of her own. With striped leggings, a tutu dress, and honey-bee wings, Lina arrived with a splash of color in Rafael's eight-year-old life.

As he watched Tía Maria drag her across the dusty road, his mother stormed into the courtyard that separated the cantina from our house.

"Rafaelito!" The sole cook at *La Sombra*, Mamá rarely left the kitchen in the middle of preparing dinner.

"You can't save him this time, Camila." Papá brushed past her. "Where is he?" He spoke in Spanish, as did everyone around Rafael. English was reserved for his lessons and the books Papá brought him.

"Rafael!" he boomed.

"I'm over here."

"Get down. This instant."

Rafael descended from his perch, branch after branch, and jumped off the tree.

"Señor Gonzalez just told me you skipped your exam today. Is that true?"

Head bowed, Rafael stared at the slabs under his feet.

"Answer me."

"*Mi amor*, he must have a reason," Mamá intervened.

"Is it true?" Papá's eyes drilled holes through the top of Rafael's head.

He didn't reply.

Papá grabbed his hand and dragged him across the courtyard.

"Where are you taking him?" Mamá followed.

"Somewhere I should have taken him a long time ago."

He marched Rafael past the bullet-riddled walls of the dining room, down the stairs to the front of the cantina. When they reached the alley where Papá parked his truck, their paths crossed with Tía Maria, pulling Bumblebee Girl behind her.

Papá and Tía Maria tipped their heads—neighbors, guardians, squelchers of young agitators. The sun was on Rafael's face as the girl's wings brushed past him. He caught a glimpse of a magnificent scowl. The pom-poms capping her antennae bounced as she passed. Still being led away by Papá, he looked over his shoulder the same time she did. With her arm in Tía Maria's grip, she stared back as they went in opposite directions. Scrawny legs. Brown skin. Eyes stinging with unshed tears. Then she disappeared behind the wall that separated the cantina from Tía Maria's home.

"Get in." Papá opened the truck door and waited for Rafael to climb inside.

They took the rubble road that ran through Paza del Mar. Papá was silent as they passed small homes and shops. Village elders napped in the shade. Kids kicked up dust storms as they chased a ball. When they got to the intersection at the edge of the village, Papá turned toward the hills. They drove until the air grew cool and the landscape turned lush with fruit trees. Orchards of mango, papaya, and lime grew along a river swollen with run-off from the rains.

"Look." Rafael pointed to the vines growing on the hardwood trees. "The same ones that grow on the tamarind tree." Delighted to have come so far beyond the boundaries of their home, he broke the silence between them.

"*Si*, Rafaelito." Papá smiled and ruffled his hair.

Rafael didn't know where they were going or why, but he knew everything was going to be okay. When Papá veered off-track and stopped outside a fenced clearing, Rafael got out and followed him.

Papá was silent for a long time, his eyes on the patch of land beyond a barbed-wire fence.

"Right here," he said. "This is the spot my life changed forever." He kneeled and took aim through a make-believe rifle. "I shot the first one through the back of the head. The second guy turned around—pants around his ankles, gun in his holster. I got him in the chest. Graciela screamed when his blood splattered over her. I still hear the echoes of those shots." A nerve ticked in Papá's jaw. "I would do it again, Rafaelito. I would kill those bastards again for laying their filthy hands on my sister."

Dirt and weeds surrounded the remnants of the small home before them. Rafael stared at the abandoned land as Papá told him the story of how he became one of the cartel's key players.

Seven

IT WAS JUAN PABLO ROZA'S TWENTY-FIRST BIRTHDAY. He had just returned from a hunting trip with his father when they saw two men dragging his sister Graciela to the field. They turned out to be El Charro's men, sent to collect tribute for the cartel he ran. They called it protection money, but the only thing Juan Pablo and his family needed protecting from was them. The organization was gaining a foothold in the area, but with barely enough to feed themselves, farmers had remained unaffected until then. Graciela had nothing to offer when the men showed up, so they decided to collect in another way.

The police came for Juan Pablo that night. They locked him and his father up, claiming it was pre-trial detention for murder, but there was no trial, no judge, and no legal proceeding. The police were on El Charro's payroll. Juan Pablo and his father were to pay for killing his men by rotting in prison for the rest of their lives.

One night, a guard came to get Juan Pablo. He told him he had a visitor. Juan Pablo prayed Graciela had found a way to see them, but it was a man he'd never laid eyes on. From the cut of his suit and the cane resting against his chair, Juan Pablo knew his visitor was Raúl Ángel Hernández, better known as El Charro.

Visiting hours were over and the chairs had been cleared, except for the one he sat on. A bare bulb cast a circle of light around him.

"Welcome, Juan Pablo Roza." El Charro stared into his drink.

A hard nudge propelled Juan Pablo forward. Glancing over his shoulder, Juan Pablo discerned the shadow of his bodyguard.

"You killed two of my best." El Charro studied him. "Clean shots. From quite a distance, I hear. With this antique." He slid Juan Pablo's rifle toward him.

"Do what you want with me." Juan Pablo knew he was about to pay for his actions. "But let my father go. He's an old man. He had nothing to do with it."

"Your father isn't the only one you should be worried about." El Charro swirled his glass. "I met your sister today. A ripe, juicy mango, ready to be plucked." He took a swig of amber liquid and eyed Juan Pablo over the rim.

Juan Pablo's fists clenched into tight balls.

"Such fury." El Charro laughed. "Anger rolls off this one, Leonardo." He spoke to his bodyguard, but his icy smile was for Juan Pablo. "You'd finish me right now *if you could. With your bare hands."* El Charro feigned disappointment and rested his hand on his cane.

El Charro's walking stick was as infamous as him. The tip held his stamp—a gold blade molded into the letter "C." He used it to mark the bodies of those he killed. Juan Pablo could feel the razor-sharp metal cutting into his skin, but he denied El Charro the pleasure of seeing him squirm.

"Do you like games?" El Charro asked.

When Juan Pablo didn't answer, Leonardo pistol-whipped him to his knees.

"Let's play something fun," El Charro said. "Pick up your rifle and aim it at me."

With Leonardo's gun digging into the top of his skull, Juan Pablo crawled to his rifle.

"I respect a man who does what it takes to protect his family." El Charro continued. "It speaks of loyalty, of guts, of passion—all qualities I value. Unfortunately, you killed two men who were very dear to me, so I must take two people who are very dear to you: your father and your sister. Unless..." He swallowed the rest of his drink and balanced the glass on his head. "You shoot this without touching a hair on my head."

"And if I miss?" Juan Pablo glared at him.

"You want to be the messiah? The man who killed Raúl Ángel Hernández?" His laughter filled the room. "You won't make it past Leonardo and the guards, but it will be a glorious death. Your father won't live to see the morning and your sister... Well, she'll be put to rest after she's paid the price for your heroism."

Juan Pablo picked up his rifle, convinced it was a ruse. Leonardo would shoot him the moment he took aim. "If I get this right, you'll let me and my family go free?"

"If you get this right, you'll prove your worth. I'll take you under my wing. Your father and sister will never want for anything."

Whatever the outcome, Juan Pablo's life belonged to El Charro, but he could still save his father and Graciela. Calling on his departed mother to steady his hand, Juan Pablo made the sign of the cross. He hadn't missed a mark in years, but he wasn't used to shooting at close range. He wiped the sweat off his brow and took aim. Staring down the barrel of his rifle was like looking into a long, dark tunnel. Everything was dark except for the orb of light at the other end, where El Charro sat. The empty glass on his head moved in and out of focus. The glass was life: his life, his father's life, and Graciela's life. Steeling himself, Juan Pablo aligned the shot and fired.

The sound of glass exploding was the sweetest thing Juan Pablo had ever heard, but his eyes squeezed shut.

Not a hair to be harmed. That was the deal. If the bullet grazed El Charro, or if the glass pierced his skin, it was over.

Juan Pablo's blood roared in his ears. He heard the scraping of a chair, then footsteps. It wasn't until Leonardo pried the rifle away from him that he opened his eyes. El Charro stood before him, dusting shards off his jacket.

Juan Pablo fell to his knees, adrenaline leaving him in a rush.

"I knew the moment I saw you," El Charro said. "I have an eye for natural-born killers. Some I mold, some I contain, and some..." He tapped Juan Pablo on the shoulder with his cane. "I awaken."

Eight

*L*EARNING ABOUT THE PAST SHIFTED R*AFAEL*'S PERSPECTIVE on his father. It made Papá bigger and stronger, yet more human.

"My life is a sham, Rafaelito." Papá's gaze refocused on him. "The cantina is a front for the cartel. Mamá and I tell you not to come into *La Sombra* because we want you as far removed from our world as possible. Not even the shadow of El Charro should touch you.

"This is not the life I wanted, but it is the life I was dealt. Mamá's only downfall was falling in love with me before my life changed. She has been my rock through it all—when your grandfather died, and when we lost Graciela. I want to give her the world, to make all her dreams come true: a home on a hill, from where she can watch sunsets and never have to put on an apron again. But we both know it will never be. What keeps us going is knowing *you* have what we never did—a chance to break free of the web we're caught in. If I'm hard on you, it's because I want you to excel, to make something of yourself, to get as far from this place as you can. Do you understand?"

Rafael nodded, although his mind was rearranging the landscape of reality, fitting in the new pieces so he could walk the terrain again.

"So, tell me why you skipped your exam." Papá squeezed his shoulder. "Is someone bullying you in school?"

"No."

"Outside of school?"

"No."

"Are you sick? Headache? Stomachache? Fever?"

"No."

"Then explain to me why your teachers keep calling? Why are they concerned about your behavior? Why does Señor Gonzalez say you're cheating on your tests?"

Rafael blinked back the tears, his mouth tight with protest.

"*Mijo*." Papá's hug pushed him over the edge.

"I'm not like the other kids." Rafael clung to him. "I can't do what they do. I can't think like they think."

Papá held him until he stopped sobbing. He gave Rafael a handkerchief to wipe his face. Mamá sprinkled rose water whenever she ironed it. The scent was comforting.

"We've always known you're different, Rafaelito." Papá kneeled, so they were eye to eye. "You know answers to questions that we need a calculator for. That's why I don't understand why you're failing your math class or why you skipped the exam today."

"Because!" Rafael's hands shot out, trying to explain. "Señor Gonzalez wants us to show our work, and I don't follow the steps he teaches. I know the answer, but he wants to see how I got to it. I didn't take the exam because he would fail me or tell you I'm cheating again, and I don't want you to get mad at me."

"Okay. That's good, Rafaelito. If you share what's bothering you, we can fix it together. So tell me how you know the answers, and I will explain to Señor Gonzalez."

Leaning against the front tire of Papá's truck, Rafael tried to describe how his brain worked.

"I see numbers as shapes. Even before I went to school, every number had a shape. One is like this..." He drew a circle in the dirt with his finger. "Two is a line. Three is a triangle. Four is a square." He traced out the progression of shapes. "Bigger numbers have more intricate shapes, like triangles inside octagons. Some are circles, some are spirals.

"If I multiply or divide numbers, they merge into a new shape. When I look at that shape, I know the number. It's like recognizing someone's face. You automatically know their name. The first time I see a shape, I have to learn it. The next time I automatically recall it. The more problems I do, the faster I get.

"I've been finishing my math tests earlier, but I pretend I'm still working. Sometimes, I put down the wrong answer because I don't want to draw attention to myself. When I'm working on a problem, it's hard to keep my eyes on the paper. The shapes dance around me. If I follow them with my eyes, my teachers think I'm not paying attention. If I look around during an exam, they think I'm cheating. I've learned that if I close my eyes, I can see the shapes in my head, but I still can't show my work, so I keep failing."

Papá nodded, like he could see pieces of a puzzle fall into place.

"It's not you that's failing, Rafael," he said. "It's us, failing you—me, your teachers, the system. It's no one's fault. Just the way the world works. Imagine you're driving along. It's a nice day. The sun is shining. You roll down your windows. Your intersection comes up, so you join the line of cars waiting to make the same turn. You wait a long time and just when you get to the end of the line, some crazy guy butts in. You're mad as hell because he's going from A to C without going through B. You honk. All the cars behind you honk too. Everyone's mad. They yell, they curse, they think he should be punished.

"You're that crazy guy, Rafaelito. You look at a problem and go to the answer without any of the steps the rest of us have to take. Can you see why it annoys Señor Gonzalez? He wants to see how you get from one point to another, but you..." Papá laughed. "You're not following the rules. You're not even on the road. You're zipping around with jet-propelled wings, so fast that he can't even see you."

Rafael squealed as Papá made buzzing noises, his hands attacking from all sides. A pinch, a poke, a tickle, and Rafael was on his back, laughing so hard his sides hurt. With his head on Papá's lap, Rafael lay on his side and watched the sun set over the abandoned land that had been Papá's home. On the spot where his life changed, Rafael's did too. He no longer felt like a freak, heavy with the secret.

Papá stroked his hair until the stars came out, one by one.

"Once in a while, an extraordinary mind comes

along," he said. "Use it well, Rafaelito. Don't ever dim your light to fit in. Mamá and I will fight for you. We'll fight your teachers, your school, the whole world if we have to. Just promise me one thing."

Rafael looked up from his lap and saw his father's face against a canopy of stars.

"Promise me you'll leave this place the first chance you get."

Nine

THINGS WERE BETTER AT SCHOOL AFTER PAPÁ MET WITH Rafael's teachers. He took a series of tests, which caused a stir among the staff. Fortunately, their attention was quickly diverted by a new student—Bumblebee Girl.

Evelina Flores went by the name written on her arm when she was found: Lina.

The only things in her possession were a letter and the bumblebee costume she wore. A grade below Rafael, Lina wore the costume like a cocoon around her. She woke up in it, wore it to school, and went to sleep in it. It wasn't long before a foul odor surrounded her. No one sat with her, talked to her, or played with her.

Whenever someone tried to get her out of the

costume, she held her breath. The first time Tía Maria rushed over with Lina in her arms, she was limp and unresponsive. Papá drove them to the doctor, but Lina recovered on the way. The next time it happened, Tía Maria was trying to coax her into taking a bath. She held her breath for so long, she lost consciousness again. No amount of threatening, cajoling, or punishment worked. Stripping Lina of her costume brought on breath-holding episodes that got longer and longer until she either passed out or was left alone.

In the battle of kids versus adults, kids always lost, so Rafael was both impressed and intimidated by Lina. She liked to sit under the tamarind tree. It grew on Tía Maria's side of the property, but its branches dangled over Rafael's courtyard.

Rafael enjoyed having the tree to himself, so he made up a story that it was haunted by a boy who climbed to the top and saw the entire world for a moment, before falling to his death. Tía Maria's foster kids came and went, but the story stuck. If Lina knew it, she didn't care, which made her cool. If she didn't know it, Rafael figured all she wanted was to be left alone, which was cool too.

Things changed when a tamarind pod slipped from Rafael's hands and bounced off Lina's head. Round came her face, brown eyes scanning the tree—up, up until she spotted his feet. She scowled when she recognized him, annoyed at being spied on by a boy—dead or alive. Rafael thought she would leave, but she stayed. After a while, she threw him a cautionary look. Satisfied he was doing his own thing, she reached for the tamarind pod, cracked the shell open, and sucked on the pulp. One by one, she spit out the seeds. Then she placed them on her toes, so they looked like dark, glossy nail polish. When she glanced at Rafael, he ignored her, but she persisted until he realized she didn't have enough seeds for all her toes. Plucking another tamarind pod, he threw it to her. When all her toes were adorned, she wiggled them and started over.

"Lina," Tía Maria called.

Lina threw Rafael a warning look, in case he was thinking of ratting her out.

Rafael placed a tamarind seed over his tooth and grinned, holding it in place with the tip of his tongue.

From where Lina sat, it looked like someone had knocked out his front tooth. She tilted her head back and giggled through her nose.

From then on, she looked for Rafael whenever she came out. If he was around, he dropped some tamarind pods to signal his presence. She stayed at the base of the tree, and he stayed in the branches. They spent hours ignoring each other until one of them was called in.

Lina liked to sketch. On windy days, her art littered the courtyard. Tía Maria cursed as she collected the papers with a pointed stick. She gave Lina extra chores, which Lina accepted without argument. But her breath-holding spells continued. She would not be separated from her costume.

"She is the devil's daughter," Tía Maria declared when Mamá invited her over. "I mean it, Camila. Who takes their child to the mall and abandons her? He sent her into the changing room with that costume and left. I know she's holding on to it because it's the only link she has to her father. Maybe she thinks he won't be able to find her if she takes it off. I don't know what goes on in her head. Every time I try to coax her out of it, she just clams up until her lips turn blue."

Rafael squirmed on his perch. Mamá and Tía Maria didn't know that he and Lina could hear their conversation.

"What about her mother?" Mamá asked. "Lina was placed in your care until they tracked her down."

"That's the tragedy, Camila. Her mother died six months ago in a car accident. She was living with Lina's father for years. Her family disowned her. They didn't even attend her funeral. Her landlord said the man traveled a lot but turns out he doesn't live in Mexico. He was here for work. When his contract expired, he left. Not only that, but the letter they found on Lina was from her father. It said he couldn't take her with him because he has a wife and kids back home."

"He has another family, so he just abandoned her?"

"He knew she wouldn't be able to walk out of the store alone in that costume, but to just leave her? My heart breaks for her, Camila. He didn't even give her his last name. How do I tell that little girl her father doesn't want her? That he is never coming back?"

In the silence that followed, Rafael witnessed the shift in Lina. Like a leaf left in the cold too long, she curled over, hugging her knees. From the top, all he could see was the line of her back flanked by torn, bent wings. The pom-poms on her antennae bobbed as she cried in the crook of her elbow.

Hold your breath, Lina. Fight back.

But Lina sobbed, tight gulps of air.

Rafael couldn't stand the sound of her heart breaking, so he scaled down the branches. He didn't know how to comfort her, so he sat next to her and let her cry. One of her drawings stirred on the ground—a crooked house with a half-finished path that led to a flower. A butterfly rested in the center of the flower.

Lina raised her head and looked at him through red-rimmed eyes.

"Is this your house?" Rafael asked. "Did you live here before you came to Tía Maria?"

Wiping her nose with the back of her hand, she glanced at the sketch. When she blinked, more tears slid down her face.

"You did, didn't you? Wher—" He broke off as she stood and walked away, the smell of her dank costume trailing behind her.

Staring at her drawing, Rafael realized it wasn't a butterfly on the flower. It was a bee. There was no one else around—no stick-figured family, no smiley faces, no smoke curling out of the chimney.

In that moment, a dark, glossy seed rooted in the bedrock of Rafael's soul. Evelina Flores became his first unselfish emotion.

Ten

WHEN THE FIRST BUDS APPEARED ON THE VINE IN THE courtyard, Rafael collected what he needed for his plan: one of Mamá's scarves, a blanket, and a flashlight. Every day, he watched the buds. He could tell when they would bloom with a knowing he couldn't explain even to himself. It was a different night every year. Mamá said he possessed magic, that he made them bloom when he wanted, but his brain was tuned in to their symmetry, the direction they faced, how heavy they hung on their stems.

Rafael felt bad for not telling Mamá that year. Instead, he snuck out of bed, propped a ladder against Lina's window, and knocked on the pane. When the curtains parted, she stared at him, surprised and intrigued.

"Let's go." He waited for her to put her wings on.

The moon was big and full as they climbed down the ladder. Rafael led Lina through the alley that separated their houses and unlatched the door to his courtyard. In the center was a tiered fountain. Water trickled from one level to the next, splashing onto cobalt tiles. Spreading a blanket, Rafael sat cross-legged and waited for Lina to join him. She sat at the edge, sparing him the cloud of odor that enveloped her. For a while, she followed his lead and stared at the wall before them. Rafael had propped a flashlight on a cardboard box and layered a scarf over it to create a blue spotlight on the wall. The stage was set, but with nothing happening, Lina shot him a questioning look.

"Over there." He pointed to the vining cactus growing off the branches on his side of the tree. With flat, leathery stems that draped down, it was a gangly, awkward-looking plant. The buds gleamed in the moonlight with the promise of white blooms.

Slowly, imperceptibly, the magic unfolded. Creamy petals peeped out, unfurling into a flower as big as the saucers in the cantina. Another blossom followed, then another, like candles being lit, one by one, to a nocturnal symphony. A thick fragrance filled the courtyard as they swayed softly, heavy with sacs of pollen. Moths fluttered to delicate flowers that started wilting all too soon.

Rafael reached under the blanket for Lina's sketch and held it out. "Blue like the house in your drawing, see?" He pointed to the spotlight on the wall. "A flower..." He motioned toward an open bud. "And a bee." He tugged her wing.

Lina glanced from the paper to him. Her eyes strayed to the flowers on the vine.

"Mamá says they're beautiful because they're

fleeting," Rafael said. "Blink and they slip away into the moon."

Lina sat beside him until the last bloom drooped. Then she plucked her sketch from his fingers, ducked into the alley, and took off.

"It only happens once a year," he called after her, wondering if she was mad because he'd woken her.

Disappointed that she didn't enjoy what he thought was really cool, Rafael tidied the courtyard and went to sleep.

In the morning, when he went to Tía Maria's to move the ladder, Lina was waiting under the tree. If it wasn't for the sketch she held out, he wouldn't have recognized her. Wearing a dress and knee-high socks, she got up when she saw him. Her hair was in two braids, the ends tied with ribbon. Not only had she changed out of her costume, but she'd also let Tía Maria do her hair.

Wondering why she was giving back the sketch she'd snatched from him earlier, Rafael noticed the new additions.

"Rafael." She pointed to a brown stump with a green top.

It was the first word she'd spoken to him, so he pretended to see the likeness.

She saw right through him and gestured to the branches above.

"Ah, okay. That's me." Rafael pointed to the tree she'd drawn. "And that's you." His finger hovered over the bee. "What's all this stuff falling on you?"

Picking a tamarind pod off the ground, she waved it in his face.

"No way." He laughed. "It looks like it's raining poop."

She looked at the sketch, then at him. Her mouth

wobbled. Rafael kicked himself for teasing her. A sputtering sound escaped her. Then laughter bubbled and broke free.

"You scared me." Rafael was in awe of the way her face transformed when she laughed. "I thought you were going to clam up and hold your breath again."

"You're afraid of me?"

"Of course not. You're much shorter without your antennae."

They re-assessed each other.

"Can you climb all the way to the top?" Lina asked.

"Not yet."

The sky peeked through the leaves as they gazed at the spiraling branches.

"Must be nice sitting there."

"Want me to teach you how to climb?" Rafael asked.

"No, thanks."

"You're afraid you'll fall?"

She shook her head.

"Then what?"

"I don't want anything from anyone," she said. "Everybody leaves. And they never say goodbye. One day, you'll leave too."

"I promise I'll never leave without saying goodbye."

With her hands clasped tightly behind her back, she turned to him and thought it over. "Fine. But a promise is a promise."

Eleven

INA TURNED OUT TO BE A BETTER CLIMBER THAN RAFAEL. When she turned nine, two years later, she was as tall as him, but longer limbed. Most days, she beat him to the top of the tree, from where they could see all of Paza del Mar. That's where they were on the last day Rafael saw her—the day that marked the end of his childhood. At the time, they thought the worst thing that could happen had already happened. One of them was leaving.

It was quiet in Rafael's head that afternoon. Lina's departure hushed all the distractions.

"You think I'll like it?" Legs dangling off the branch, she wiggled her toes. She asked Mamá to paint her nails because she wanted to look good for her new foster parents.

"Not a chance. You better pray Tía Maria gets better soon or you'll die from missing me."

She didn't take the bait. Instead, she slipped her hand through the crook of his elbow. "I don't think Tía Maria is going to come back from the hospital."

Being separated from her best friend was bad enough. Having to say goodbye to Tía Maria was equally painful. Lina kept losing everyone she got close to.

"Look." She pointed below. "There's Miguel."

A few years older than them, Miguel did odd jobs around the cantina in exchange for food. It wasn't uncommon for kids to grow up without parents. Orphans were collateral damage in the escalating drug war between El Charro and the Zamora cartel, but Miguel was different. He shunned company and moved like he had things to do and places to be. Papá told them to stay away from him, which made him even cooler.

"He runs errands for El Charro." Papá's face was grim. "I don't think the kid knows the kind of business he's involved in. I warned him, but he keeps coming back."

"What do you think his real name is?" Lina asked, as Miguel disappeared into the cantina.

They called him Miguel because he hung around the church of Archangel Michael.

"Why? Do you like him?"

Lina gave Rafael a strange look, tucked her hair behind her ear, and glanced away.

"You have a crush on Miguel." A strange weight settled on Rafael's chest.

Swinging around, half annoyed and half petrified, Lina leaned over and kissed his lips.

Rafael's heart ricocheted from despair to a kaleidoscope of colors. Shapes and patterns flashed before him in an adrenaline-spiked rush: the spirals on a snail's shell, waves on a dune, the arch of a chameleon's tail. His inner screen lit up, so beautiful and perfect that he didn't want to open his eyes.

I'm seeing happiness, he thought.

When their lips parted, Lina gazed solemnly at him. "Now you're my boyfriend. We don't have to say goodbye."

Rafael nodded, acknowledging the privilege and responsibility.

Their status as a couple felt like it was missing something, so he broke open a tamarind pod and gave her half. They sucked on the pulp with dappled sunlight on their faces.

"I like Miguel," Rafael declared, when the catalyst to their kiss re-appeared.

"I like him too." Lina grinned.

Miguel swept the alley between the cantina and Tiá Maria's house. Then he swept the other side, which flanked the fish shop. Mamá and Papá were happy to fill his bowl, but he was too proud to accept charity. He left with a container of leftovers, as a large sedan pulled into the alley.

"They're here." Lina recognized her foster parents from an earlier visit.

"Fancy car." It was too wide to open both doors in the alley, so the man backed out, let his wife out, then returned to park. She waited until he came around so they could enter the cantina together.

Lina and Rafael exchanged a glance. It was time.

"You'll come visit?" she asked.

"Of course. Mamá and Papá promised Tiá Maria we'd check in on you."

"You know where I'm going?"

"Papá knows. He said it's about two hours away. We'll see you in a few weeks."

"I'll wait for you."

They took one last look at the world from their perch. Rafael wanted to hold her hand because he knew she was nervous despite putting on a brave face.

"Kids." Mamá came into the courtyard. "Señor and Señora Morales are here."

"Stay," Lina said, when Rafael started climbing down with her. "I'll wave to you when we leave."

She scaled down the trunk and put her shoes on. Halfway inside, she paused and backtracked. Sifting through the leaves on the ground, she collected a handful of tamarind seeds and slipped them into her pocket.

When she emerged from *La Sombra* with her new guardians, Rafael waited for her to turn around. She stood with Señora Morales, facing the street, while Señor Morales brought the car around. Her life was packed in a suitcase, just large enough to manage on her own. It was more than she'd arrived with, but she was being uprooted again. Shoulders squared, she lifted her chin as the sedan rolled up to the curb. Putting her suitcase in the trunk, she said goodbye to Mamá and Papá. Then, without glancing at Rafael, she got in the car.

Hey. Wait.

But the dark interior swallowed her frame.

As the sedan turned into the road, Lina rolled her window down, stuck her head out and looked for Rafael. He crawled further along the branch, where the leaves were not as dense, and waved. Putting off her goodbye to the very end, Lina waited until they were almost out of each other's sight. Hair whipping around her face, she waved back.

Then, like a bee flitting from flower to flower in the wind, Evelina Flores disappeared from view.

Twelve

THAT EVENING, AFTER SEEING RAFAEL MOPE AROUND, Mamá and Papá broke their cardinal rule.

"How would you like to have dinner with us at the cantina tonight?" Mamá asked. "Papá won't be serving, so we can have a bite before anyone comes in."

Although Papá waited tables, Mamá used the word *serving* for his cartel work. Paza del Mar was one of El Charro's bases, and it was Papá's job to protect him when he was in town. Deep in his own territory, El Charro traveled without security guards. He enjoyed the confidence and notoriety it projected. He also enjoyed cold beers, Mamá's cooking, and the celebrity-like attention he attracted while conducting meetings from the cantina.

Papá posted dinner specials every night, but *La*

Sombra's reputation as El Charro's hangout kept the lo-
cals away. Most of the customers had connections to the
cartel, so Papá carried a gun under his apron. It was better than his earlier assignments, and Mamá was grateful
they could stay in one place. Once in a while, El Charro
called Papá away. When he returned, Papá would sit on
the stairs at the entrance and smoke his demons away.

There were no cigarettes in sight that evening. An
hour before the cantina opened for dinner, Papá drew
the curtains while Rafael set the table. Mamá brought
out a platter of french fries piled high with shredded beef,
guacamole, cilantro, jalapenos, and lime. They attacked
the platter, trying to balance as many toppings as they
could on each fry.

"I win," Papá declared.

"Of course, you win. You have a mouth as big as the
moon." Mamá opened her arms in a wide gesture.

"You love this mouth." Papá grabbed her wrists and
kissed her. "Come, *mi reina*." He drew her to the center
of the dining room. "Rafaelito, clear the table. I have not
danced with my wife in a long time."

Turning on the record player, Papá pulled Mamá into
his arms. Wearing stained aprons, they swayed between
Formica-topped tables. As Rafael watched them, little triangles appeared on the inner screen of his mind, each a
snapshot of the day. His first kiss. His first dinner at the
cantina. The crackle of the music. The halo of Mamá's
hair. Bugs swarming around the lamppost outside. Dusk
seeping into the sky. The triangles coalesced and grew
outward, detail by detail, until a perfectly symmetrical
snowflake crystallized in the archive of his senses.

"It's beautiful," he said, in awe of each gleaming facet.

"Then why the long face?" Mamá stopped dancing

and sat beside him. She could tell when he disappeared into his head.

"He misses his friend." Papá pulled up a chair. "We miss her too."

When Tiá Maria fell ill, Mamá and Papá offered to look after Lina. Mamá wanted to assume guardianship, but Papá wouldn't have it, not as long as he worked for El Charro. If there was a safer place for Lina, that's where she belonged.

"She's not just my friend," Rafael said. "She's my girlfriend."

"Ay, my little Romeo." Mamá laughed, but Papá kept a straight face.

"It's serious then?" he asked.

"Yes." Rafael nodded. "We kissed."

"Hmm." Papá drummed his fingers on the table. "I'll drive you and Lina to pick up a marriage application form. Camila, talk to Father Andres about the ceremony. We'll have the reception here. You and Lina can work on the guest list when we go to see her."

Rafael's jaw dropped little by little until it was hanging open.

Papá stared at him for a few ticks, then roared with laughter.

"So this is what *La Sombra* is like when I'm not around." A voice boomed from the door.

"Señor Hernández." Papá turned the record player off and greeted the man known as El Charro. "We weren't expecting you today."

"A last-minute meeting." Shrugging off his coat, El Charro lifted his walking stick, giving his driver permission to leave. "Camila." He tipped his hat and set it on the table. When his eyes fell on Rafael, Mamá's toes curled in her sandals.

"I forget you have a son, Juan Pablo." The chair scraped as El Charro sat across from Rafael. "Do they hide you away, little rabbit? Do you run to your burrow when you see me coming?" He leaned forward and stared into his eyes.

Face-to-face with a legend, Rafael stared back. El Charro was the name parents invoked to get their kids to behave.

Go to sleep or El Charro will put you in his sack and carry you away.

Mapping El Charro's face against his own projections of the man was like holding a traced image against the original. Rafael was still adjusting the ratios and curves when El Charro's expression changed.

"He looks at me without flinching." El Charro broke eye contact and glanced at Papá. "Grown men piss in their pants and this little rabbit... It's like he's dissecting me." He chuckled. "Two beers, Camila. One for me and one for your boy. He will remember the night he proved himself a man."

"I don't like beer." Rafael scrunched his nose. "May I have a sweet empanada instead?"

Mamá's expression signaled he was out of line. He had offended a powerful and dangerous man.

Gripping Rafael's neck in the crook of his cane, El Charro pulled him forward until he was staring at him through the end of his nose. Every pore of El Charro's skin came into focus. Cold, dark eyes. Narrow ears. His breath, like fumes licking his face. Throat tight with dread, Rafael gulped.

El Charro howled with laughter and sat back. "Give the boy his empanada. He's earned it."

Before Mamá could respond, a floorboard creaked by the entrance. Papá spun around so fast, Rafael didn't see him draw his pistol until it was pointed at the man in the doorway. El Charro's laughter faded. A triangle of tension stretched between the three men. They held still, like cobras waiting to strike.

The stranger raised his arms. "I'm unarmed. I just want to talk."

"I thought I was meeting Sánchez tonight," El Charro replied. "Is he one of yours now?"

"No. He just wants us to make peace."

"Is that what you want, Alfredo?" El Charro stood. "To make peace?"

"I have no other reason to show up here, alone and unarmed."

Seconds ticked as El Charro assessed the man.

"What do you have to lose?" Alfredo prompted. "Hear me out. If you don't like it, we continue the way we are."

"Or I could kill you and end this war right here."

"You could. But we can make a lot of money together. I think you'll like what I have to say."

El Charro rested his hands on his cane, pondering the options. "You have ten minutes, Alfredo." He gave Papá a nod.

Keeping his gun trained on Alfredo, Papá crossed the space between them and patted him down. "He's clean."

"I will take those two beers now, Camila." El Charro motioned Alfredo to join him.

"How about we sit here?" Alfredo picked another table. "Out of respect for the lady and the child."

"Always the gentleman." El Charro's words were barbed with sarcasm, but he picked up his hat and moved to the other table.

"Come, Rafael." Mamá rose. "Time to go."

"What about my empanada?" Rafael asked.

Grabbing his wrist, Mamá pulled him into the kitchen.

"Alfredo Ruben Zamora is the head of a rival cartel. Two of the most dangerous men in Mexico are sitting in our cantina and you want an empanada?" She squeezed his hand so hard that his fingers prickled with pins and needles.

Rafael didn't want an empanada. He wanted to watch Mamá and Papá dance instead of going to his room every night. He wanted to be part of whatever they were part of. He wanted to stop being afraid, and he wanted them to stop being afraid for him. He wanted them to look at him like they did the first time he made it to the top of the tree.

"I'm sorry," he said.

Mamá sighed and let go. "Hold on." Placing two beers and some tostadas on a tray, she called Papá through the serving window. When he didn't appear, she served the men herself and put something on the stove.

"The perimeter is clear." Papá slipped into the kitchen through the side entrance. "Call Ricardo. Tell him to bring backup. Zamora is up to something. I can feel it in my bones."

"Wait." Mamá handed him a bottle of ketchup. "El Charro always asks for this. Food will be ready soon."

On high alert, Papá brushed past Rafael, then paused and turned around.

"Rafaelito." His expression softened.

"Papá."

They understood each other. Rafael had to get out of his hair.

Papá gave him a nod and headed into the dining area. Mamá prepared toppings for a pizza. Not wanting to bother her, Rafael left. At the far end of the hallway was a door that opened to the courtyard, but he stopped to wash his hands in the bathroom first.

"Rafael?" He heard Mamá calling.

Turning off the light, he peered into the hallway. Mamá stood outside the kitchen, holding a plate of empanadas. Face lit up, Rafael stepped forward.

A crack of gunfire pierced the air. In the dining area, Papá dropped the bottle of ketchup. It splattered on the floor and over his sneakers. For a moment, he stood motionless. Then he stumbled back, clutching his pistol. Alfred Zamora fired another shot. Papá fell to his knees, dropped his weapon, and collapsed.

Mamá spun around, mouth open, but never got to call his name. The bullet ripped through her as she held the plate. A wet stain spread down the back of her dress. She made a horrible gurgling sound. The empanadas slipped off, one by one, before the plate shattered at her feet. Clutching her throat, she shuffled silently toward Papá.

"Carnage. Everywhere you go," Alfredo Zamora said to El Charro as Mamá collapsed on the floor, a few feet from Papá. "Such a pity." He turned his gun to El Charro. "You want to know who planted a weapon for me under this table before you die?"

Hidden in the hallway, Rafael knew what he had to do.

Run, said Papá.

Hide, said Mamá.

But Rafael couldn't move. He watched as dark puddles grew around them. Their blood seeped in straight lines along sun-bleached planks. Rafael's legs crumbled. He huddled against the wall, hoping death would come for him, groove by groove, and take him wherever it had taken Mamá and Papá.

Something moved in the kitchen. A face appeared in the serving window. It was the kid Rafael and Lina called Miguel. Having used the side entrance, he was oblivious to what he'd walked in on. The moment he spotted Mamá and Papá, he froze. Eyes wide, he saw Alfred Zamora about to shoot El Charro.

Rafael expected him to take off, but Miguel crawled out of the kitchen and crept silently across the floor. He moved slowly over shards of glass and the sticky filling that had spilled out of the empanadas. Alfred Zamora had his back to Miguel. If El Charro saw him, he gave no indication. With each step Miguel took toward Papá's gun, Rafael retreated further into the hallway.

Miguel picked up the gun. His hands shook as he took aim.

Rafael ducked into the bathroom and squeezed his eyes shut.

Not again. Curtain after curtain opened to the same nightmare.

When the boom came, blood and ketchup splattered across the pristine snowflake-memory in his mind. He peered around the corner, not knowing who had shot whom.

Alfred Zamora's body lay beside a toppled chair. Miguel dropped the gun like it was smoldering. El Charro crossed the room and kissed him on the cheeks.

Rafael started shaking uncontrollably.

Mamá was dead.

Papá was dead.

His insides trembled, his fingers trembled, the ground under his feet trembled. The overwhelming urge to run exploded through him. He bolted out the back door and into the courtyard, not stopping until he was high in the branches of the only solid thing in his world.

Thirteen

EL CHARRO DID NOT FORGET ABOUT RAFAEL. IN THE morning, he sent his men, but Rafael would not come down from the tree. The upper branches were not strong enough to support their weight, so they bribed him with cheese and pop, but nothing persuaded him from his safe place. When their shadows grew short under the noon sky, they drove away.

From Rafael's lookout, everything was the same—stray dogs sniffing piles of garbage, sewing machines whirring in the tailor's veranda, men playing cards in the village square. Yet nothing was the same. Resting his head against the tree, Rafael traced the familiar patterns of gnarled bark and closed his eyes.

The men returned in the evening with a message

from El Charro: "If you stay where you are, you'll miss your parents' funeral."

Rafael climbed down, scaled the branch hanging over the courtyard, and jumped off. Opening the back door, he stepped inside the cantina. It took a moment for his eyes to adjust to the dark hallway.

Mamá stood by the kitchen with a plate of empanadas.

Rafael walked through his last memory of her with an ache in his gut.

The floor was mopped, no sign of blood or bodies or broken glass. The smell of bleach was so nauseating that Rafael gagged. Keeping his eyes on the front doors, he crossed the space with his head high. He was Camila and Juan Pablo Roza's son.

As he left the cantina, Rafael had a razor-sharp vision of Papá smoking on the entrance stairs, and watching the wispy tendrils disappear into the sky.

Rafael walked past him, got in the car, and shut the door. When the engine started, he pictured Papá stubbing his cigarette out.

Promise me you'll leave this place the first chance you get.

A sob rattled in Rafael's chest, but he squeezed his fingers until his knuckles turned white.

❀

On the day of the funeral, El Charro sent a suit, new shoes, and a car to collect Rafael from his guest house. The driver took him to a building with a "Bolerama" sign flashing outside.

"Look at you. What a handsome boy." El Charro

signaled the man at the door to escort him to his booth. "I'm sorry about your parents."

Rafael didn't thank him for his condolences. They were dead because of him.

"Have something to eat." El Charro pushed a bowl of chilaquiles across the table. "It's going to be a long day. I don't know what you like, so I got you a little of everything."

All the dishes reminded Rafael of the cantina.

"Your father will be laid to rest a hero today. He took a bullet for me and did what no one had the balls to do. He killed Alfredo Zamora." El Charro assumed Rafael had left the cantina after Alfredo Zamora arrived. He had no idea Rafael had witnessed everything.

Rafael didn't know why he was pinning Alfredo Zamora's death on his father, when it was Miguel who shot him, but he knew enough not to contradict him.

"I look after those who are loyal to me," El Charro said. "Today, you become part of my family. I have a special gift for you. Come." He stood and waited for Rafael to follow.

Weaving through the billiard tables, he led him to the bowling lanes. There was no one else around except two of his men.

"Do you know how to bowl?" El Charro picked a ball and rolled it toward the pins, knocking down all but one.

Rafael shook his head.

"It's fun." He picked another ball and held it out. "You put your fingers like this, hold the ball here, then swing your arm back and release the ball. Let your hand follow through with the shot." He let the ball go and watched it head for the pins. "Don't worry about knocking those down. Just try to get the ball straight down the lane."

Handing Rafael a ball, he stepped aside.

"I want to see my parents." Rafael craved their faces.

"Do you think I emptied this place out on a whim?" El Charro replied. "This *is* for your parents."

Rafael didn't understand what he meant, but did as he instructed. His ball veered into the gutter.

"Try again." El Charro gave him another ball. Then another.

When Rafael had rolled the ball down the center of the lane a few times, El Charro called one of his men. "Pedro. The box."

Pedro brought a gift-wrapped box and placed it on the table.

"I promised you a gift," El Charro said. "Go ahead. Have a peek."

Untying the bow, Rafael opened the box. His stomach turned over.

"A masterpiece, isn't it?" El Charro grinned. "I asked Pedro to pour some pig's blood on it. Nothing like making a big splash." He laughed, slapping his palm on the table. "Now, here's what you have to do before we attend your parents' funeral."

Rafael kept his eyes on the back of the driver's seat and gripped the canvas bag into which El Charro transferred his gift. They picked up Miguel and drove to a place Rafael had never seen before.

"You know what to do." El Charro reminded him when they stopped outside a church. The spires were so tall, Rafael strained to see the tops through the window.

Fingers clenched around the bag, he nodded.

"Damian," El Charro addressed the boy Rafael referred to as Miguel. "You wait for him by the door."

The stairs leading into the church were wide and high. Rafael took one at a time until he was inside. The smell of aged wood and candles surrounded him. The priest stopped speaking as he marched down the aisle. Alfredo Zamora's photograph was propped in the front. His family and friends sat in the pews.

Pulling his severed head from the bag, Rafael sent it rolling down the aisle. It weighed the same as a bowling ball but made a sickening, thudding sound. Someone screamed when it came to a stop. The "C" carved into his forehead was crusted with blood.

"For my parents," Rafael repeated the words El Charro had coached him to say.

"Not many kids get to avenge their parents' death," he told Rafael. "Alfredo Zamora killed Camila and Juan Pablo. Now, you get to deliver his head to his memorial service. When you walk out of there, the scales of justice will be restored."

Rafael walked out to cries of "El Charro!", realizing he was nothing but a pawn in El Charro's game. He sent Rafael to the rival camp to warn those who tried to harm him. This was not about Rafael or his parents. They were all disposable in El Charro's world.

Rafael walked past Damian, who stared at him, then the chaos left in his wake. Sliding into the car, Rafael wiped his bloodied hands on his shirt and went back to gazing at a neutral spot. He didn't want El Charro to see any of the emotions overwhelming him. Pain. Despair. Rage. Horror.

"Well done, little rabbit." The smoke from El Charro's cigar was thick in the car. "One more funeral before the day is done. Let's go put your parents to rest."

It was stifling in the small church, but Rafael kept his jacket on to hide the blood on his shirt. Staring at his shoes, he forgot Papá wasn't by his side, and found himself aching for his nudge, calling him back to attention. When the wind caught his hair at the cemetery, Rafael thought of how he hated Mamá smoothing it down with her spit. Not having them by his side felt like someone had erased the parentheses that held him together. There was nothing to stop him from drifting into chaos.

"Rafael." Damian lay his hand on his shoulder.

Tearing his eyes from the soft earth where his parents lay buried, Rafael realized they were the only ones left in the cemetery.

"I'm so sorry." The sincerity in Damian's eyes relayed he was no stranger to loss. Pain recognizes pain; Damian's reached through the thick cloud of grief and embraced Rafael's.

"Camila and Juan Pablo were good to me," he said. "They were good people."

For the first time that day, a tear rolled down Rafael's face. He wiped it away with the back of his sleeve. If he had a younger brother, he would have held his hand, like Damian held Rafael's. Slowly, they walked to the car.

"Look at you two." El Charro rolled down the window as they approached. "You've already worked your way into my family, little rabbit."

Rafael knew that family meant something entirely different in El Charro's world. The cartel used kids to smuggle drugs and weapons, to kill, to spy, or to take the fall. Kids without family were the easiest to target. Rafael had no one left to look out for him.

"You get to pick a new name," El Charro said. "A cool name. A strong name. Tell me, what would you like to be called?"

"Rafael."

"You want to keep the same name?"

"It's the only thing I have that my parents gave me."

Wiping his sunglasses with a silk cloth, El Charro put them on and peered at him through whiskey-tinted lenses. "Do you know who the first Rafael was?"

"No, sir."

"God's own. Archangel Rafael." He laughed, slowly at first, then in surging, maniacal bursts. "The thing is..." He swung the door open for Rafael and Damian to get in. "There is no God where we're going. It's where boys go to become men. The next generation of *sicarios*, *halcones*, *traficantes*. The possibilities are endless. Find your strength and you'll find your place. A new world awaits you in Caboras."

As they rounded the intersection out of Paza del Mar, Rafael leaned his head out the window and looked back. Disjointed memories spiraled in his head. Mamá boiling milk in the kitchen. Warm rain on the window. The slap of wet denim on his face as they raced to take the laundry down. Sitting at Papá's feet, getting his hair dried with a towel. Spicy hot chocolate. Laughing at Papá's toenails. Laughing at the wet cat. Laughing. Laughing.

Rafael closed his eyes, letting the wind soothe his damp lashes. When he opened them again, he looked for the dome-shaped tree behind *La Sombra*. Beams of light slanted on branches that he had loved and climbed. And shared.

I'll wait for you, Lina said.

A flicker of hope surged through Rafael. He wasn't

alone. Lina was out there, his signpost in a desolate landscape.

As Paza del Mar receded from view, Rafael made a vow.

I will find you, Lina. Wherever you are, whatever it takes, I will find you.

PRESENT

Fourteen

"DO YOU RECOGNIZE THIS PERSON?" DETECTIVE Burke slid a printout across the table. "It's from security footage that we obtained the night of the incident."

Vee stared at it, but the face was blurry and pixelated.

"Maybe this will help." Detective Burke turned her screen toward her and played the recording.

Vee's pulse quickened as she watched a figure walk down her street. "That's her. That's the person I saw through the window. The hood. The raincoat. The same silhouette."

Detective Burke scrolled forward. "She disappears from the frame here, outside your home. Then she runs back out to the street a few minutes later. The time coincides with your statement. I was hoping you could identify her."

"I've never seen her before."

"Maybe your husband can come in and review the file. Is he back?"

"No, but I received a text from him."

"So, you've reconciled?"

Feeling like Detective Burke was taking mental notes on her marriage, Vee pushed her chair back and stood. "I'll let him know you're looking for him."

"No need. I'll get a hold of him myself." Detective Burke rose and ushered her to the door. With her hand on the handle, she paused. "I wonder, though... Should I be?"

"Should you be what?" Vee asked.

"Looking for your husband."

Before Vee could answer, a wave of morning sickness hit her. She clenched her teeth, waiting for it to pass.

Detective Burke studied her face. "Good day, Mrs. Roza."

She shut the door behind Vee, but Vee felt her piercing stare follow her all the way to the exit.

Fifteen

"Mr. Roza, this is Detective Laura Burke again. It's important that you call me back."

Laura left her number again and finished her coffee. Caffeine fueled her days. Insomnia plagued her nights. For all the cases she solved, her personal quest eluded her. At times, she was tempted to abandon it, but the pursuit of truth was like a pack of dogs gnashing at her heels.

Laura tossed her empty cup into the wastebasket and replayed the security footage she had just shown Vee. She prided herself on being able to read people, and something about Vee did not sit right with her. Scrolling to an earlier timeline, she paused and frowned.

"What the hell?" Noting the date stamp on the

footage, she referred to Vee's statement. The discrepancy was glaring.

Grabbing her phone, Laura called Rafael again. Once again, she was directed to his voice mail.

Hanging up, she made another call. "I need to track the location of a cell phone, and I need it right away. I believe one of my investigations just turned into a missing person's case."

Sixteen

"Is this the woman you saw with Rafael?" Vee unfolded the printout from the police station.

Jeanne put on her reading glasses and studied the image. "It's hard to tell."

"This is the person they caught on camera from the other night."

"And you think it's the woman Rafael brought home?"

"I don't know what to think. Maybe I'm making connections that aren't there."

"Stop agonizing over this. The police are on it, so let them do their job. Your job is to look after yourself and the baby." Jeanne put her glasses away and rose.

"Have you eaten since you got back? How about a turmeric latte?"

She turned on the stove and steeped the milk, humming softly.

"What is that tune you're always humming?" Vee asked.

"A lullaby I made up for my daughter." She stirred in honey and turmeric powder.

"It's beautiful."

"I'll teach you if you like. Fair warning, though. The words are a little grim. Like all the best fairy tales." She handed Vee a cup of golden milk. "Finish it. I'll make us something to eat."

"I remember the first time you made this for me." Jeanne's turmeric latte had seen Rafael and Vee through coughs, colds, and the heartbreak of repeated miscarriages.

"It took a while for you to get used to it." Jeanne chuckled. "Rafael loved it from the start."

"He poured it down the sink when you weren't looking."

"He did not."

"He didn't want to offend you."

"Rubbish." Jeanne plated some sandwiches and pulled up a chair. "I don't believe that."

"It's true, although we both love it now. When you moved in, we called you Queen Jeanne. The way you talked, the way you walked. We had bets on who could mimic your accent best, but we still can't get it right." Vee bit into her sandwich and gave it a shot. "Could you please pass the water?"

"Oh, fo fawk sakes. It's wotah. And don't talk with your mouth full." She shot Vee a stern look.

"See?" Vee grinned. "I never know with you."

"Oh, my darling girl." Jeanne laughed. "I could never be angry with you."

"Aren't you having any?" Vee asked.

"You know, if my daughter were alive, I'd want her to be exactly like you." Jeanne's mouth twitched as she bit into her sandwich. "You and Rafael are my family. And now there's a little one on the way. I can't wait until I'm done at the hospital."

"How much longer?"

"A few more weeks. The other nurses are throwing me a retirement party, but what I'd really like is a small celebration with you, Rafael, and some close friends."

Jeanne studied their ongoing chess game and advanced her knight.

Vee sat back and considered her move. She had yet to defeat Jeanne, but she was learning fast.

"I need to get going." Jeanne rose and placed her plate in the sink. "My shift starts in an hour."

"Would you mind getting rid of these for me?" Vee handed her a stash of amber vials. Seeing her antidepressants lined up next to the prenatal vitamins reminded Vee of all the times she'd failed to carry a baby to term. It was time to clean the slate. Even though the baby was no larger than a lima bean, Vee felt its presence every moment of the day.

"Of course, dear. I'll dispose of them at the hospital." About to let herself out, Jeanne motioned toward the chessboard. "I'll be back to checkmate you."

"Don't be so sure. I'm getting better every day."

"I'm going to beat you." Jeanne flashed a cheeky smile. "For the gazillionth time."

"That's not even a word."

Vee mulled over the chessboard after she left, but her thoughts kept straying. Walking into the sunroom, she looked out of the newly replaced window. A layer of jacaranda blooms covered Rafael's car.

So your husband left on foot after your argument?

Why Rafael stormed off without his car was a mystery. Especially in the middle of a thunderstorm.

Unless... Vee's breath caught. *Unless someone picked him up.*

Pieces of a puzzle she didn't want to put together were becoming impossible to ignore.

Studying the printout, Vee gazed at the blurred planes of the woman's face.

Was she the one? Did all the heartache send Rafael running into her arms? When did the end of their marriage begin?

PAST

Seventeen

THE SECOND TIME RAFAEL FELL IN LOVE, HE WAS twenty-four. His gift with numbers was the only reason he survived El Charro. Life in San Diego was a far cry from his cartel days, but he still woke up drenched in sweat. He had unfinished business in Paza del Mar, and until that was sorted, his demons continued to haunt him. He met Raven on one of his trips to Mexico. With hair the color of a moonless night, she was whiskey kisses and twisted sheets. Intense, unsettling, and corrosive.

She captivated Rafael the moment she strutted onto the stage, a tank top knotted tight under her breasts. Wearing shorts and military boots, she was flashes of glistening skin under a smoky spotlight.

"That one is off-limits," the bartender said. "Arturo

Bernal's woman. But if anyone else catches your eye..."
He gestured toward the other ladies in the dimly lit space.

"I'm here for a meeting with Arturo, but your boss is late." Rafael glanced at his watch.

"Nice piece." The bartender assessed its value. "I'll give Señor Bernal a call. Who shall I say is here?"

"Rafael Roza."

The girl on stage bent forward and caressed her skin, thigh to ankle. Every man in the room was mesmerized as she undid her boots. She was an alchemist, transforming the mundane into magic. With laces loosened, she flipped her head, tossing her hair in the air. As it settled around her shoulders, the doors flung open. Daylight flooded the bar with its harsh glare.

Before Rafael could blink, chaos erupted. Armed men stormed inside and fanned out, scanning the room with their guns. Panic rippled through the bar. In a scramble for safety, a woman rushed toward the exit.

"No one leaves." One of the men intercepted her. "Calm down or we shut you up permanently."

Grabbing his captive by the hair, the man spun her around. "Tell me, which one is Raven." When she didn't answer, he tightened his hold. "Someone show me Raven or you all die, starting with her."

The girls exchanged looks but said nothing.

"Loyalty among whores?" He laughed. "Have it your way."

"Let her go." The girl on stage intervened. "I'm Raven." She retied the laces on her boots.

"Good girl. Walk over to me. Nice and easy." When Raven was within arm's reach, he let go of his hostage and clamped his arm around Raven's neck. Holding a gun to her head, he retreated toward the door.

From the corner of his eye, Rafael caught the

bartender reach under the counter. A shot whizzed by, splattering the bartender's blood on amber bottles of liquor. He dropped the gun and fell, clutching the wound on his neck.

A high-pitched ringing filled Rafael's ears. The sound of gunshot incapacitated him. He squeezed his eyes, but all he saw was Mamá and Papá's blood collecting in the grooves of the cantina floor. Grappling with the crushing weight in his chest, he flexed his fingers and focused on them instead.

"Move out." The man dragging Raven away instructed his team.

As they filed past Rafael, Raven's eyes locked on him. She motioned toward the gun the bartender had dropped on the counter. It was inches from Rafael. All he had to do was lean forward and retrieve it, but he remained frozen. A flash of loathing crossed her eyes. A man who literally wouldn't lift a finger to save her.

As she stumbled past a table, Raven grabbed an ashtray and flung the ashes in her captor's face. Momentarily disarming him, she swung the ashtray in a wide arc and slammed it into his throat. He clutched his neck and let go. Charging toward Rafael, Raven slid across the counter and swiped the gun.

"Don't." She pointed the muzzle at the only other armed man in the room. The rest had moved out when orders were given. "Arturo will kill you. Then he'll hunt down your whole family, one by one." Holding him at bay, she moved toward the back exit.

"If I don't bring you in, my boss will do the same." The man kept his pistol on her.

They measured each other, fingers ready on the trigger.

"No one wants to hurt you," the man said. "Arturo

skipped a payment. He brings the money, we let you go. It's a simple exchange."

Raven held her ground.

Closer to Rafael, the man she brought down with the ashtray staggered to his feet. "Get back in here," he alerted the rest of the team.

"Drop the gun." His buddy inched toward Raven. "You can't escape."

"Run, *bonita!*" A customer smashed a bottle over the guy's head.

Grabbing the split-second opportunity, Raven bolted for the back door. Rafael caught a glimpse of her silhouette against the afternoon light as it shut behind her. Chunky boots, toned legs, a glossy curtain of hair swinging behind her as she sprinted away.

Eighteen

RAFAEL GOT INTO HIS CAR, DROPPED HIS BRIEFCASE IN the passenger seat, and let out a deep breath. The piercing note in his ears subsided to a whooshing sensation, but his head throbbed with pain.

"Drive." A woman spoke from the back seat.

Startled, his eyes darted to the rearview mirror.

"You should lock your car if you don't like surprises." Raven leaned forward, pressing a gun into the back of his seat.

"Where to?" Rafael turned on the ignition.

"Make a left at the end of the street and keep driving." She crouched lower when they got to the traffic lights.

"They're gone," he said.

"They're never gone. They'll keep coming until Arturo squares up his debt."

"You should call Arturo."

"Screw Arturo. Screw them all. Keep driving."

Taking the road that ringed the bay, Rafael headed toward the mountains. Houses and shops grew sparser between palm-fringed views of the ocean. As they climbed higher, ancient trees formed a giant canopy above them. Trucks hauling sugar cane from the fields lumbered by in the opposite direction.

When Rafael turned into a winding driveway paved with crushed stones, Raven jolted to action.

"Get back on the road." The muzzle of her gun pressed into his temple as a small villa came into view. "Now."

"I won't drive aimlessly until you figure things out." Rafael parked and turned the engine off. "You're in trouble, and I'm in the middle of a business deal with Arturo. Come inside and call him. If those thugs are after you because he owes them money, he needs to sort it out. You won't be safe until that's resolved." Grabbing his briefcase, Rafael got out, planting one foot on the ground. "If you plan on shooting, this would be a good time."

Their gazes locked and held.

"You're not a killer," he said.

"You're wrong."

The stillness in her eyes sent a chill down his spine. Then, as they stared at each other, something strange happened. Little sparks started flickering on Rafael's inner screen. Shifting focus, he gazed at her through it. The points of light mapped out like stardust across her face.

"I'll take my chances." He exited the car and walked into the house.

A few moments later, the squeak of rubber-soled boots followed him into the kitchen.

"For a man who couldn't lift a gun to help a girl out, you've got balls."

Rafael poured two shots of whiskey and slid one across the counter. "I don't know about you, but I could use a drink."

She gulped it down and scanned the space. "Nice setup."

Rafael's best option was to contact Arturo and tell him she was with him, but it was her call to make. She wandered through the house, room by room, while he made dinner. After a while, he heard the shower running.

"Raven?" He plated the food, but she didn't respond.

Walking into the bedroom, he picked up a trail of clothes—shorts, wispy underwear, a scrunched-up top, one boot discarded by the foot of the bed, another by the shower stall. The curtains were drawn, but the bathroom light illuminated her sleeping form. Wet strands soaked the pillow as she slept, elbow tucked in the dip of her waist. Scrubbed free of makeup, she looked soft and vulnerable.

Rafael put her things away and retrieved his briefcase. Punching in the passcode, he opened the safe and transferred the cash. He stacked the bundles neatly and tossed the empty briefcase into the closet.

"You had all that money on you when those men burst into the bar?"

"You're up." He shut the safe.

"And they thought I was their cash ticket." She laughed and propped herself up. "This is the business deal you were talking about? With Arturo?"

"We signed off on the deal already, but Arturo wanted

something extra on the side, something off the record. I was there to fulfill my end of our agreement."

"And his end of the agreement?"

"He sold me a cantina he owns." It had taken fourteen years, but Rafael finally had *La Sombra*—the cantina his parents ran, the home where he grew up, the courtyard where Mamá's dresses fluttered on the clothesline.

"A cantina." Raven seemed relieved but bolted upright when the doorbell chimed. Clutching the sheet to her chest, she shot Rafael a wary look. "Are you expecting someone?"

"Stay here. I'll see who it is."

When Rafael returned, the sheets were tossed aside, and the bed was empty. He opened the safe and got his passport. As he turned to leave, he caught Raven's reflection in the mirror. Wearing one of his shirts, she was pressed up behind the door, clutching her gun. Damp hair, bare legs, buttons undone. Smooth skin against crisp cotton.

"It's the police," Rafael informed her.

Her body tensed. For a second, it looked like she was about to bolt. Then she slumped against the wall. "It was only a matter of time. I didn't think they'd come for me so soon."

"They're not here for you. They're here about the incident at the bar. They want to see my ID, but maybe you should talk to them."

Raven shook her head. "They could be working for the guys who tried to kidnap me."

"Suit yourself."

After the police left, Rafael returned to the bedroom and put his passport back in the safe.

"You didn't tell them I was here." She stepped out from behind the door and twisted her hair into a knot.

"They didn't ask." Her simplest moves turned Rafael on.

"You're not from around here." She circled him. "You have an American passport."

"I was born in Mexico, but I live in San Diego."

"You like it there?" She flicked an imaginary speck of dust from his shoulder, her fingers lingering.

"My father told me to leave the first chance I got. I'm keeping the promise I made to him." His skin prickled as her breath fanned the back of his neck.

They were dancing around a charged field. One wrong move and Rafael would be sucked into her world.

"Are you ready to call Arturo?" he asked.

"Later." She took her time coming around to face him. "I'm famished, and something smells absolutely irresistible."

Rafael broke free of the sultry web she was weaving around him and led her to the dining room. "You don't mind if I watch TV, do you?" He needed the distraction to keep his head straight. She was Arturo's girl. He'd do well to remember it.

A few bites into their meal, they froze at the mention of his name.

Eyes glued to the anchorwoman on the evening news, Raven dropped her fork and walked toward the television.

"Local business owner, Arturo Bernal, was found dead in his home following a shooting at one of his establishments earlier today. Eyewitnesses say a gang of armed men swarmed the place in an attempt to kidnap a member of his staff. One person sustained a fatal gunshot wound."

The news channel switched to another story, but Raven kept staring at the screen. She took a step back and sank into the couch.

"Arturo is dead." She hunched over and buried her head in her hands.

Rafael sat beside her as she slowly fell apart. Sobs wracked her body.

"I'm sorry." The pain of losing a loved one was unbearable. Rafael still felt a deep hollow where Mamá and Papá once lived.

"You don't get it." She turned her tear-streaked face to him. "He's gone. It's over. I'm finally free."

"Your boyfriend was abusive?" She wasn't sobbing. She was crying with relief.

"Boyfriend?" Her laughter was laced with irony. "Arturo wasn't my boyfriend. He owned me." Tucking her legs under, she sat back and clasped her hands.

"Nine years." She had a faraway look on her face when she spoke. "I was fourteen when I met him. A runaway. Over the moon at having landed a job at his father's restaurant. On my second day, Arturo came into the kitchen and told me I was too pretty to be washing dishes. He was eighteen—handsome, worldly, and charming. He brought me candles, hand lotion, nail polish— things I couldn't afford. He looked out for me, held my hand, made me feel like I was the most beautiful thing in the world. He told his father he wanted to marry me.

"I didn't stand a chance. I was young and naïve—fifteen, when I got pregnant. That was the first time Arturo hit me. He drove me to see a woman who performed abortions from her home. I remember the smell of open sewers, the plaster peeling off the walls, the rusty instruments on her tray. I saw Yolanda three more times after that. She told me Arturo brought all his girls there. He came from a family of sex-traffickers that pass their tricks on from generation to generation. First you find a vulnerable target, then you charm, isolate, abuse, reward, lie, beg, coerce, mistreat...whatever it takes to break them.

"When I tried to leave, Arturo drove me to the multi-storied homes his family owned—pink and tangerine buildings with barricaded windows and finials shaped like angels. They force the women inside to service clients. If they have children, the kids get used as leverage. Arturo promised to hunt me down and lock me up with them if I ever left him.

"He kept me for himself, but he whipped me back in line whenever I got too gutsy. His father told him the best way to control me was to get me pregnant again. By then, I was taking birth control pills. When he found out, I ended up with a busted lip and broken ribs. Afterward, he begged for forgiveness, claiming he only did it because I made him look like a fool in his father's eyes. He swore I was the only woman he loved. His favorite. His life. His soul. All that changed when I refused to have his baby. He made me dance on stage. He got off seeing men lust after me. The hotter they were for me, the bigger he felt having me on his arm.

"Three days ago, Yolanda called. She botched up an abortion and couldn't stop the bleeding. I rushed over, but the girl was already dead. She was sixteen. One of Arturo's recruits."

Raven pointed the remote at the TV and turned it off. "Arturo asked me to go over to his place that night. He needed consoling for all the effort he put into a lost asset. When I got there, he had his kit out—all the stuff he needed to shoot up. He asked me to inject the heroin. I'd done it before, but that night, I pumped more into him than I should have. He signaled for help, and when I didn't intervene, he realized it wasn't an accident. He reached for his gun, but I got to it first. I was terrified. If he survived, he wouldn't just kill me. He would make me suffer the rest of my life.

"I backed off, but he kept crawling toward me. When his fingers wrapped around my ankle, I pulled the trigger and took off, not knowing if he was dead or alive."

Crawling to Rafael's side of the couch, Raven curled up beside him and drew her knees into her torso. "I killed Arturo three days ago. I haven't stopped looking over my shoulder since then."

Nineteen

RAVEN FELL ASLEEP ON THE COUCH—THE EXHAUSTED slumber that follows an emotional outpouring. Not wanting to disturb her, Rafael closed his eyes and drifted off.

Sometime during the night, she woke in unfamiliar surroundings and panicked. Rafael reached out to reassure her, but she lashed out in defense.

"I'm sorr—" The words died on her lips as he scooped her up and carried her into the bedroom.

"Sleep." Tucking the covers around her, Rafael turned to leave.

"Stay." She grabbed his wrist.

Rafael hesitated, but only for a beat. Sliding next to her, he turned on his side and found her watching him.

"Do you think they've figured out that I shot Arturo? With his own gun? I should get rid of it." Her thoughts unraveled in the dark. "It won't make any difference in the end. There is no happy ending for women like me."

Pain flickered in her eyes before the thick curtain of her lashes came down. When she met Rafael's gaze again, it was replaced with defiance. "They can have my body, but they'll never touch my spirit."

A slew of emotions hit Rafael as she slid into his arms.

"Can you do something for me?" She lifted her face to him. "Tomorrow, I'll go back to that world, but tonight, can you pretend you care?"

Throttling the dizzying need to consume her, Rafael gathered her close. When his lips grazed the crown of her head instead of her mouth, she pulled back. He smoothed the hair from her face and followed its length down her back. Her eyes widened when he didn't stray further. With each stroke, she softened. After a while, she buried her nose in the crook of his neck and surrendered to the feeling of being held.

When Rafael woke up the next morning, she was gone.

"Raven?" He searched the house, but she was nowhere to be found.

Pouring a cup of coffee, Rafael scrolled through the financial news. His thoughts kept getting side-swept by an undercurrent of disappointment. Raven left without saying goodbye. All Rafael saw when he looked at his screen was the musk-rose flush of her lips.

When his phone rang, he was grateful for the interruption.

"Damian." Rafael pulled up the portfolio he was monitoring for him. "We're almost there."

"How much longer?"

"Six months, maybe a year."

"Good. I can't wait to take the bastard down."

"We'll have his company. His personal finances may be another matter."

"I'll figure it out when we get there, but that's not the reason I called."

"No?" For as long as Rafael could remember, Damian had one burning quest in his life—to destroy the man who had taken everything away from him, a man who scarred him before El Charro got to them.

"I called to congratulate the new owner of *La Sombra*."

"Thanks." Like Damian, Rafael was working on his own bucket list. "Drinks tonight?"

"Make it Friday. I'm fixing up my new boat, courtesy of my investment advisor."

"You're not listening to your investment advisor. I suggested a suit, a tie, and a decent haircut."

"Who needs that when you've got the sun, the sea, and a fishing rod?"

"Living the dream, huh?" Rafael grinned, then grew serious. "I still have nightmares about El Charro's ranch. If it wasn't for you..."

"I'll always have your back, Rafael."

"And I'll always have yours."

Hanging up, Rafael squeezed his eyes shut and waited for the memories to subside.

When the glass door to the terrace opened, he spun around.

"Good morning." Raven wiped the sand off her feet and stepped inside.

"You're still here." Relief rippled through Rafael.

"You still haven't turned me in." With his shirt tucked into her shorts, she crossed the floor and stole his coffee. "I went for a walk." Hopping onto the counter, bare legs dangling over the edge, she pinned him with a sultry stare. Flecks of seaweed clung to her ankles.

"Breakfast?" Rafael poured himself another cup of coffee. He wanted nothing more than to taste the salt on her skin.

"I'll look after it." She placed a pan on the stove. "You look like you're in the middle of something."

"Work." Rafael circled back to his laptop while she rummaged through the fridge.

"Cantina stuff?" She cracked an egg and glanced over her shoulder.

"No, the cantina I bought from Arturo is a personal project."

"So, what kind of work do you do?"

"I'm an analyst for a wealth management firm. Market research, stocks, bonds, financial models. That kind of thing."

"You must be good with numbers."

"You could say that." Rafael smiled. His brain was wired for it. He could pick up patterns before they affected prices. One look at a company's indices and he knew whether to buy, sell, or hold. After graduation, he invested in the financial market and built a portfolio with a stellar track record. Rafael was making a killing, and every investor wanted in on the ride.

"Shall we sit outside?" Raven carried their plates to the terrace.

High on a cliff, with steps traversing to the beach, it had boundless views—from the rainforest-carpeted mountains to the ocean below.

"It's beautiful here." Raven scanned the beaches glimmering around the bay. Bougainvillea and cactus dotted the landscape. "Not many rentals like this in the area."

"It's not a rental. I bought it when I closed the deal on the cantina."

"I thought you live in San Diego."

"I do, but I fell in love with this place the moment I saw it." Rafael's father had been robbed of his dream, but his words remained etched in Rafael's soul.

I want to give her the world, to make all her dreams come true: a home on a hill, from where she can watch sunsets and never have to put on an apron again.

"You always get what you want?" Raven regarded him over the rim of her mug.

He wanted her, and she knew it.

"You intrigue me." She speared a grape and popped it in her mouth.

"How so?" Every nerve in Rafael's body crackled around her.

"You could have taken what you wanted last night— what we both wanted—but you didn't."

"I was tempted. I won't deny it. But my thoughts are occupied by someone else."

"She must be very special." Raven reached for his hand and stroked it.

Rafael's pulse leaped at her touch, but he pulled away. "She is. Always has been, and always will be."

"I've never met a man I couldn't seduce. Until you. She's a lucky girl." Her lips were soft as they grazed his cheek. She rose and started clearing the table. "I'll get out of your hair. It will look suspicious if I go missing right after Arturo's death."

"You think that's a good idea?" Rafael followed her

into the kitchen. "The guys that came after you are still out there, and the investigation is ongoing."

A round of sharp knocks on the front door stopped them in their tracks.

"Go." Rafael motioned toward the bedroom. "Stay there until I come and get you."

More rapping followed. Rafael waited until Raven was out of sight before opening the door.

"Rafael Roza?" the man on the other side asked.

"Yes."

"Martín Bernal. Arturo's older brother."

"Is the doorbell not working?"

"You heard about Arturo's death?" He walked into the house.

"It was on the news last night."

"Not everything makes it on the news." Martín held out a photo of Raven. "Have you seen this woman?"

"Yes. She was at the bar yesterday."

"She was also the last person to see Arturo alive. His neighbor saw her leave his place in a hurry, you know? The autopsy puts his death around the same time. Whether someone put her up to it or not, this bitch killed my brother. When I smoke her out of wherever she's hiding, she's going to wish she died with him."

Martín walked to the counter and picked up a cup. "You have company." He sniffed it, picked up the other one, and did the same. "You should know I'm like a bloodhound. Once I pick up a scent, I follow it through. I'll leave this here to jog your memory." Smoothing Raven's photo over the chopping board, he staked it with a knife.

"Oh, and one more thing." He paused at the door. "If I find anyone protecting her, I'll skin him alive."

Rafael waited until he got into his car and drove away.

"Everything all right?" Raven asked when he walked into the bedroom.

"That was Martín Bernal. I thought he was here to collect the cash I had for Arturo, but apparently Arturo kept our side deal to himself."

"Martín was here for me." She sat on the bed, her knees giving out. "He knows."

"You have to get out of town. The sooner, the better."

"And go where? Arturo's family has eyes everywhere."

"Then leave the country. Lay low. Do whatever you need to shake them off."

"Spoken like a man with choices." Raven laughed with no trace of humor.

"There was a time I didn't have any either." Rafael thought of the time his life belonged to El Charro.

"I'm sorry," she replied. "You've shown me nothing but kindness, and now you're in the line of fire because of me. If Martín finds out I'm here, he'll come after you too."

"He knows someone else is here, but he doesn't know who. I'm on his radar, though, so whatever we do, he'll be watching."

Silence stretched as they played out all the ways things could end.

"What are you doing?" Raven asked when Rafael reached for his phone.

"I'm getting you out of here. Martín won't stop until he finds you. As long as you're in Mexico, you're in danger."

Twenty

"TOMORROW." RAFAEL TORE OFF THE NOTE AND circled the address. "We'll get your passport photos before we head here."

"You think it'll work?"

"If Damian says this guy is the best, then no one will be able to tell you're traveling with fake documents."

"Your friend has a pulse on people like that?"

"There was a time when *we* were people like that."

"You? I don't believe it."

"We worked for El Charro."

"Yeah, right. You wouldn't even touch that gun to help me out."

"Guilty as charged. It's a good thing El Charro had other uses for me."

"I remember the headlines when he and all the key players in his organization came down."

"I was there when it happened."

"You survived?" She shook her head in wonder. "You must have been very young."

"I was fourteen. But that's another story, Damian's story. I was along for the ride and let me tell you, it was one hell of a ride. I was lucky Damian looked out for me and saw me through business school. The point is, I got out, and so can you."

Raven stared at the note on the table. The plan was for them to leave on different days, for different places. Rafael caught a flash of loneliness in her eyes when she looked up, the kind that sneaks up when it's least expected.

"Don't mind me." A hint of sadness tinged her smile. "I'm just a sucker for green eyes." Averting her gaze, she scrolled through the flight list. "So, where shall I go?"

"Anywhere you like. Just say the word and I'll book the ticket."

"I'll pay you back. As soon as I'm on my feet."

"You can pay me back by staying safe." Rafael rose and collected his keys. "I have to take care of something. Think you can stay out of trouble until I'm back?"

"I'll be an angel." She shot him a sassy look.

"I mean it. Stay put."

Rafael drove to Paza del Mar with flashbacks of the night before—the velvet warmth of Raven's skin, the surge of her breasts against his body, her hair spilling over his arms.

Rubbing his eyes, he laughed. He'd spent the entire night fighting the urge to touch her.

The steps to *La Sombra* were worn with time. Cement peeked through flaking paint. The fish shop next door still had the same fly zapper over its display. On the other side, Tía Maria's house stared blankly through boarded-up windows. Sadness squeezed Rafael's heart as he stepped inside the cantina. It no longer smelled like Mamá's cooking.

"Señor Roza." Alma and Carlos, the couple that ran *La Sombra*, greeted him. "We hope you've come hungry." They led him to a table covered with dishes.

"You went to a lot of trouble," Rafael said.

"A sample of what's on the menu."

"It looks wonderful. Please." Rafael gestured to the chairs. "Sit."

"Señor Roza..." They glanced nervously at each other. "We've worked at *La Sombra* for many years."

"I'm not here to replace you."

Alma shot Carlos a relieved look.

"I didn't buy this place to run it. I just want to reclaim a part of my history. I asked to meet you because I had something else on my mind. When was the last time you took a vacation?"

"Señor?"

"I spent the first ten years of my life here. My parents never took a day off. You have a son around the same age as I was when I left Paza del Mar. Take him to the mountains. Show him the beaches. I'm giving you a paid leave. Rest. Relax. When you come back, pick up where you left off."

"Thank you. That's very generous of you."

"It's not completely selfless. While you're away, I'll

have the contractors come in to renovate the place. I'd also like to rename it *Camila's* in honor of my mother's memory. If there's anything particular you'd like, we can discuss it."

"We have many suggestions." Carlos grinned, at ease about his family's future. "You might regret asking."

"Let the man enjoy his lunch," Alma chided. "Please, dig in before it gets cold."

They left to attend to their customers. Picking up his fork, Rafael took his first bite of Carlo and Alma's cooking.

Papá came inside and lay his cigarettes down. Mamá walked out of the kitchen, untied her apron, and draped it over the chair. Holding hands, they stood in the doorway, their silhouettes framed in the light. For a few moments, they gazed out silently. Then Papá turned to Mamá, his face glowing with tenderness. Smiling, they disappeared into the sunshine.

The sounds from the street seeped back in. Rafael sat for a while, at peace. When he rose and walked into the kitchen, he no longer felt he was trailing blood over the floor.

"Mind if I look around?" he asked.

"You barely ate." Alma glanced at his table. "Something wrong?"

"Quite the opposite. It was exactly what I needed, but I'll take it to go."

While Alma filled the takeout containers, Rafael got re-acquainted with the kitchen. Walking into the storage room, his eyes fell on a half-open, dusty box.

"Everything okay, Señor Roza?" Carlos popped in.

"Call me Rafael." He dragged the box out of the corner and wiped the dust off. "If you have no use for this record player, I'll take it."

"Of course." Carlos held the door to the alley open so he could load it into his car. "And this just arrived for you." He handed Rafael another box.

"Thank you." Rafael put both in the trunk and went back inside the cantina. "There's a car parked on the street." He pointed it out to Carlos. "It's been following me all day."

Carlos studied the driver. "He works for the Bernals."

"I thought so. Martín Bernal put a tail on me."

"Would you like me to distract him?"

"No. I was counting on him to do just that." Rafael dropped the vinyl slat of the window blinds. "There's just one more thing before I go."

The fountain was dry, its tiers ringed with grime and dead leaves. The courtyard looked smaller, but the crown of the tree was wider, casting a mosaic of shadows. The branches Rafael scaled almost touched the ground. He picked up one of the tamarind seeds on the ground and held it in the palm of his hand.

A boy placed it over his front tooth and grinned.

A girl giggled through her nose.

"I miss you so much, it hurts," Rafael said to the glossy black seed.

His throat seized whenever he thought of Lina.

"I'll see you in a few weeks."

It was a promise he never kept. A few weeks turned to ten, then fifty, then a hundred. By the time he was free of El Charro, Rafael had lost trail of Lina. He'd pulled himself from branch to branch, city to city, but the view from the top was desolate without her. She was the fleeting bloom of the vining cactus, coiled around the notches of his memory.

Reclaiming *La Sombra* wasn't just about getting his home back. It was also about getting back a piece of Lina.

I'll wait for you, she said.

"I'll wait for you too." He traced a stem, hoping that one day she would come to *La Sombra*, if only to call out the boy who broke his promise.

Twenty-One

A BLUE TRUCK FOLLOWED RAFAEL UP THE MOUNTAINS as he drove from Paza del Mar. When he turned home, it lumbered by, slowing at the bend in the road. Tucked under a canopy of trees, another car flashed its lights at the driver as he drove by.

Martín Bernal had two men tailing Rafael. One followed him from *La Sombra,* and the other was stationed outside his villa.

"Raven?" He swung the door open. When she didn't answer, he dropped the boxes and raced to the bedroom. "Raven?" he checked the bathroom, the study, the kitchen. Looking out to the terrace, he came to a halt. Raven stood barefoot, holding a pair of scissors. Her dark strands scattered around her like fallen leaves.

Rafael slid the door open and stepped out.

"What do you think?" She turned around, rubbing her palm over the shorn clumps.

He stared, speechless.

"That bad?" She laughed.

Handing him the scissors, she walked inside and assessed her reflection in the bathroom mirror. With a strange gleam in her eyes, she traced the outline of her butchered hair in the glass.

"My hair was easier to grab when it was long, so Arturo never let me cut it. He could drag me across the floor, rip it out by the roots, and no one would know. He doesn't have a hold on me anymore." She stepped back from the mirror, a little unsteady.

"Have you been drinking?" Rafael asked.

"I'm fine, but you're out of whiskey." She gave him a lop-sided grin.

He steered her to the couch and moved the boxes out of the way.

"What did you bring?" she asked.

"Food." He opened one of the takeout containers. "Clothes." He gestured toward the box delivered to the cantina. "Short notice, but I think you'll find what you need."

"You don't like me in your shirt?" she teased, popping the buttons open, one by one.

"I like you just fine." *Understatement of the year.* "Here." He handed her a takeout container. She was tipsy as hell. "Get some food in you."

"What about you?" She sat, resting it on her lap.

"I want to see if this record player still works." He plugged it in and lifted the dust cover. The record Mamá and Papá danced to was still on the turntable. Rafael lowered the stylus, turned up the volume, and walked to the terrace.

The last rays of the sun were soft on his face. Beaches cooled in the shadow of the mountains. He closed his eyes as a melancholic ballad played, the dust and scratches filling him with nostalgia. He saw the gauzy fabric of Lina's wings, Mamá's toes curling in her sandals when El Charro spotted him, the fury in Papá's eyes when he skipped the exam. His throat clenched with the bittersweet beauty of fleeting, ordinary moments.

Heading back in, Rafael stopped in his tracks. Another moment seared itself on the pages of his memory: Raven dancing, a fork in one hand and a takeout container in the other. Eyes half-closed, she moved to the music, lips gleaming with grease and spice. Buttons undone to her navel, she was bare-thighed sensuality, swaying between despair and defiance.

She caught him staring and joined him outside, her movements slow and slinky. Keeping a sliver of space between them, she danced around him, a spinning coin in a tilted universe. Her nearness was overwhelming. Rafael's skin prickled each time her body shifted. Flushed and breathless, she paused and scraped the bottom of the takeout container.

"Last bite." She offered it to him.

The air crackled as they faced each other.

Rafael's phone buzzed, but he remained motionless. When it rang a second time, he glanced at the screen.

"Yes?" he answered. Everything else fell away as he waited for the voice at the other end.

"We have a hit on Evelina Flores," the man said.

A ringing impulse of hope flared in Rafael's chest. Over the years, he had cast a wide net for her, but all he knew of the couple that picked her up was their last name and the car they drove. That, and the lack of accurate records thwarted him at every turn, so he hired a team of investigators to help him.

"Tell me." Rafael walked to the edge of the terrace and steeled himself.

"One of my guys found school records in Tecolán. The timeline coincides with the information you gave us. A property search of the area led us to a home belonging to Hector and Teresa Morales."

"Good work." He calculated how long it would take for him to get there. "Are they still there?"

"Rafael..."

He held his breath. Years of tracking Lina hinged on what came next.

"The house is no more. It burned to the ground. I'm sorry, Rafael. Lina died in the fire with Hector Morales. Teresa Morales made it to the hospital but didn't survive. The neighbors said that..."

The man's voice drifted off as a curtain of darkness fell around Rafael. All the lights guiding his inner screen shut down. All the shapes drifted off.

"Are you okay?" Raven asked.

Rafael blinked, bringing her back into focus. His phone buzzed with a disconnected line.

"She's gone," he said.

"Who's gone?"

Rafael stared blankly, without responding.

"The person you were talking about?" Raven followed him inside, but he needed to be alone.

Shutting the bathroom door, he stripped and stepped into the shower. When the first icy blast hit, Rafael bowed his head to its numbing grace. His Bumblebee Girl was no more. The ray of hope he woke up to each morning was snuffed out forever. The pain was as sharp as a punch to his gut. Resting his hands on either side of the panel, he let the water cascade over him. As the temperature warmed, steam rose and condensed around him.

The door to the shower stall slid open. Raven stepped inside. Wrapping her arms around him, she hugged him from behind, her cheek between his shoulder blades. For a while, it was enough—two broken pieces fitting into each other's edges. Then her lips grazed his skin. Rafael sucked in his breath and turned the water off. She licked his earlobe, pressing her breasts into his back.

Rafael spun around and pulled her close. Their lips met, urgent and demanding. She fell back against the wall as he explored her back, her waist, her hips. When he lifted her, she clasped her legs around his hips. He carried her to bed and lost himself in her embrace.

Raven stirred against him, nestling her feet between his. Somewhere between the first kiss and the heady rush of release, they started moving like partners in a dance that was instinctually familiar. Each touch, each turn, built up to the perfect rhythm.

"I knew." Raven traced his collarbone. "Even in the beginning, when Arturo was trying to win me over. I knew it wasn't the way sex should be. The bed was always a place of negotiation."

Rafael drew her in, tucking her closer.

"If I kept even one girl from Arturo's clutches, it was worth it. Even if they get me."

"No one's going to get you."

"Don't make promises you can't keep."

"My plan is foolproof."

Pulling her head back, she gazed at him. "I'm listening."

"Martín is having me followed. He also has someone watching the house. We can use that to our advantage. Tomorrow, we'll take the stairs to the beach. A car will pick us up from the resort down the bay. We'll get your passport photos taken and meet the guy preparing your travel documents. From there, I'll drop you off at the marina. Damian docks his boat there. You can lay low until it's time for your flight. We can't book anything until we have your papers."

"But Martín knows someone is here with you. He's waiting to see who."

"Tomorrow, after I drop you at the marina, I'm meeting someone at the resort. We'll walk back to the house. In the evening, we'll step out. I'll make a show of taking her out for dinner. Martín's men will report back that it's not you. My return flight to San Diego is the day after. I'm sticking to my itinerary, so it won't raise any flags."

"What if they talk to her? The woman you're bringing to your place?"

"She knows what to say. She's classy, expensive, and discreet. Her story will check out."

Raven thought it through. "It's a good plan. Now all I have to do is figure out where to go."

"Pick a big city, somewhere no one can find you. When the heat is off, I'll come and get you."

Her eyes flew up, searching his face. "I thought we were going separate ways."

"I want to see more of you." Lina's death had ripped a hole in Rafael's heart. Being around Raven made him feel alive again.

"You don't even know my name."

"Your name's not Raven?"

"Raven is my stage name."

"So tell me." He stroked her midnight-black hair. The cropped length exposed the bones of her face.

"What's the point? Tomorrow, my name will be whatever it says on the passport. I'd rather be her. Unsoiled and untainted. I'd rather you call me by her name."

Rafael brushed a kiss across her forehead. "Get some sleep. Tomorrow's a big day."

She settled into his arms, but her lashes rose and fell against his skin.

"Tell me about her," she said.

"About whom?"

"Whoever's got you so torn up."

"She was my first love. My first kiss." Rafael closed his eyes and saw Lina standing on the curb, a suitcase by her side. "She moved away, but I never stopped searching. Turns out, she died years ago. She died thinking that like everyone else, I abandoned her."

Everybody leaves. And they never say goodbye. One day, you'll leave too.

"Love is a bitch." Raven propped her head on her elbow and traced his brow. "It stings when someone hurts you, and it stings when you hurt someone. But I have to say..." Her gaze roved over his body. "I'm not the slightest bit sorry for whatever led up to this." Throwing her leg over his hip, she snuggled into his chest.

"I just realized," she said, as they drifted off to sleep. "I don't know your name either."

"It's Rafael. My name is Rafael Roza."

When Rafael reached for her in the morning, she was gone. Glancing at his watch, he smiled. She had a thing for early morning walks, and it was starting to show.

Slipping into jeans and a T-shirt, he walked into the living room and tried the terrace door. Just as he expected, it was unlocked. Rafael turned on the coffee machine and made breakfast. When it was done, he set up the patio table. The air was crisp with the promise of a new day. Warm rays kissed the tops of mountains. The ocean colored under the rising sun.

Firing up his laptop, he completed his morning scan through the financial markets, then sat back. Raven was taking her time. The coffee was cold, and they had to leave soon. Leaning over the balcony, he searched the beach, but he was too far up to locate her. With one eye on the steps leading up to the terrace, he made his calls. Half an hour later, Rafael paced the floor. Something was wrong.

About to check if Martín's man was still outside, he grabbed his keys, then glanced back at the table. The note with the passport forger's address was gone. Rafael rushed to the bedroom and lifted Raven's pillow. Her gun was gone. He scanned the room and froze. The safe was open and all the money was gone.

Raven had taken off. She had enough cash to buy a new identity, get out of the country, and start a new life. And that new life didn't include him.

"Fuck." Rafael sat at the edge of the bed, not knowing whether he was crushed, amused, or offended. Raven had played him like a pawn on a chessboard. Picking up a stray hair from her pillow, he held it to the light.

Dark hair, dark eyes, dark heart.

He was reeling with just one hit. Maybe he'd got off easy. Maybe having her in his life would annihilate him.

PRESENT

Twenty-Two

"I BELIEVE YOUR HUSBAND IS AT RISK, MRS. ROZA." Detective Burke helped herself to more coffee.

"You mean he's in danger?" Uneasiness twisted in the pit of Vee's stomach. "From what?"

"That's what we're trying to find out." Detective Burke gestured toward the officers trailing through the house. "Thank you for cooperating. There have been some recent developments in the investigation, but before we proceed, I'll remind you again that you have the right to legal counsel."

"Detective Burke, if Rafael is at risk, I'm not going to waste time seeking legal advice."

"Noted." She pulled out a logbook and pen. "Has your husband been in touch since we last spoke?"

"No."

"So, the last time you saw him was Monday night, and the last time you heard from him was...?"

"Thursday. He sent me a text on Thursday."

"Have you tried to locate him?"

"No. He said he needs some time to himself."

"Is that something he does often?"

"No, but our argument got pretty heated. I said some things I regret."

"Any idea where he could be?"

"If this was the middle of the academic year, I'd tell you exactly where, but he's not teaching this summer. He's working on a research project. His schedule is erratic."

"What kind of research?"

Vee thought back to her conversations with Rafael. "Too technical for me to understand."

"Is it true that your husband has a neurological condition that allows him to do things beyond the rest of us?"

"Rafael has synesthesia. His brain has more connections than the average person; his senses are more intertwined. When you reached for that coffee, your brain sent a signal to your arm. In a synesthete's brain, these signals branch out into other areas and cause unusual combinations of senses. They might see sounds or taste words. A dog's bark could evoke the taste of oranges. Different musical notes could be perceived as different colors. There are as many kinds of synesthesia as there are potential connections in the brain. Rafael has number-form synesthesia, but it overlaps with other sub-classes."

"Meaning?"

"Rafael sees numbers as shapes or patterns. They're

also arranged spatially in his mental space, like a map. Just as you and I navigate through physical objects around us, Rafael navigates through them in his mind."

"Fascinating." Detective Burke flipped to a fresh page. "Your husband has an interesting history. Born in Mexico. An obscure connection with a now-deceased drug lord. He made a clean break, as far as I can tell. A model citizen, a self-made man. He made a fortune as an investment advisor. How did he end up as a professor at Caltech?"

"A mind like his craves expansion. He got bored and enrolled in some courses. One of his professors took him under her wing, and he ended up changing careers."

"What about you, Mrs. Roza? You had a successful start-up, but you gave up controlling interest. Would you say you're financially dependent on your husband?"

"Excuse me?"

Detective Burke rose from the table and fiddled with the magnets on the fridge. "Did you solve this?"

"Not yet."

"I wouldn't have pegged your husband for someone who plays word games, not when he has a gift for numbers."

"It's something we started when we moved in, and we've kept playing ever since."

"Are you any good with anagrams?"

"I like to think so."

"What can you do with this?" Detective Burke tore a page from her logbook, wrote her name, and handed it to Vee.

"Laura Burke." Vee thought about it for a few moments. Then she penned the rearranged letters.

"Bureau Lark," Detective Burke chuckled. "Touché, Mrs. Roza. Another reason I need to revert to my maiden name. I can see why your husband enjoys sparring with you. We're still trying to figure out the note. Would it be possible to see your garden?"

"It's not much of a garden." Vee led her through the living room. A row of windows opened up to spectacular vistas of the San Gabriel Mountains. "We're the last house on the hill. The valley cuts away from here, so unlike our neighbors, we don't have a garden, but the view makes up for it." Opening the doors to the deck, Vee stood aside and let her pass.

"Not much of a garden?" Detective Burke scanned the sweeping views. "Mrs. Roza, you have the Rose Bowl and Arroyo Seco for your backyard. What I would give to watch the Fourth of July fireworks from here."

"I'm not complaining." Perched on a hill, the deck had sealed the deal for her and Rafael.

"This is your garden, I assume?" Detective Burke inspected the cedar boxes secured to the wall. Cascading with flowers and trailing plants, they created a small but striking vertical garden.

"Any idea why someone would allude to your garden in the note?" Detective Burke asked.

"I've been thinking about that myself. I wish I knew."

Taking one last look, Detective Burke nodded and stepped inside.

"We're done, Detective," a police officer commented. "Nothing to report."

"What about that?" Detective Burke nodded toward the computer as she walked past the study room. "Is that yours or your husband's, Mrs. Roza?"

"It's Rafael's. I use it on the rare occasion."

"I'd like to bring it in to the station, if that's okay."

"Is that necessary?" Vee asked.

"It could be."

"If it helps, sure. You said there's been a recent development in your investigation?"

Detective Burke waited until the officers left with the computer. "It seems we've gone from investigating a vandalism to a missing person's case."

"Rafael isn't missing. I didn't hear from him for a couple of days, but..." Vee frowned. "Does this have something to do with whoever broke the window?"

"I didn't say the two are connected, but now that you mention it, did you and your husband argue because he's involved with another woman—perhaps the person from the security footage?"

"No, we argued because..." Vee fumbled, feeling like disclosing the pregnancy would somehow jinx it. "Well, Rafael didn't want me to get pregnant."

"You got pregnant against your husband's wishes because you thought he was leaving you for another woman?"

"We had a disagreement, a major one. Why do you keep insinuating it had to do with another woman?"

Detective Burke walked around the desk and sat. "I tried to reach your husband several times to come in and view the footage from your neighbor's security camera, but he hasn't returned any of my calls. That strikes me as odd, given the damage to his property and a pregnant wife, home alone. So, I reviewed the footage from an earlier date and caught something rather interesting. The night of your argument, your husband left in his car."

"That doesn't make any sense. His car is in the driveway."

"That's because your husband came home the following night."

"You're mistaken, Detective Burke. Rafael left on Monday night and hasn't been back since."

"The camera doesn't lie, Mrs. Roza. Your husband left Monday night, came home Tuesday night, parked in the driveway, and hasn't left since."

"You're saying Rafael has been here this whole time?" It was so absurd, Vee wondered if she'd heard her right. "Where is he, Detective Burke? Do you see him?"

"No. That's why I brought my team in today."

"You came here looking for my husband?" A sharp laugh escaped Vee. "You must have the recordings mixed up. Check the dates again."

"What was the date Mr. Roza texted, saying he's taking some time off."

"It's right here." Vee pulled the message up on her phone. "Read it for yourself."

Detective Burke glanced at the screen and nodded. "That was the last time your husband's phone was on. I got a warrant to access his location. We know where that message was sent from."

"Well?" Vee prompted.

"Do you know how triangulation works when tracking a phone, Mrs. Roza?" Detective Burke grabbed a pen and illustrated. "A cell phone accesses the network through signals transmitted by cell towers. Each tower provides a circle of coverage. If a cell phone's signal is picked up by three towers, the place where those circles overlap is the user's location, or at least, the best approximation. Care to guess where your husband texted from?"

Vee met her gaze with expectant silence.

"Right here." Detective Burke marked the intersection of the three circles with an "x" and slid the paper toward her.

When Vee stared at it blankly, Detective Burke rapped her pen on the "x."

"Right here, Mrs. Roza. Your husband's phone was in this house when you received that message."

"That's impossible."

"That's a fact. And here are some more facts: Rafael Roza left home on Monday night. He returned on Tuesday evening. On Wednesday night, we received a call about a disturbance. Neither the responding officers nor I saw your husband when we arrived. You stated the two of you had an argument before he left. We canvassed the area and obtained footage of the person who damaged your property. On Friday, you viewed the recording at the police station. When asked about your husband, you said he had not returned, but you had received a text from him. Yet both the footage from your neighbor's security system and your husband's cell phone records place him right here." Detective Burke gestured around the room. "Home, sweet home."

Vee stared at her, trying to wrap her mind around things. "I haven't seen my husband since last week and you're telling me he's been home this whole time?"

"Correct."

"Detective Burke, when you said my husband's at risk, did you mean he's at risk from me?"

"It's my job to consider every possibility."

"Including the possibility that I sent myself a text from his phone? To what end?"

"To assure us he's okay. To keep anyone from looking for him. I don't have the answers, Mrs. Roza. I'm just trying to make the pieces fit, and right now, the facts are telling me one thing and you're telling me another."

"But *I'm* the one who called you."

"On a different matter. We're still trying to figure out the motive behind that incident. Maybe someone was trying to save your husband."

"That's insane."

"Maybe someone was trying to distract us from what was really going on."

"You think I had someone break my window?"

"Maybe you cut someone off in the parking lot. Maybe your husband did. Maybe someone doesn't like your face. Like I said, it's my job to consider every possibility, but I have to tell you, things aren't looking good for you. The two of you have an argument. Your husband comes home the night after, and nobody's seen him since. Mr. Roza has amassed quite a fortune. A penthouse in New York, a vacation home in Mexico, this little jewel in California, sizeable investments, and numerous other assets. As the sole beneficiary, you stand to gain the most."

Vee's face turned to stone. "Get out of my house, Detective."

"As you wish." Detective Burke ambled out of the study. "A word of advice, Mrs. Roza." Pausing at the door, she regarded Vee with steely eyes. "Get yourself a good lawyer."

Twenty-Three

VEE STARED AT THE CEILING, SEARCHING FOR A WAY OUT of the labyrinth. Every question led her deeper into the maze. Shadows crept along the walls as the moon journeyed across the sky. The world was spinning, and Vee was spiraling into a void where nothing made sense. The heaviness was back. Death roamed the house, but it wasn't for her or her child. Her shroud swept the floorboards for Rafael.

When the first rays of the sun seeped through the window, Vee flung the curtains open and stood in the dusky light.

Her hand circled her belly. Each day she woke with her baby still in her womb was a miracle.

"I don't know what's going on with your daddy, but I'm going to find out."

The thought of Rafael with another woman shook her to the core, but the thought of him in danger filled Vee with burning purpose. She had to get to the truth.

Gathering what she needed, Vee walked into the sunroom and got to work.

By the time the sun arced over the mountains, she had a timeline—names, places, notes, events. Standing back from the grid of sticky notes on the glass panes, Vee saw more questions than connections staring back at her. But she had a map. It was nowhere as complex as the projections Rafael saw in his mind, but it was a start.

Vee's thoughts were interrupted by the doorbell.

"Hey." Jeanne waited outside with a basket. "I made some breakfast goodies."

"You want to come in?"

Jeanne glanced at her watch. "Maybe a quick peek at our game. I'm working mornings this week." Placing the basket on the kitchen counter, Jeanne stood over the chessboard and considered Vee's move. "Sod it. You castled. I'll make my move when I get back."

"That's not fair. You have all day to think about it."

"Exactly." Jeanne laughed. "Make sure you finish everything in that basket."

"It will take me a few days." Vee peeked inside the basket and smiled.

Grabbing a muffin after Jeanne left, she walked back into the sunroom and stared at the sticky notes. Rafael's car said he was home. His phone said he was home. How could he be home, yet not home?

Vee looked out of the window at Rafael's car.

What if it wasn't him that drove the car home that night?

Detective Burke had seen Rafael's car, but she could not have seen the driver. The security footage Vee viewed at the police station barely covered the driveway.

Grabbing the spare fob, Vee dashed out and unlocked Rafael's car. If his phone was in his car, it would explain the location. It still didn't explain the text.

What if someone is trying to frame me for something? Vee thought.

It was the only explanation that made sense. If Vee found his phone, she'd be one step closer to the truth. The police had swept the car, but they could have missed it.

Vee combed every inch of the interior. A search through the trunk was also futile. Holding her breath, she called Rafael from her phone, but went straight to his voicemail. His phone was still powered off.

Slumping in the driver's seat, Vee's eyes fell on a set of keys in the cupholder. Rafael's office keys.

What kind of research is he conducting? Detective Burke's words came back to her.

He said she was on his research team, Jeanne recalled about the woman she saw him with.

Vee turned on the ignition and backed out of the driveway. Was all this connected to Rafael's work? Her fingers drummed the steering wheel as she approached the campus. Parking in the garage, she walked into the building and rode the elevator to Rafael's office. A fire drill notice was posted on his door. Letting herself inside, Vee tossed it into the wastebasket.

The smell of mahogany and books surrounded her. She picked up the frame on his desk—a picture of them on vacation, staring at a magnificent cathedral ceiling. Vee's throat ached at the wonder in their eyes. They had just found out they were having a baby. The world was wondrous and scary and exciting, all at once.

"Stop pushing me away," Rafael said, after Vee miscarried.

When she opened the door hours later, he was still there.

"I'm being punished," she said. *"I don't deserve kids after what I've done."*

"You are not to blame. You hear me?" Rafael cradled her face.

Breathing around the painful knot in her chest, Vee traced Rafael's face through the frame. "I'm going to find you. We're going to get through this, like every other storm we've weathered."

Vee needed something to point her in the right direction, but rifling through Rafael's papers was like grasping at air. The scientific jargon was beyond her. She searched through his drawers, flipped through books on his shelf, and scoured his office. Nothing jumped out. Then again, she had no idea what she was looking for.

About to power up Rafael's laptop, Vee felt a wave of dizziness. It had been hours since she'd eaten. Tucking the laptop under her arm, she cast one last look around the room. Then she turned the light off and opened the door.

"Sorr—" About to apologize for running into the person outside Rafael's office, Vee froze. The pixelated photo she'd pored over came into sharp focus. Dark hair. Dark eyes. Oval face.

"Hey, you're the one who broke my window."

Color drained from the woman's face. For a single, suspended moment, they stood face to face in the hallway. Then, urgency kicked in.

"You need to come with me to the police station," Vee said.

The stranger stared back with a horrified expression.

"Detective Bu—" Before Vee could finish, a loud, shrill fire alarm sounded.

The woman pivoted and fled down the hall.

"Hey." Vee chased after her. "Wait."

The woman turned sharply at the end of the corridor. Emerging around the same corner, Vee saw her weave around a janitorial cart and duck into the stairwell. She followed, chasing her down the stairs. The sound of footsteps bounced off the walls as more people poured into the stairwell for the fire drill. Vee pushed through, anxious not to let the woman out of sight. She got to ground level before Vee, flung the door open, and sprinted for the exit.

Separated by throngs of people in the lobby, Vee lost track of her. Adrenaline surged through her veins as she scanned the crowd. The stranger was her only lead. She couldn't afford to lose her. Catching another glimpse of her, Vee jolted into action.

A group of students darted out of Vee's way as she gained on the woman. She reached out to grab her, but a sharp pain ripped through her. Gasping, Vee doubled over. Her fingers lost their grip on the laptop. She fell to her knees with a sickening sensation.

"Are you okay?" someone asked.

"Call an ambulance." Vee clutched her belly as another spasm overwhelmed her. "I'm losing my baby."

Twenty-Four

THE SUNROOM FELT BARREN WITHOUT THE CANOPY OF jacaranda blooms in the front yard. Purple flowers littered the driveway, wilted and spent. On the other side, a grid of sticky notes marred the view of distant mountains.

"Still looking at your crazy wall?" Damian brought Vee some hot water with lemon.

"Is that the technical term for it, or are you calling me crazy?"

"This is enough to drive anyone crazy. You had a close call, Vee. You were in the hospital for four nights. It's a miracle you and the baby are okay. Come with me to Mexico until this thing blows over."

"Leaving the country is just going to make me look

guilty. I'm not going anywhere. Not until I figure out what's going on."

"I need to find Rafael." Damian's jaw set with determination.

"You have eyes on the cantina, as well as the villa in Mexico. You hired a private investigator. You've spent hours going through his reports." Vee gestured toward the papers strewn on the coffee table. "You need to get back to your family."

"Why do I feel you're trying to get rid of me?"

"I'm a tough cookie, Damian. There were times I thought I'd never see Rafael again. This time is no different. I would feel it if something happened to him, but that space feels the same." Vee placed her hand over her heart. "It would feel empty, right? You can't lose someone you love and not feel it. Tell me Rafael is all right," she implored.

Face twisting with pain, Damian embraced her. "Of course, Vee. Of course, he's all right."

"You have a message from Detective Burke," Damian said when Vee woke the next morning. "She asked if you could call back, but you're not talking to her without a lawyer."

"I've already retained a lawyer."

"A good one, I hope." Damian drained his coffee and folded his paper. "I'm off to pick up some groceries. I won't be long."

"You don't have to stock the fridge before you go. I can get my own groceries."

"Doctor's orders. Eat. Rest. And do as you're told."

"That's never worked with your wife, so what makes you think it'll work with me?"

"Rafael and I sure know how to pick our women." Damian's brooding features softened into a chuckle.

Home alone for the first time after being discharged from the hospital, Vee sat down to breakfast, but kept thinking about her run-in with the mystery woman.

Who was she?

What was she hiding?

Vee shut her eyes and pictured Rafael with her.

He slid a bra strap off her shoulder. His tongue dipped between her collarbones.

Vee rushed to the sink and retched.

Rafael was missing. The police suspected her. She had almost lost the baby. And she had just pictured Rafael with another woman.

Vee had to find a way to cope with the emotions that assailed her throughout the day. At the same time, not doing anything was sending her deeper into despair.

She turned Rafael's laptop on and gazed at the lock screen. Two weeks ago, Vee would have entered the code without a shred of doubt. Now, she wasn't sure. She entered the password Rafael used for all his devices and held her breath.

The system accepted it.

Staring at the home screen, Vee noticed a group of shortcuts separated from the rest. They were arranged in a spiral, radiating from a central file. Each file was dated. She clicked on the earliest, at the center. A video started playing.

The mystery woman appeared on camera. Rafael was off-screen, prompting her. She was hesitant, but let him coax her into doing things. The connection between them was undeniable. A part of Vee felt wrong watching, but she remained glued to the screen.

When it was done, Vee clicked on the next file in the

sequence. It was more of the same. With each recording, the woman grew more comfortable and confident—video after video—until Vee had watched them all.

She sat back, trying to wrap her mind around what she'd just seen. This wasn't an affair. Rafael's connection with the woman was deeper.

PAST

Twenty-Five

*G*ETTING INVOLVED WITH YVETTE ADAMS WAS A BAD IDEA, but Rafael did it anyway. The first time he saw her in class, he did a double take—third row, dead center. Her head was bent over the exam. A razor-sharp bob obscured her face, but something about her stirred his senses. He caught the sweep of dark lashes as she flipped a page. Then, as if sensing his gaze, she swung her eyes his way. They stared at each other, flashes of light caught in the water. A wild thrill flared in Rafael's chest.

"Thank you for coming to oversee the exam on such short notice, Rafael." Professor Bustamante snapped him back to reality.

"Happy to step in." They spoke in hushed voices. "How is your husband?"

"They've taken him in for surgery. I'll know more when I get to the hospital. If you need anything, message me."

Rafael faced the lecture hall after Professor Bustamante left. It took all of his will to keep his eyes from the third row. She was a radar signal on his screen, as impossible to ignore as an oncoming attack. Synching his watch with the countdown timer for the exam, Rafael looked where he shouldn't. Their gazes locked again. Her lids drew quickly over her eyes, but a rush of color stained her cheeks.

At thirty-two, Rafael was used to students having crushes on him. He could read the signs, and he knew how to handle them. But this wasn't one-sided. It was demanding and insistent, resonating beyond the crackle of attraction and recognition. Her presence disturbed and excited him. Even when he wasn't looking, he was aware of her every move: the way she tucked her hair behind her ear, the way she crossed her legs, the way she put her pencil in her mouth. She aroused an aching curiosity and longing in him.

Gritting his teeth, Rafael reminded himself of all the reasons he should ignore her. One by one, the students dropped their completed answer sheets on his table. When she rose to hand in hers, he kept his eyes on the paper. She held on to it long enough for him to unravel. He looked up. Leggings, a drawstring hoodie, and bold, defiant eyes.

She wasn't sorry for any of it. Her gaze dropped to his ring finger and her nostrils flared. Surprise? Excitement? Challenge? Rafael couldn't say what, but it flickered briefly as she handed him her paper. Then she swung the door open and walked out.

Her answer sheet scorched his hands.

Don't look. Her name will get buried in the pile and you'll never be tempted to look her up.

Rafael dropped her exam and let out a long exhale. There were eight students left in the room. When the last one turned in his exam, he knew exactly how many papers to sift through to get to hers. It annoyed him that he'd kept track. He slid all the answer sheets into an envelope and sealed it shut.

His phone rang as he was leaving.

"How did it go?" Professor Bustamante asked.

"Fine. I'm just wrapping things up. How's your husband?"

"I'm afraid Fred's not well. I need to take some time off until he recovers. Professor Hastings has agreed to take over the class, but he has a schedule conflict. Can you cover the sessions he can't?"

"Of course." Professor Bustamante wasn't just Rafael's mentor. She was also the reason he was an Assistant Professor. "I'll work it out with him."

"Thank you, Rafael. I appreciate it."

After they hung up, Rafael's eyes swept the empty room. Third row center was trouble—the kind of trouble he hadn't seen coming. He had to make sure she didn't get under his skin again.

Twenty-Six

PROFESSOR BUSTAMANTE'S CLASS WAS RELATIVELY SMALL. It didn't take long for the students to introduce themselves.

"Yvette Adams," she said, when it was her turn.

Rafael nodded and moved on to the person beside her. He was more prepared; he'd fortified his defenses.

"I'm Assistant Professor Rafael Roza." He introduced himself when everyone was done. "I'll be teaching this course with Professor Hastings until Professor Bustamante returns. So…" He clapped his hands. "Let's pick up where she left off: Introduction to Waves." he projected the first slide of the lecture on the board.

"You're reading these words because of electromagnetic waves in the visible light spectrum. Light waves reflect off the board, enter your eye, and hit the retina at the back of your eye. The nerve cells in your retina transform these waves into electrical impulses that your brain processes into an image: the text you're reading, the colors in this room, the person sitting next to you...

"My voice is reaching you because of sound waves traveling through the air.

"When you look up at the sky and see extraordinary patterns in the clouds, you're seeing gravity waves in action.

"Waves race across the surface of our oceans. They ripple out from earthquakes and alter the fabric of our planet.

"At the other end of the spectrum are waves that operate at the heart of an atom, where matter behaves like a wave one moment, and a particle the next.

"As different as they seem, all waves have something in common—they are oscillations that carry energy from one place to another.

"In this course, we are dissecting various types of wave phenomena. My approach is a little different from Professor Bustamante's. I want you to see it in action. I want you to observe sound waves shattering a wineglass. I want you to watch a fluorescent tube light up on its own in an electromagnetic field. I want to take you behind the scenes and raise the curtain on the unseen so you can see how it works." Rafael paused when a student raised his hand. "Yes?"

"Are we shifting away from the mathematical focus of this course?"

"On the contrary. We will delve deeper, but in a fun, experimental context. Mathematical principles don't just affect what you see or touch or hear or smell. They permeate the universe around us.

"We just talked about how your eyes convert light waves into electrical signals that your brain translates into an image. So in effect, it's your brain that does the seeing, not your eyes. Now imagine if your brain was wired differently, by the tiniest fraction. You would see something completely different. The way the light gets to you would follow the same mathematical rules, but your entire world would shift. There are people that experience the world differently. They see things others don't see and hear things others don't hear.

"Reality isn't as concrete as we believe. Evolution has shaped our perceptions to ensure we survive. That means hiding stuff from us we don't need to know, stuff that would otherwise overwhelm us. If we had to process the entire spectrum of visible and invisible light to detect a tiger in front of us, we'd be dead. So, for our own good, our senses are pared down. We don't see what really is; we see what we need to. That makes reality a magnificent illusion, based solely on our perceptions.

"It is important to understand the physics or mathematics or biology of our world, but in order to understand the truth, we have to look at our perceptions, because that is the lens through which we view reality. Let's do a simple exercise." Rafael walked around the desk and stood before the room. "Where do you see me right now?"

"At the front of the class."

"A few meters away."

"Okay, now close your eyes," he instructed. "Where do you see me now?"

There were a few laughs.

"You don't see me?" He smiled.

"We can hear you," someone commented.

"All right. Now open your eyes." Folding his arms,

Rafael leaned back against the desk. "I ask you again. Where do you see me?"

A guy in the back row scoffed. Another student rolled her eyes.

"Inside." The voice was silky cool. "I see you inside."

Rafael's eyes flew to Yvette. He had the sensation of the floor falling away from him.

"Very good. You see me inside." Untangling his gaze from hers, he pointed to another student. "You see me inside. As do you. And you.

"What you think of as reality is a perception. Your environment presents the data, but your understanding and interpretation of that data happens inside. When you expand perception, an interesting thing happens. Your reality expands with it.

"I want you to leave this class not just with an under-standing of wave phenomena, but with awe and wonder, knowing you're part of something much larger. I want you to see the magic in the ordinary, whether it's a grain of sand floating in the ocean or the goose bumps you feel when you look at the night sky and realize there are bil-lions of galaxies still to be mapped in the cosmos.

"Our lives are a flash in eternity, so witness, revere, appreciate, dissect, question, discover... You are not a bystander in reality. You are the lens through which re-ality exists. Any questions?"

The room was silent.

"Good." Rafael snapped the laptop shut, not having ventured beyond the first slide. He had their attention. "Don't forget to sign up for the field trip. I'll post the de-tails tomorrow."

As the class shuffled out, a student stopped at his table.

"I really enjoyed your lecture, Professor Roza." She leaned in.

Giving her a nod, Rafael packed up the rest of his things.

She lingered, fidgeting with her bag. "Do you have a minute to go over a question from the exam?"

Dilated pupils, lips parted like she was about to kiss the air, she was intellectual excitement transformed into erotic longing.

"I'll be putting aside some time during class to go over the exam. I'm sure other students have questions too, so let's wait until the results are out and do a group recap."

"Of course." She brightened when he made eye contact.

Sometimes all it took was an acknowledgment coupled with a firm brush-off.

"Anything else?" he asked.

"It's Michelle." She peered at him through a fan of lashes.

With an inward sigh, Rafael braced himself. Level Two. Time to be ruthless. He was about to speak when Yvette Adams walked by. Her knowing sideward gaze immobilized him. She glided by like a whisper—feet, legs, hips, arms. Then, as if she knew he was holding his breath, the corner of her mouth tilted. She looked over her shoulder as she left, and he hung suspended in the moment.

"Professor Roza?"

Ripping his eyes away, Rafael turned his attention to Stephanie. No. Denise? Shelly?

"Well..." There he was, standing before her with an inappropriate, incapacitating crush of his own. "I'll see you, next class."

When the room emptied, Rafael shut his eyes. A tangle of naked skin flashed before him.

"Dammit." He knew better than to fantasize about Yvette. It wasn't that he was powerless to resist. What killed him was that he didn't *want* to resist. If she came on to him, his defenses would turn to ashes, and she'd walk away with dusty feet.

Run. Hide. Fight it all you want. The look she gave him over her shoulder said it all. *You see me inside, too.*

Twenty-Seven

RAFAEL SKIPPED HIS MORNING WORKOUT TO DROP OFF the papers Professor Bustamante needed.

"Room 326," she said when he called from the hospital lobby.

Knocking softly on the door, he let himself in. Professor Bustamante gave him a weary smile.

"Thank you," she said. "I'm sure you have better things to do on a Saturday."

"It's no trouble." Rafael handed her the files. Her husband was still unconscious—hooked to machines—but she was determined not to let her work pile up.

"This is going to take some time." She reached into her bag for her reading glasses.

"Anything I can do to help?"

"Coffee would be great. And maybe a bite to eat."

"Of course. I'll be right back."

Rafael turned down the hallway and waited for the elevator. When the doors opened, he bumped face-first into a bouquet of flowers.

"Sorry." He backed, letting the person exit.

As she brushed past him, goose bumps pricked the back of his neck. White peonies obscured her face, but he knew that voice, that hair, that walk. Spinning around, he caught the swirl of a summer dress. Long legs. Velvet skin.

In a sky-blue dress that flared from her hips, Yvette Adams was a rush of sweet air in the sterile corridor. Rafael turned back around, intent on getting away, but the elevator shut before he could get in. He pushed the button in rapid succession as he waited.

As if that will summon it any faster.

Yvette paused at the nurse's station and chatted to the staff.

Come on. Come on. Rafael glared at the elevator.

She placed the flowers on the counter.

The doors slid open. He stepped inside, selected his floor, and rested the back of his head against the wall.

"Hold the door, please." Footsteps rushed toward the elevator.

Rafael pushed the button to shut it. With barely a slit of space left, Yvette stuck her hand between the doors and pried them open.

"Thanks a lot." Sarcasm turned to surprise when she saw him.

They stood at opposite ends, eyes locked. As the elevator descended, a cocktail of sensations ricocheted between them. Adrenaline coursed through Rafael's veins. He was up on his toes, running on all cylinders.

When the doors opened, he gestured toward them, inviting her to exit. She strode out, crossed the lobby, and disappeared through the revolving doors at the front.

Rafael placed Professor Bustamante's order at the cafeteria. As he waited, he spotted Yvette re-entering with two more bouquets. She left the bigger one in the hospital chapel, then took the elevator again. Rafael collected Professor Bustamante's order and took it up to her. They chatted for a while, then he let her get to work.

Standing by the elevator, Rafael scanned the hallway, hoping to see Yvette again, hoping *not* to see Yvette again. When the door opened, he held his breath, but it was empty. His heart pounded when the elevator stopped on the second floor. A family of four entered. The kids spilled out the moment they got to the lobby. He stopped by the information desk to retie his shoelaces.

Don't be a fool, a part of him warned.

I'm just tying my laces, the other part chimed in.

You're waiting for her...

Rafael straightened and left the building. Halfway to his car, he passed a beat-up hatchback. Something was seeping out and collecting on the ground. Brake fluid? Coolant? Gas? Getting on his knees, he sampled the liquid and sniffed.

"May I help you?"

Leaping to his feet, Rafael wiped his hands on his jeans and stared at Yvette.

"Water." He pointed to the puddle under the car.

"I know." She swung the rear door open. "A bucket tipped over."

The trunk was packed with utility buckets—some filled with flowers, others stuffed with towels to keep the vases from moving.

"You work for a florist?" Rafael asked.

"I *am* the florist." She mopped up the water on the floor of her trunk. "It's a new business venture." Wringing out the water, she shook the towel dry and placed it back in the trunk.

"Landing a hospital contract is a pretty good deal for a new venture."

"I'm not getting paid for this." She balanced two vases in her arms and attempted to nudge the door shut.

"What about these?" Rafael motioned to the remaining vases.

"One more trip will do it."

"I've got them." He shut the door and waited for her to lead the way.

She hesitated, then started walking toward the building.

They left flowers at the information desk, the gift shop, and the geriatric wing before heading to the maternity ward.

"The happiest place in the hospital," Yvette said when they got off the elevator. "Also where I get the most referrals."

"So, you leave complimentary bouquets with your business cards, hoping someone will call you with an order?"

"Short answer, yes. Long answer? Flowers have an expiration date. Leftovers are given away or destroyed. I pick them up for next to nothing. It's nice to know they're cheering someone up and it gets me a few customers." She handed a bouquet of hydrangeas and roses to the nurse at the station.

"Thank you, dear." The nurse brightened. "Oh, and someone from the hospital committee left her number in case you're interested in collaborating on the next fundraiser."

"Thanks." Yvette tucked the note into her dress pocket. "Everything okay? You seem down today."

"It's been a rough shift. We lost a newborn this morning. The parents are heartbroken. Would you mind if I put these flowers in their room?"

"Not at all." Yvette squeezed her hand.

"I take it back," she said, as they walked away from the nurses' station. "It's not always the happiest place in the hospital."

In the game of attraction, she was an adversary, but when her defenses were down, Rafael wanted to lay it all down. Stifling the urge to hold her hand, he curled his fingers into his palm.

"Wait a sec." She peered down a hallway.

A woman stood outside the newborn intensive care unit. Dressed in scrubs, she held her face in her hands.

Yvette returned to the nurses' station and pulled out a rose. Placing her hand on the woman's shoulder, she gave her the flower. The woman stared at it, then at Yvette. She continued staring with red-rimmed eyes as Yvette walked away.

When Yvette got to the end of the hallway, she glanced back at the woman. They exchanged a silent look. Then Yvette smiled and turned the corner.

"You think that's the mother who lost her baby?" Rafael asked.

"Whoever she is, she's having a rough day."

They took the elevator to the lobby and exited to the parking lot.

"It's so strange," Yvette said when they got to her car. "I thought I'd cheer that woman up, but she's the one who turned my day around."

Their eyes held, even though they had no reason to linger.

"You've been very kind, too." She kissed his cheek.

Her lips were whisper-soft, but a thousand volts buzzed through Rafael's body. He stood, stiff and still, as she slid past him and got into her car. He wanted to watch her drive away, but he crossed the lot to his car. The imprint of her mouth burned his skin as he turned on the ignition.

Weaving out of the parking lot, Rafael saw Yvette bent over her car with the hood propped.

"Something wrong?" He pulled into the spot next to hers.

"It won't start."

"You have roadside assistance?"

"Roadside assistance? For this?" She tugged a strip of the rust under the hood. It peeled right off.

"I'll get someone to have a look at it." Rafael scrolled through his phone.

"You're not even going to pretend to have a look?"

"Know your strengths, know your weaknesses, and build a kick-ass contact list accordingly." He dialed out and waited.

"Tony," he said. "I need your help." He gave him the details and hung up.

Yvette folded her arms and stared at him.

"What?" Rafael asked.

"How much is this going to cost?"

"Don't worry about it. Open the trunk."

"The trunk? I'm pretty sure the problem isn't with the trun—" She broke off as Rafael transferred the remaining flowers from her car to his. "What do you think you're doing?"

"Taking you home."

"But my car." She gave him an exasperated look.

"Tony will look after it. I don't know if he'll be able to fix it or how long it will take, so I'll take you home and let you know what he says."

"Just like that? You've decided?"

"Okay, then. You decide."

She glared at him for a few beats. Then she reached for her handbag, swung it over her shoulder, and marched to the passenger side of his car.

"I've been up since the crack of dawn. I appreciate the ride home, but I can't afford a mechanic, so tell your guy not to bother. I'll figure something out."

"Tony's not g—"

"I can't accept your help. Just a ride, please."

Rafael opened the passenger door and let her in.

"For the record…" He slid into the driver's seat and fastened his seat belt. "Tony's not a mechanic, and I wasn't offering to pay for his services. It doesn't cost me anything extra."

"Are you saying you called a guy who's not a me-chanic to fix my car, and he jumped to do your bidding? What kind of arrangement is that? Did you bump up his grade in class or what?"

"I'll give you points for imagination." Rafael chuck-led. "Tony, or Antonio, as he was known before, is an ex-con with a heart of gold. He runs a personal concierge service. If I need a ride to the airport, someone to pick up my laundry, redecorate my home, or arrange a caterer, I skip the headache of vetting professionals and call Tony. He has a fleet of specialists ready to go, and he always gets the job done. Having him send someone to look at your car doesn't cost me anything because I'm already paying for that tier of service."

"Must be nice. Now I don't feel so bad, but I can't accept anything more from you."

"We all need a little help now and then."

"A little help?" Her head snapped, eyes blazing. "We both know this is more than that."

She was right. There was more to it. A hell of a lot more. Rafael wanted to kiss her, pull her into his arms, and taste every inch of her. She wasn't immune, either. Being around each other was heady and exhilarating.

"When I first saw you in class—"

"When I first saw you in class—"

Their words collided with startling synchronicity.

"You first," she said.

"Well, I felt like someone zapped me. The odds of a student signing up for my class, cross-referenced with the odds of that student being Yvette Adams, are incomprehensibly slim."

"Well, technically, I signed up for Professor Bustamante's class."

"True. But here we are."

"Where exactly *are* we? Didn't we drive through here already?"

"We did. We went around in a circle. I started driving, we started talking, and I didn't get your address."

She laughed and entered her address into the navigation system. "Tell me something. How did you end up in academia?"

"A sequence of choices—step by step, day by day. You know those moments of anxiety where everything is fine, but you still feel you're missing something? I was on top of the world. A penthouse suite, New York at my feet. But I'd wake up feeling like there was more. The voice in my head kept saying, 'This isn't it, this isn't all.'

"One day, someone left a course catalog in my office,

and I ended up enrolling in a class. Every Wednesday night, I attended a lecture. The Big Bang, the formation of elements, dark matter, dark energy, anti-matter. How the universe formed. Where is it going? The voice in my head grew quiet. Excitement creeped in. For one hour every week, I was spellbound. I wanted to dig deeper, so I applied for graduate school, got into Caltech, and moved to Pasadena."

"And the voice? What does it say now?"

"Most days, it says, 'This is good. Keep going.' Other days it says, 'Call Tony. We need chocolate-cherry ice cream.'"

"You have a personal genie, and you ask for groceries?" She laughed.

"What would you ask for?"

"I'd ask to go back in time. I've done many things I'm not proud of, but if I had to pick one, I know exactly what I'd change."

Rafael shot her a questioning look.

"I met a good man, and I sabotaged it." She had a faraway look as she combed through the tangles of the past. "I didn't think I was good enough for him, so I left. I came to Los Angeles for family, but they made me feel even less worthy. No one can make you feel good about yourself, except you. So that's what I'm working on.

"I never finished high school, so getting my diploma, then saving enough for college took a while. I'm thirty-one now, so it's intimidating being surrounded by younger minds, but starting college *and* my own business feels good. Next time I meet someone, I won't let the weight of my past get in the way. I'll stand my ground and not feel like I don't deserve to be loved."

Rafael's throat ached with unspoken words, but he kept his eyes on the road. It didn't matter what he said.

Memories had teeth, and sometimes they took a big chunk out of you.

They were quiet the rest of the way. Water sloshed in the buckets in the trunk.

"This is me," Yvette said, when Rafael pulled into her apartment complex.

His phone buzzed as he parked in the spot she showed him.

"It's Tony," he said. "He says it's the transmission. His guy can replace it, but it'll cost more than what the car is worth. He can have it towed to the garage."

"Can he have it towed here until I figure things out?"

"Of course." Rafael sent the directions to Tony.

When he looked up from his phone, he caught Yvette watching him with a strange expression.

"When I first saw you in class..." She averted her gaze. "Well, before I saw you, I felt you. The air shifted. My skin prickled. I knew that if I looked up, I'd find you. I've dreamed of you—your face, your eyes, your voice. And there you were, all the details filled in, even better than I remembered. My first thought was unashamedly selfish. I wanted you. No matter what. But now..."

"Now what?"

"Now, nothing. Truth is, I'm all secrets and lies. Do yourself a favor." She opened the door. "Steer clear of me."

"Is that what you want?" Rafael's fingers clamped around her wrist.

"No. But don't say I didn't warn you." She walked around to the trunk and waited for him to open it.

They carried the buckets up the stairs to her apartment. A blast of cold air hit Rafael when they stepped inside.

"Sorry." Yvette pulled the blackout curtains aside to

let the light in. "I leave the air conditioning on full blast. The flowers last longer when it's cool and dark. You can put the buckets here." She cleared the clutter on her dining table—scissors, foam, pins, pruning shears.

There wasn't much room in the apartment. Rafael found Yvette's nearness was ten times more intoxicating. When her arm brushed his, the sensation was like a match striking his skin. He withdrew to the other side of the room. It was sparsely furnished, but cozy. Floor pillows substituted for a couch on a thin rug. Her bed was a mattress on wooden pallets. Clean, white sheets. A sweater tossed over the chair. Floral cutouts pinned to a board. A pair of socks rolled into a ball. Plants trailing toward the light.

In a flash, all the mundane, beautiful pieces of Yvette swarmed his defenses. Stepping inside her personal space was a mistake. She was working on herself. A man of honor would walk away. The last thing she needed was to be derailed just as she was getting started.

"I should head home." Rafael turned to find her holding drinks.

Blue dress, pillow-soft lips, sunlight in her hair.

A shadow of humiliation swept across her face. "Of course." Placing the drinks on the counter, she opened the door.

"Yvette, I'm sorry."

"No. *I'm* sorry." She stared at his shoes. "I don't know what I was thinking. You're a good man."

It should have made him feel better, but as he drove home, Rafael had the curious sensation of being held down by steel weights.

Twenty-Eight

"*H*ave you ever wondered what it would be like to *see* sounds?" Rafael addressed the class. "Some of you may visualize it like this." Drawing a graph with a standard wave function, he jotted down the parameters. "Frequency, amplitude, wavelength. But today, we're going to take it a step further." He gestured toward the setup on his table.

"Here, we have a metal plate mounted on a speaker. When we play a sound through the speaker, the plate moves up and down, creating a vibrating platform. We're going to sprinkle a layer of salt on the plate. Let's see what happens when we play different sounds through the speaker." Rafael turned on the tone generator and cycled through different frequencies, starting at the lower end of the dial.

Grains of salt danced on the plate, coalescing into patterns. They broke apart when Rafael turned the dial up, and reassembled into more intricate, symmetrical formations.

"As the plate vibrates, waves set off from the center to the edges. Waves are also being reflected inward from the edges and interfering with the outgoing waves. When two waves cancel each other out, they create a standing wave—an area where there is no vibration. The salt collects in those areas, and we see the formation of these fascinating geometric patterns."

White grains of salt shimmered in a star-like motif against the dark plate. "We will now shift to higher pitches. It won't sound pleasant, but I promise it'll be worth it."

Pouring more salt on the plate to accommodate more complex patterns, Rafael scanned the room. His eyes fell on Yvette. Riveted by the demonstration, she leaned forward, her hair obscuring all but the line of her nose. Every night, her face echoed in the stillness of his mind, in the extraordinary void that had no business taking up so much space.

"We are reaching the upper limit of the auditory range," Rafael said. "Hands up if you can still hear the sound."

Stunning patterns arranged themselves on the plate. Kaleidoscopic structures, reminiscent of mandalas, continued forming on the plate. One by one, students dropped their hands.

"The sound is now out of our hearing range, but we know it's still there because we can see its effect on the salt. Just because something moves beyond our perception does not mean it ceases to exist."

Turning the speaker off, Rafael walked around the desk. "We are on the cusp of new discoveries every day. New tools help us examine what we could not comprehend before. What we think we know today may be obsolete tomorrow. Maybe the students sitting in this room five, ten, fifty years from now, will laugh at this." He gestured toward the projector. "Shaking salt on a plate. Things you do at Sunday brunch."

His comment was met with a round of chuckles.

"My point is... We are constantly assembling and re-assembling beliefs about ourselves and our world. There is no such thing as getting it wrong. Every day is a building block, even when we have to dismantle something and start anew.

"It's a privilege to be part of the pool of thoughts, ideas, and desires that shape humanity, whether in science, art, business, or on a personal level. Everybody counts. Every dream. Every attempt. Like a grain of salt in this intricate formation, we can't see the whole design from our limited perspective, but every day you get up, you're expanding it. Think about that next time you're feeling small or unworthy."

Like a note struck on a piano, Yvette's gaze swung to Rafael.

I met a good man, and I sabotaged it. I didn't think I was good enough for him, so I left. I came to Los Angeles for family, but they made me feel even less worthy.

She remained seated as the other students filed out of the room.

"That was amazing, Professor Roza." The student, with a not-so-subtle crush, brushed her hand against Rafael as she trailed past his table.

Subtle hints were not working. "Michelle, I think we nee—"

"Sorry to interrupt." Yvette thrust some papers under his nose. "I need this signed right away."

Michelle gave her a withering stare. "I'll catch up with you later, Professor."

"I had it under control," he said, after she left.

"I wasn't trying to save you," Yvette replied. "I need this form signed before the office closes."

Rafael scanned the first page. "You want to withdraw from the course?"

"Yes."

"The deadline for withdrawal was weeks ago."

"Which is why I need your signature."

"Is there something wrong with the way I'm teaching this course?"

"No."

"What, then?"

"I don't need this course to graduate. It's an elective."

"You aced the midterm exam. You're on your way to a good grade. Drop the course now, and not only will you lose the credit, but you also won't get a refund on your tuition either."

"I know."

Their eyes held and battled.

"This is about me, then?"

"It's about me." She stared at her hands. "I find it hard to be around you."

A lump lodged in Rafael's throat. Her hands had multiple scratches. He pictured her working with roses, her skin so cold from the air conditioner that she didn't feel the thorns as she arranged them.

Little things about her affected him in grand ways.

"I may not be around much longer," he said. "Professor Bustamante's husband is better. She'll be back soon, and all of this will be for nothing. I deny your request for withdrawal."

He started dismantling the equipment on his table. About to wipe the salt off, Rafael was struck by the last pattern on the plate. It imprinted on his inner screen and turned maze-like, so he could walk through it in his mind. He took a mental step forward, surveying the pathways around him.

"What are you seeing?"

Reeled back, Rafael fixed his eyes on Yvette. "How do you know I'm seeing something?"

"You're one of those people, aren't you?" she said. "You mentioned them in class—people who experience things differently, who see things or hear things others don't. I noticed it a while ago. Your eyes flit to the side. Your gaze softens. Sometimes you stare right through the class. It lasts a few seconds, then you're back. Most people would miss it."

"But not you. I didn't realize you watched me so closely."

"I'm sure you're used to it." She shrugged. "Half the class is smitten. Michelle was about to rip my hair off for interrupting."

"Yet, you're the only person to deduce I have synesthesia."

"Is that what it's called? Synesthesia?"

Rafael searched her face. She was genuinely interested.

"It varies from person to person, but that's the umbrella term for it," he said. "It was a relief when I found out there's a name for it, but I've kept it mostly to myself."

"Then we both have things we keep to ourselves. It must be hard seeing the world differently from everyone else. Tell me, what did you see when you looked at that pattern on the plate?"

"It's hard to explain. Where you see a flat surface, I see a three-dimensional rendering that I can walk into. Think of a cube. Now imagine the interference of waves from a setup like that. When the salt collects in areas of no vibration, it hovers. Researchers are using the same concept to levitate objects with sound, to build a lexicon of dolphin language, to understand atomic processes within a star, to gi—" Rafael broke off at her expression. "I've bored you."

"Not at all." She smiled, a little sadly. Picking up the withdrawal request, she shot him a questioning glance. "You still won't sign this?"

"You still haven't given me a valid reason to do so."

She leaned across the table, lips a breath away from his. "You really want me to?"

A shiver ran through Rafael. Her nearness was a challenge, the sweetest kind of warfare. Meeting her gaze, he stretched out the moment until the tables turned and she was on the receiving end. A telltale rush of blood stained her cheeks.

"Well." She straightened and stuffed the form into her bag. "I'll be on my way."

The air stirred as she walked away. Honeysuckle and magnolias. She smelled different each time, depending on the flowers she worked with.

"Rafael..." She held the door half open and looked over her shoulder.

When their eyes met, she struggled with what she wanted to say. Then she gave him a wistful smile. "You have a beautiful mind."

He stared at the door after she left.

Rafael, not Professor Roza.

His name felt like it belonged on her lips.

Twenty-Nine

*Y*VETTE DIDN'T SHOW UP FOR THE NEXT CLASS.

In the class after that, Rafael demonstrated how to shatter a wineglass with sound. It was always a crowd-pleaser, but he couldn't shake off the knot in his gut. Third row, center, remained empty.

"As I mentioned earlier, today is my last day," he said. "Professor Bustamante is back tomorrow. I am still conducting the field trip tonight, but it's optional, so if I don't see you, good luck with the rest of the semester. You can always look me up if you have questions or need help with course material."

It made no sense that the absence of one person could extinguish all the light in the room. The thought of not seeing Yvette again was like snuffing out the moon.

"I can't make it to the field trip tonight." Michelle lingered after everyone left. "I hope this isn't goodbye, though." She handed Rafael a note.

He glanced at it, then held it back out. "I'm sure there are many people who would love to have your phone number. Give it to someone who'll use it."

She made no move to reclaim it. "Not even the slightest possibility?"

Rafael didn't respond.

"Fine. No coffee, no dinner, no romantic entanglement. How about a swim? Just dip your toes in the pool with me."

Of all the propositions, this was the strangest Rafael had ever received. "Now I've heard it all."

"Wait," she called, as he turned away. "You know that site where students rate their professors? Well, there's one that rates how hot they are. Your page gets a lot of buzz. I mentioned I was in your class and ended up taking a bet that I could get a shirtless pic of you."

"Okay. *Now* I've heard it all."

"You'd be surprised how many people want a peek at the six-pack you're hiding."

"Exactly how much did you wager, Michelle?" Rafael's expression turned to disbelief when she disclosed the figure. "What's the name of the website?"

"Why?"

"I'm going to look after that bet for you."

"Oh, I could kiss you! Tag me when you upload the image. This is the name of the website. And this is my username." She jotted it down for him.

"Got it."

"Wait." Her smile faded when she noticed his expression. "That's not what you're going to do."

"No. I'm going to have it shut down."

"You said you were going to help me."

"I *am* helping you. No website, no bet."

"But I like that site. They have pictures of all the hot professors."

"Allow me to share something with you." Rafael steered her toward the door. "There's a wave phenomenon we didn't cover in class. To understand it, you need to take a few steps that way." He pointed to the hallway.

"Here?" She stopped and turned around.

"Yes, that's perfect." Rafael raised his hand and waved goodbye.

It took a few seconds for the gesture to sink in.

"Ha," she said. "I see what you did there. A wave. You are so lame, Professor Roza."

"See you around, Michelle." He chuckled and headed back inside the lecture room.

"One more thing," she called.

"Yes?"

"Gotcha." She grinned and snapped a photo. "Don't worry. It's just for me, so I can look back and say, 'Hell. At least I tried.'"

Her words hung in the air as she walked away.

What regrets would Rafael have when he looked back? Getting involved with Yvette was a mistake. So why did it feel like a part of him was snagged on her and he couldn't move on without unraveling his being?

Rafael led a small group on the field trip that night. As they approached the power lines at the top of the hill, the crackle of electricity got louder. Handing out fluorescent tubes, Rafael went over the instructions and safety measures.

When held perpendicular to the overhead cables, the bulbs started glowing, one by one, on their own.

"So cool!" someone exclaimed.

"That's sick." A pair of students used them as lightsabers in a mock fight.

Another student broke away from the group. "Check it out. The further I go, the dimmer it gets." She kept walking until the bulb stopped glowing.

When everyone was done experimenting, Rafael collected the fluorescent tubes and dismissed the group.

"So, we're supposed to figure out how the bulbs light up without being hooked to a power supply?" One of the students lingered.

"If it intrigues you, yes. That's what these field trips are about—to get you to look up things on your own. Basically, power lines create a magnetic field around themselves as they carry electricity from one place to another. When we place a fluorescent tube in that electromagnetic field, it sets up a voltage across the bulb which makes it glow. The higher the current carried by the cables above us, the brighter it glows..." Rafael trailed off as a figure approached.

By the time she reached the top of the hill, he was the only one left.

"I'm late," she said.

"I wasn't expecting you to come at all."

"Years ago, I walked away without saying goodbye. I live with that every day. So here I am."

"Well, then." Rafael held out a fluorescent tube. "Here's to proper goodbyes, Yvette Adams."

His throat ached as she accepted it. A current zapped between them, buzzing like the power lines above.

She lifted the tube to the sky. It flickered for a few moments, then lit up. Eyes to the stars, she marveled at the silver light. Her face moved him the same as the night sky, when a window opened to the universe and galaxies tumbled overhead. She was the waxing and waning of the moon, walking into his life, walking out of his life. All he could do was watch her turn pirouettes around him, then disappear in the light of day.

Rafael walked toward the edge of the canyon. Sticking one end of a fluorescent bulb into the ground, he stood it up vertically. It glowed with a pearly sheen. Planting a row of lights on his left and right, he sat between them and stared into the valley. Ancient oaks and sycamores blended into the darkness. Gnarled trunks, ravaged by wildfires, stood defiantly under the moon. In the distance, arteries of light snaked through the city.

"Nice." Yvette stuck her light bulb at the end of the row. "It's like a mini-runway into the valley."

She settled next to him, resting her chin on her knees.

An indescribable softening came over Rafael as they gazed at the vistas below—barren rock carved by wind and water, bushes clinging to walls of silt and clay. It swept him back to the top of the tallest tree in Paza del Mar. His mouth filled with the sour taste of tamarind pulp. Lina's legs dangled next to his. The world lay at their feet.

"Where did you go this time?" Yvette asked.

Under the shadow of the night, her eyes were Lina's eyes. The tip of her nose. The shape of her mouth. A face time had erased, a face he would never look upon again.

"I went back to a time when the world was pure and sweet. A girl whose kiss made everything shimmer." Rafael's voice turned thick with emotion. "A promise I couldn't keep."

Reflecting on a loss that she too must have known, Yvette took his face in her hands. Her kiss was so tender, an ache sprung from his heart. He was a river meandering through the canyon, and she was the ocean. For a moment, they melted into each other under the vast indigo sky.

"Goodbye, Rafael." Her eyes filled with sadness. She took two steps and halted, as if she'd come upon an electric boundary. Rafael hung on the chance that she'd turn around. Then she continued, her head bobbing as she marched down the hill.

Power lines buzzed overhead. Constellations dotted the sky like grains of salt flung across the heavens. An orchestra of nocturnal insects played in the darkness. Everything was in its place, yet emptiness stretched from one end of Rafael's being to the other.

Humbled that he could feel as dark as the chasm below when the world was so full and alive, Rafael stayed on the hilltop until the sun came up.

Thirty

"PROFESSOR ROZA, YOU CAN'T SHOW UP WITHOUT YOUR significant other and not expect me to take advantage." Mrs. Singh, the chair of the hospital fundraising committee, linked her arm through his. A networking genius, she steered them toward the event coverage personnel in the ballroom.

"Smile." She angled her head, turned, and smiled again. "There. Now my husband will be jealous and shower me with attention all week."

"One week?" Rafael leaned in, kissed her cheek, and paused long enough for a few more flashes to go off. "You should be adored every day."

"After forty years, I need to up the ante." She offered her other cheek.

Rafael laughed and obliged.

"I think that'll cover me for the month." Her eyes twinkled as she showed him to his spot. "Your other guests have already arrived."

"My other guests?"

"Daniela Bustamante and her husband, Fred." She gestured toward the couple at his table.

"Yes, of course." Rafael glanced at them. "Thank you, Mrs. Singh."

"Thank *you* for being a valued donor. You still have an empty seat at your table. It would be a shame to let it go to waste. Can I send someone to fill in?"

"Absolutely." Unbuttoning his jacket, Rafael sat across from his guests. "The more, the merrier. Right, Professor Bustamante?"

"Right." The woman gave him a bright smile.

"Are you feeling better, Fred?" He asked her companion.

"Oh yes. Much better." He smoothed the sleeve of his cardigan. "A bit chilly, though. It's the air-conditioning, you know? Hot outside, cold inside. One never knows what to wear."

"Let's cut to the chase. You're not Professor Bustamante," Rafael said to the woman. She was at least a decade older. "And you're not Fred."

"No. We're not." They stared back at him.

"Did the two of you crash the gala?"

"Well." The man leaned over and lowered his voice. "It's our first time in Los Angeles and..."

"We just wanted to see what was going on," his partner piped in. "We were walking on the beach and spotted the car by the entrance. Flowers spilling out of the hood, the windows, the trunk. So bright and whimsical. Everyone was flocking to take pictures, so we thought we'd take a few shots too. Then we spotted Marwan Hussein." Hand on her heart, she closed her eyes and sighed.

"And Diane Bergen," the man continued. "And that singer... What's her name? The one who toppled off stage because her headgear was so heavy."

"We just wanted an autograph. When the lady asked if we were on the guest list, l mumbled something, and well...here we are. I'm Judy, by the way. And this is my husband, Ken."

"Rafael." He extended his hand.

"Rafael, we'll leave as soon as your guests arrive."

"No need," Rafael replied. "Fred is recovering from surgery, and Professor Bustamante didn't feel like attending without him."

"So, we can stay?" Judy stuffed her handkerchief back inside her purse. "I don't have to turn on the waterworks, Ken."

"We were all set to play absentminded seniors," her husband confided. "It gets us out of sticky situations."

"No doubt you get into a lot of those." Rafael grinned. "So, did you get any autographs?"

"No," Judy replied. "We don't want to risk getting kicked out. We've been sitting here like good little children, soaking it all in."

"Well, we have a few minutes before the ceremonies begin. Would you like a photo with Diane Bergen?" he asked.

"*Her*?" Ken's eyes zipped to the star's table. "You can get us a photo with the grand dame of Hollywood?"

"I made her a lot of money when I was an investment banker. Come. I'll introduce you."

Diane was a delight and happy to take a photo with Ken and Judy.

"Have you met Marwan?" she asked, after they re-treated. "I'm working with him on a new project." She turned to her co-star, but his seat was empty. "Ah. He's gone off again. Enamored by someone he spotted earlier. Keep me company till he gets back, darling? Ida Hudson and I aren't the best of friends. Apparently, I shouldn't have dated her ex. I don't know whose idea it was to put us at the same table."

While the gala hosts made introductory remarks to kick the evening off, Diane scanned the room. "Where the hell is Marwan? We're up next and he's off chasing skirts again."

"He's over there." Rafael pointed to the sweeping staircase. Marwan was chatting with someone at the top. He caught the look Diane sent him, grinned, and tilted his head toward the stage.

"He wants me to meet him there." Diane gathered her gown when the hosts announced her name.

Her co-star took his time. He raised his companion's hand and kissed it before making his way down.

With the spotlight on the presenters, the woman Marwan was talking to went unnoticed. Face obscured by a crystal chandelier, she descended one step at a time. The way her hand swept over the banister captivated Rafael. As she came into view, she paused and tucked her hair behind her ears.

Unprepared for the sight of Yvette, his heart stilled, then slammed against his ribs. In a sea of ruffles and rhinestones, she wore a black jumpsuit with simple flats. A single magnolia adorned her hair. She was the spring breeze descending on frozen ground.

Her eyes settled on someone, and she smiled. Jealousy surged through Rafael. He followed her gaze, expecting Marwan Hussein at the receiving end. But

Marwan was on stage and Yvette headed the opposite way. Unable to see, Rafael cursed the sea of tables in the way.

Diane and Marwan's speech faded into a jumble of words. It was only when everyone started applauding that Rafael realized they were done. Excusing himself, he made his way back to his table, but all the seats were taken.

"There you are." Mrs. Singh vacated his seat. "I brought one more guest to complete your table. Allow me to introduce you."

Mrs. Singh's guest turned in her chair. Her smile froze when she saw Rafael.

"Rafael Roza, this is Yvette Adams, the mastermind behind this evening's showstopper—the flower-filled car at the entrance."

Her words hung in the air as Yvette and Rafael stared at each other. Two months had passed since they kissed. There were no power lines overhead, but the space between them thrummed and sparked.

"A pleasure to see you again, Yvette."

"Likewise," she replied.

"You know each other?" Mrs. Singh exclaimed. "This worked out better than I thought."

Neither of them noticed when she left, nor when dinner arrived.

"Well." Judy cleared her throat. "The two of you can eat each other up with your eyes, but some of us need something more substantial."

"We weren'—"

"It's not like tha—"

"Of course not." Judy grinned. "I'm always wrong about these things. Eh, Ken?"

"Always." He dug into his food.

"So, tell us," Judy said between mouthfuls.

Yvette and Rafael exchanged a glance.

"I don't mean the charged field, darlings." Judy gestured between them. "Don't get me wrong. If I thought you'd share, I'd be all over it. I was wondering if you'd share what inspired the showstopper, Yvette."

"It was a bit of a misfortune that turned out to be a blessing," Yvette explained. "I was delivering flowers to the hospital when my car broke down—the same day Mrs. Singh left her number to see if I'd like to work with her on the fundraiser.

"It wasn't worth getting my car fixed, but I held on to it. When I was brainstorming ideas for the event, I realized my old hatchback was the perfect accessory. A good scrub and a fresh coat of paint is all it took. I sprayed the word *Bloom* for the theme of the gala, and loved it so much, I named my new business after it."

Flowers by Bloom Girl. The centerpiece at every table had a discreet logo. The Os in Bloom were white flowers with yellow centers.

"Clever," Judy said. "It adds a touch of whimsy."

"With everyone taking photos with the car, it's clever marketing too." Ken raised his glass. "To Bloom Girl."

Rafael's eyes met Yvette's as glasses clinked.

"Congratulations." He felt a sense of pride he had no right feeling.

"Thank you." She cut into her dinner like she hadn't eaten all day.

"This is breathtaking." Judy pointed to a large flower in the centerpiece. "I've never seen anything like it."

"It's a killer," Yvette replied.

"It's poisonous?" Judy pulled her arm back.

"Not that kind of killer." Yvette laughed. "I use four kinds of flowers in every arrangement: thrillers, fillers,

spillers, and killers. Thrillers are star-quality favorites—
big, lush peonies, or roses, or tulips. Fillers add mass
and cover up empty spaces. Spillers soften the edges,
cascade over the sides, and keep the design from looking rigid. And finally, killers, for intrigue and an element
of surprise. They are usually lesser-known blooms like
this protea."

"Let's see if I have this right." Ken finished his dinner and sat back. "Judy and I are Fillers. We aren't even
meant to be here. We're just filling up empty seats."

"Speak for yourself," Judy replied. "I'm more of a
Spiller." She leaned forward to showcase her ample cleav-
age with a hearty laugh. "Rafael here? He's most definitely
a Thriller. Star-quality. Big, bold, beautiful."

"And Yvette?" Ken asked.

"Hands down, a Killer."

Yvette choked on her drink.

"Heavens, I only meant you could slay any man in
this room," Judy teased after she recovered.

"I'll vouch for that."

Rafael's hackles rose as Marwan Hussein interrupted.
He stood beside Yvette's chair, hand extended.

"You promised me a dance."

Renowned for both action and dramatic roles,
Marwan had a persuasive charm coupled with brooding
good looks. He escorted Yvette to the dance floor, his
hand on the small of her back. Rafael averted his gaze.
He had no desire to witness how close he held her.

"They're playing that song we've been hearing on the
radio." Judy rose and tugged Ken's arm.

"I can't. My knee is acting up."

"I bet it would heal miraculously if Diane Bergen
wanted to dance."

"I'm telling you, it's not happening."

"May I?" Rafael offered Judy his arm. "With your permission, Ken?"

"Please." He made a shooing motion with his hands.

"Ha." Judy shot him a triumphant look. "This Spiller's still got it." She thrust her chest out and parted her way through the couples on the dance floor.

"Don't tell Ken, but I'm ready to pack it in. All the excitement has done a number on me. There's just one more thing I have to do. Would you mind steering us that way?" She tilted her head in the direction she wanted to go. "And now a little that way. Not that much. Good. That's it. Almost there. A few steps to the right. My right. Yes. Now, before I go, thank you for how graciously you handled Ken and me crashing your table. If you're ever in Canada, you must look us up." She tucked a card into Rafael's chest pocket. "And be sure to bring her with you."

"Bring who?"

"My goodness." Judy butted into another couple and feigned surprise. "Marwan Hussein. I'm your biggest fan. My husband and I have come a long way to be here. Would you mind terribly if I cut in?" Switching partners before he could respond, she whisked him away.

Yvette and Rafael faced each other as the music played on. Couples milled around as they stood in silence. The moment stretched to eternity.

"I'm sorry. I have to go." Brushing past Rafael, Yvette crossed the floor and stumbled toward the exit.

On Rafael's far left, Marwan Hussein excused himself and chased after her.

Rafael headed for the terrace and hunched over the balcony. Perched on a cliff, it had sweeping views of the coastline from Malibu to Palos Verdes. The sun had set, but watercolor hues lingered in the sky. Rafael kept his eyes on the gentle waves rolling in. The suffocating sensation eased, but burrowed deeper, into the space where heartache collected, where every loss still lived and breathed.

Skipping the silent auction and the rest of the festivities, he said his goodbyes and left. As he crossed the lobby connecting the ballroom to the hotel, he caught a glimpse of Marwan Hussein in the elevator. He was locked in a passionate embrace with someone Rafael couldn't make out through the closing doors.

Jealousy raged through Rafael. He pressed his thumb into the hard edges of his keys. As he waited for the valet to bring his car, he spotted a figure at the service entrance.

Yvette wasn't in the elevator with Marwan Hussein. She was stacking pails into a van.

"What are you doing out here?" Rafael was ridiculously relieved.

She spun around, caught off guard. "I have to return the rental van before midnight. I meant to leave hours ago, but Mrs. Singh insisted I stay for dinner. Then Marwan wanted to dance. I'm not going to make it." She glanced at her watch. "I still have to go home and empty the van."

"You'll make it." Rafael jumped into action. "We'll move this stuff to my car. I'll drop you home and have someone drive the van to the rental place."

"This feels like déjà vu. You're going to call Tony? At this time?"

"That's what twenty-four-hour service is for—times like this."

"You can't keep swooping in and fixing things. I don't like it."

"Is it me you don't like, Yvette, or my help?"

She wavered, but Rafael already knew the answer.

She didn't like accepting anything from anyone, but especially him, because he got under her skin.

"Fine. Call Tony," she conceded, hands on hips.

Rafael's mouth quirked at her gracious stance. "Wait here. I'll get my car."

By the time he pulled in, she'd emptied the van. They loaded everything into Rafael's trunk.

"Leave the key in the ignition. Someone's on the way." Rafael let her in his car and hopped into the driver's seat. "We just need to send the address where the van needs to be driven." He handed her his phone.

His eyes flew to her fingers as she entered the address. Everything about Yvette turned him on: the fine hair on her cheek, the sweep of her lashes, the dip in the center of her mouth. The pulse in her throat jumped when she caught him watching her. She was equally affected.

Rafael accepted his phone and turned on the ignition.

Between the orange glow of streetlights, their faces fell into shadow. The silence was different. Loaded. They weren't driving toward her apartment. They were driving toward a decision.

It took six trips to carry everything from the car to her apartment. By the time Rafael set the last of the buckets in the kitchen, they were both on edge. The air crackled with promises.

"I thought I lost you," he said. "I thought you went with Marwan to his room. When I saw you outside, I almost dropped to my knees. I don't want to feel that way again. I don't want to lose you."

Her eyes watched his mouth as he spoke.

"Yvette? Did you hear what I s—"

Her kiss was breathless. Clasping her fingers behind his neck, she drew him close. The air expelled from Rafael's lungs. He angled his mouth to taste her. His lips trailed to her throat, to the pulse under her skin. A wild surge of pleasure gripped him when her hand slipped under his waistband and untucked his shirt. The butterfly play of her fingers on his heated skin made him ache with raw hunger. He pulled back with a sharp intake as she unbuttoned his shirt, grazing his nipple with her thumb. Yvette stared back, her eyes dark pools of desire.

They undressed in a rush of passion, stumbling toward the mattress. Unwilling to interrupt the achingly sweet exploration of her mouth, Rafael stripped blindly. They landed on the floor pillows in a tangle. His hands caressed the planes of her stomach, her back, the flare of her hips. He pulled her onto the spread of his legs, gasping as she parted. The sound of sex filled the room. She rose and fell, hunger flaring as he stroked her clit through the triangle of soft, curly hair. Her orgasm was sharp and sweet, a swift intake of breath. She was the glowing image of fire and lust and passion. With a strangled moan, Rafael flipped her over and drove into her with the heady rush of release.

Afterward, she peeked at him through half-hooded eyes, lazy and content. He propped himself up and stroked the curve of her mouth, running his thumb over her lip.

"In the morning, you'll leave me," she said. "Forever."

Rafael stilled and raised his brow.

"I've been keeping something from you, Rafael. I want you to know that I'm sorry."

"Yvet—"

"Just hold me." She snuggled into the crook of his shoulder.

Rafael pulled a blanket over them and settled in. He'd battled his attraction to Yvette as long as he could, but now that it was done, he was all in. There was nothing she could do or say to throw him off.

"What are you doing?" Yvette squinted.

"Recording how beautiful you look." Morning illuminated the lines of her neck and shoulders.

"Do you think that's wise?" She pulled the blanket over her face.

Rafael laughed and tossed his phone aside. "Falling in love is never wise."

"Don't fall in love. Not with me."

"Why not? You're smart and strong and determined. You can do anything you set your mind to." He stroked her hair. "Why do you hate yourself so?"

Slipping out of reach, she gathered the blanket to her chest and sat. "You will too, when I tell you the truth."

"Fine. Let's have it." He grinned.

Bit by bit, she revealed the details.

Bit by bit, Rafael's world careened out of orbit.

Everything shifted. Everything changed.

By the time Yvette was done, nothing was the same again.

PRESENT

Thirty-One

"DID YOU KNOW ABOUT THIS?" VEE ASKED DAMIAN after playing him the recordings.

"I had no idea." The groceries he picked up remained scattered on the counter.

"You think he's with her?"

"I don't know, but we have to find her. Let's get these videos to the private investigator. Maybe Paul will catch something we missed." Damian reached for his phone.

"You're calling him right now?"

"I'm canceling my flight first. There's no way I'm letting you handle this on your own."

"I'm not on my own. Jeanne is next door, and you're just a call away."

"That's what you said before you ended up in the hospital."

"Damian." Vee cut his call short. "I promise I'll come running the minute I need anything. Right now, you need to make that flight. I've kept you from your family long enough."

"You and Rafael are family too."

"We are, and we always will be, but there's nothing you can do for us here that you can't do from home." Vee steered him toward his bag.

Damian wasn't big on hugs, but he enveloped Vee in his arms. "We'll find him. I promise."

Vee watched as he disappeared from view. Then she scrolled through her contacts and called Tony.

"Sorry, it's taken dme a while to get back, Tony. I was out of commission for a few days."

"Glad we connected," he replied. "I was away myself. I have the information you asked for."

"And? When was the last time you heard from Rafael?"

"Tuesday, week before last."

Tuesday. Vee's heart skipped a beat. The day after their argument. "What time?"

Tony scrolled through his records. "I have the call logged at 6:03 a.m."

"Did he say where he was?"

"No, but...uh..."

"You can tell me, Tony. You're legally bound. Rafael and I have a joint membership with your concierge service."

"He asked for a room in the city."

"On Tuesday morning? What about Monday night?" Vee had to know where he went after he left.

"No, nothing on Monday."

"This room..." Vee braced herself. "Has he used it before?"

"No."

"Anything else you can tell me about his call?"

"Well, he requested blackout blinds and a tuxedo."

Strange, but Vee jotted it down. "How long was he there for?"

"He checked out late afternoon."

"Send me what you have, including the address. Do you know if there's a video doorbell or security camera on the property?"

"I can find out."

"I'd appreciate it. My lawyer or private investigator may get in touch. If they do, you have my permission to talk to them."

"Anything you need." He noted their details. "And Vee...I hope Rafael shows up soon."

Thank you, Tony." Vee hung up and crawled into bed. A million thoughts buzzed through her head, but she needed to lie down. Her knees had taken the brunt of her weight when she collapsed, but every part of her ached, including her heart. Bone-weary, she cradled her tummy and shut her eyes.

Minutes ticked, but sleep eluded Vee.

Where did Rafael go after their argument?

What was he doing in that room the next day?

Why did he need a tuxedo?

Tossing the covers aside, Vee turned on Rafael's laptop and checked his calendar. It was clear for that day. She scrolled through the rest of the month, but there were no black-tie events or invites.

Feeling restless, Vee watered the plants in the sunroom. After days of neglect, they perked up. She tied a drooping stem of the night-blooming cactus to the lattice and stepped back. She could predict which week it would bloom, but Rafael always beat her to the exact night.

"Traitor." Vee traced the scalloped edges. "I'm the one that looks after you, but you only bloom for him. He has a way about him, doesn't he? Me, you...her." Vee's eyes drifted back to Rafael's laptop. "We all bloom for him."

She replayed one of the videos and paused at a close-up of the woman's face.

Did she have something to do with the room, the blackout blinds, and the tuxedo?

Vee had to find her. Scrolling through Rafael's contacts, she searched all the female names on the internet. Hours later, she came up empty-handed. Tired and frustrated, she took a screenshot of the woman's face, uploaded it, and searched for similar images. It was a shot in the dark, so when she appeared in the results, Vee bolted upright. Clicking the photo directed her to the woman's profile on a professional networking site. For a few moments, Vee stared at the screen. She had all the information she needed to track her down.

As Vee scrolled through her work experience, she froze. Jeanne was right. The woman was on Rafael's research team, but three years ago. The videos were recorded later, which meant they'd stayed in touch. Vee wondered if she'd been so weighed down by her miscarriages that she'd failed to look, to listen, and to observe?

She jotted down the woman's name, although it was now burned in her mind. Finding her address was easy—an apartment in Alhambra, twenty minutes away.

Vee grabbed her keys and dashed out. She had a name, a face, and an address. She wasn't going to waste another minute tracking her down.

Thirty-Two

VEE CHECKED THE ADDRESS AND SCANNED THE apartments. The building had three levels, with units facing a shared courtyard. Taking the stairs to the second floor, Vee followed the numbers on the door. As she got closer, her mouth went dry. She wanted the truth, but was she ready for it?

About to knock, Vee noticed the door was ajar.

"Hello?" She nudged it open.

The lights were off, and the curtains drawn. Vee stepped inside and peeked around the corner. A stack of dishes soaked in the kitchen sink.

Venturing further, she surveyed the living room. White walls, black shelves, a leather sofa with grid-like seats. Everything was crisp, clean, and devoid of color.

"Hello?" she repeated.

The bedroom door was partially shut. Vee tiptoed into the hallway and eased into the bathroom. One toothbrush meant the woman was alone; two would need further investigation.

White tiles. White vanity. A single white toothbrush. The placement of items on the counter was neat and precise. The only thing off was the mirrored cabinet over the sink. Its door was open, revealing a row of prescription vials. Vee picked one up, but it was too dark to read the label. Nudging the bathroom door until it was almost closed, she turned on the light. None of the pills were familiar, so she took a photo. As she moved the mirrored door back to its original position, she caught the reflection of the wall behind her and froze. Scribbles covered the entire expanse.

Vee spun around and gasped. One word, written over and over again:

Garden Garden Garden...

The writing was loud and discordant, a frenzy of black strokes. From ceiling to baseboard, every inch of space shrieked the same word. Vee stumbled back and switched the light off. The afterimage remained, an eerie inversion of white on black.

Disturbed and panicking, Vee dashed out and fled the apartment.

"Promise me you won't do anything so rash again." Jeanne placed a turmeric latte on Vee's nightstand. "What were you thinking? Going there on your own? I'm just glad you made it home safe."

"I had to know if Rafael was there. Or if she had his phone. Something. *Anything.*"

"And?"

"What do you make of this?" Vee shared the picture of the medications. "I can't tell what they're for, but I'm sure you know."

Jeanne zoomed in and studied the labels. "Neuroleptics. They're used for psychosis, delusions, hallucinations..." She scrolled to the other end of the image. "This one's for anxiety and insomnia." Handing Vee's phone back, she frowned. "You had no business confronting her. She could be absolutely nutters."

"It didn't look like that in the videos."

"You never know what's going on under the hood. Not until you pop the bonnet and have a good look. You shouldn't go poking around other people's business like that. I'll be keeping an eye on you when I'm home. You've been warned."

Vee leaned against the headboard and reached for the milk. "How is everything coming along for your retirement party? Saturday night, right?"

"I canceled. It doesn't feel right without Rafael."

"You can't let a milestone like that slide without a celebration. Give me the guest list. I'll let everyone know it's back on. It'll give me something to do."

"I have a better idea. Let's celebrate on our own. We'll dress up, order in, and to hell with everything and everyone else. The best way to say goodbye to it all."

"Deal." Vee placed the latte back on the nightstand.

"Finish it." Jeanne handed the glass back and waited until she drank it all. "Get some rest now. I'll let myself out."

Vee closed her eyes and sank into the pillow. Her

hand slid over her belly. A part of Rafael was with her, and that comforted her.

"Ha," Jeanne exclaimed from the other side of the wall. "Checkmate, girly."

Vee smiled and drifted off, listening to her hum as she rinsed the dishes.

Thirty-Three

VEE'S DREAMS WERE STRANGE AND DISJOINTED.

"Vee!" Rafael called.

Vee spun around, but he wasn't there. Everything was out of place. The sunroom was bare, except for the fridge. Vee couldn't read the anagram he left her, so she moved closer. With each step, the sky darkened. Clouds rumbled, heavy with soot and ash. Each letter on the fridge was written on a sticky note. She peeled them off, one by one: G, A, R...

Vee knew what came next: D, E, N.

"No." Then notes slipped through her hands, swirling in the air. They landed at her feet, rearranged: D, A, N, G, E, R.

The sky cracked open. Rain cascaded over the glass

ceiling. It rushed over the windows and poured in through the cracks. Water dripped on Vee's head and splattered on the notes.

As the splotches grew, Vee gasped.

It wasn't water. It was blood. Rivulets of blood ran down her legs.

"No." She choked back a cry.

Blood stained the notes at Vee's feet, but when she looked around, the notes were everywhere—on the walls, on the windows, on the floor.

D, A, N, G, E, R

D, A, N, G, E, R

D, A, N, G, E, R

The room started spinning. Gusts of wind rattled the windows.

Vee's eyes flew open. Drenched in sweat, she lifted the covers. As real as the dream felt, she had not miscarried in her sleep.

Relieved, Vee got out of bed and turned the kettle on. Morning light filtered through the windows. As she waited for the water to boil, her eyes fell on the unsolved message on the fridge:

Pi the wise one.

Vee wrote each letter of the message on a sticky note and placed them on the table. Swapping them around, she grouped them into words.

Whose nite pie.

Poise the wine.

White... Vee paused and scanned the remaining letters.

White...peonies. Her heart gave a lurch. *That's it. White peonies.*

Solving Rafael's message was anti-climactic. Vee had hoped for more than a random anagram. She wanted a peek inside his mind before he disappeared. What was he thinking? What was he feeling?

Vee crumpled the notes and tossed them into the garbage. Rafael had been gone for fifteen days. The sinking feeling in her chest grew heavier with each passing day. A breeze swept withered jacaranda blooms to the curb. It stirred a hazy memory around the edges of Vee's mind. She shut her eyes, trying to bring it into focus.

White peonies.

Vee's eyes flew open. She'd seen them. White peonies by the curb.

Like dominoes tipping one by one, a cascade of thoughts rippled in quick succession. Vee rushed to the sunroom and stared at the grid of notes. Placing an "x" on the ones that stood out, she stepped back. She was following a single strand in a tapestry—impossible to isolate, yet impossible to ignore.

Picking up the report from the private investigator, Vee noted the number and called him.

"Hi, Paul. Could you get me a background check on someone?" Vee gave him the name. "I want everything you can get your hands on. Family history, legal, criminal, financial, and employment records... I want it all and I want it fast."

Vee had barely put the phone down when the doorbell rang. Mind still reeling, she opened the door.

"Good morning." Detective Burke removed her sunglasses and slipped them into her pocket. "Sorry for showing up unannounced. I tried to get a hold of you at the hospital, but your doctor wouldn't let me visit. Said any kind of stressful situation could set back your recovery. How are you feeling?"

"I'm better now." Vee drew her robe around her body.

"Glad to hear it. Are you up to answering a few questions?"

"Not without my lawyer."

"Fair enough, but you should know that we've tracked down the person who broke your window. I was hoping you'd accompany me to the station to confirm it. There have been some other developments that you can help us clear up, but sure." She shrugged. "Bring your lawyer." She turned and walked toward her car.

"Wait." Vee's chances of finding Rafael were better if she worked with Detective Burke instead of against her. Vee also had some hunches of her own she wanted to discuss. "Give me a minute."

Changing into jeans and a T-shirt, she grabbed her handbag and got in Detective Burke's car.

Thirty-Four

"SORRY, THESE ROOMS CAN BE STARK." DETECTIVE Burke caught Vee staring at the block walls. The door was the same concrete-gray as the floor.

"Would you like something to drink before we start?" she asked.

"No, thanks."

"All right, then." Detective Burke pulled her chair up to the table. "This is my colleague, Detective Espinoza." She introduced the man next to her. "This interview is being recorded. Could you please state your full name, date of birth, and birthplace?"

Vee opened her mouth, then shut it again.

"Mrs. Roza?" Detective Espinoza prompted.

"Sorry." Vee quelled her nerves and gave them her details.

The process was more formal than she expected. Her chair was bolted to the floor. There were cameras on the walls, and two detectives interviewing her.

"Do you know this woman?" Detective Burke swiveled her laptop around.

"That's the woman I ran into outside Rafael's office." Vee peered at the full-screen image. "The same woman who broke my window."

"Are you positive? You weren't able to identify her from the security footage. Could it be two different people?"

"It's her. I'm sure of it. Her name is Charlotte Song. Her bathroom wall is covered with the same word she scribbled on the note from that night."

"So, you know her? You've been to her place?"

"Yes... I mean, I don't know her, but I tracked down her address. I went to see her last night."

Detectives Burke and Espinoza exchanged a look. "Not going to lie, Mrs. Roza. We weren't expecting that. Tell us what happened."

"Nothing. She wasn't there."

"Then how did you see her bathroom wall?"

"The door was open. I walked in, but no one was home. I ventured further and saw the writing in her bathroom. It freaked me out, so I left."

"Why didn't you come to the police?" Detective Espinoza looked up from the notes he was taking.

"The last time I talked to Detective Burke, she made me feel like I was the one under investigation."

"Confronting Charlotte Song was reckless." Detective Burke sat back and regarded Vee.

"What else was I supposed to do? I need answers. My husband's been missing for two weeks now."

"So you did confront her?" Detective Espinoza asked.

"No. Like I said, she wasn't there."

"But when you set out to see her, that was the plan?" Questions pinged from Detective Burke to Espinoza and back again.

"There was no plan. I just wanted to know if Rafael was there."

"Did you see anything to indicate he was?"

"No."

"So, you went in, looked around, and..." Detective Espinoza waved in the air. "Left."

"That's right. I don't get why you're asking all these questions. You brought me in to confirm it was Charlotte Song who broke my window, and I did."

"Indeed. Thank you for that, Mrs. Roza. We're trying to figure out her motive for breaking your window, and how it's related to your husband's disappearance, if at all.

"We discovered correspondence on your husband's computer, which indicates that Charlotte Song was misdiagnosed with a mood disorder. It turns out that she has synesthesia, just like Rafael, except a different kind. Sounds generate colors in her field of vision.

"I'd like to show you some sessions your husband recorded with her. It has nothing to do with your husband's research. This is something entirely different. See, here..." Detective Burke played a video. "Your husband is generating a sound. Charlotte is circling the color she sees when she hears that sound. Every time he hits this note, she circles the same color. Every time he hits another note, she circles another color."

"I've seen these videos, Detective Burke. Rafael's laptop is synced with the computer you picked up. I didn't realize Charlotte has synesthesia, but I see what they're doing now: mapping out Charlotte's correlations—which sounds go with which colors."

"Exactly. But it gets more interesting." Detective Burke scrolled to a later session. "Here, they are using that map to communicate words. Charlotte is translating each note to a color, then each color to a letter of the alphabet: S, U, C, C, E, S, S. The first word in a language that's all their own."

"I don't get it." Vee leaned closer to the screen. "The sounds for the three S's were not the same, so why did Charlotte pick the same letter each time?"

"We couldn't figure it out either, so we brought in an expert. It has to do with the ratio between the frequencies of those sounds." Detective Burke referred to her notes. "Middle C, or C4, on the piano, vibrates at a frequency of 262 Hertz. An octave higher is C5, at 523 Hertz. Double the frequency. Go up another octave and you have C6, at 1046 Hertz. Charlotte is picking the same letter for different sounds, because there is an algorithm connecting them. We are far from understanding the complexities of it, but it's part of what your husband was trying to break down."

"What about the later recordings?" Vee asked. "It's just Charlotte writing random words with no sounds to prompt her."

"That's what we thought, but our consultant says there *is* sound, just not the kind you and I can hear. Charlotte continues to write words because she can perceive sounds beyond the normal audible spectrum."

"I see."

"Unfortunately, that ability comes at a cost," Detective Burke continued. "Because of the way her brain is wired, certain sounds provoke reactions that are beyond her control. She's prone to anxiety, panic, rage, depression."

"You talked to her?"

"We found messages on your husband's computer. Were you threatened by their relationship, Mrs. Roza?"

"Threatened? I didn't even know about Charlotte Song until she broke our window."

"Would it be accurate to say that your husband hid his relationship with her?"

"Tell me something, Detective Burke. Do you discuss every professional relationship with your significant other?"

"It appears professional, but we belie—"

"You should be talking to Charlotte Song about her relationship with my husband. Why don't you bring her in to clarify things for you?"

"We would, Mrs. Roza. Unfortunately, Charlotte Song was found dead in her apartment last night."

Vee blinked with stunned disbelief.

"You've cooperated with us so far, Mrs. Roza. If you have anything else to share, now would be a good time."

"Charlotte Song is dead, and you think I have something to do with it?" A thread of hysteria caught around Vee's voice.

"We have unidentified fingerprints at the scene of the crime. An eyewitness saw a woman fitting your description flee her apartment. Your own admission puts you at Charlotte Song's apartment last night. We're waiting on the autopsy and fingerprint analysis." Detective Espinoza rapped his pen on the table. "We already have a motive, so if I were you, I'd start talking."

"What motive? What are you talking about?"

"Here's our take," Detective Burke replied. "Your husband was leaving you for Charlotte Song. You tried to hold on to him by getting pregnant, but he didn't change his mind. You had a row. He walked out. He came home to collect his things the following night. You argued. Things got out of hand. You killed him. A crime of passion.

"The following night, Charlotte Song came looking for him. She worried when he didn't show up. She wanted to get a note to him because he wasn't returning her messages: *Garden*. A hotel? A street name? A codeword for their meeting place? Something spooked her, so she ended up smashing your window instead.

"You knew Charlotte would stir up trouble if Rafael didn't show up. You wanted her gone. In the meantime, you had to deflect suspicion away from yourself, so you sent yourself a text from Rafael's phone.

"Charlotte grew more concerned, so she went to Rafael's office and ran into you. We don't know exactly what transpired, but you were in the hospital following that encounter. Upon your release, you tracked her down. There was no sign of a struggle or forced entry. Tell us, Mrs. Roza, what exactly happened between the two of you?"

Vee stared at the detectives in stunned silence. She was caught in a dark, sticky web, and they knew it.

"Fill in the blanks for us and it may earn you some points, Mrs. Roza. How did you kill Charlotte Song?" Detective Espinoza asked.

Vee opened her mouth, then snapped it shut. "You're pinning this on the wrong person."

"Then set us straight. What have we missed?"

"Everything. You've cooked up a theory that's so ridiculous, I don't even know where to begin."

"Here's your chance then," Detective Burke said. "Tell us why it's ridiculous."

"If Rafael was leaving me for Charlotte Song, why

didn't she come to you when he went missing? Why show up at my house instead of talking to the police?"

"Maybe she didn't think he was missing. Maybe she thought you convinced him to stay, so he was avoiding her. She tried to get his attention the night of the thunderstorm. When that didn't work, she went to his office."

"If that's all there was to it, why did she run away? Why not just talk to me?"

"The woman was having an affair with your husband, Mrs. Roza. I think it's safe to assume that coffee and a bagel with you wasn't on her list of things to do."

"You keep pushing this alleged affair." Vee's voice surged with emotions. "You have no proof that Rafael's relationship with her was anything but professional."

"It's only a matter of time before we find it, but you did. Didn't you, Mrs. Roza? Either Rafael told you or you found out. That's why Charlotte ran from you. What did you say to her? Did you threaten her?"

"If I threatened her, she had plenty of time to lodge a complaint. I was in the hospital, for Christ's sake."

"Even if she came forward, it would be your word against hers. Charlotte has been in and out of the hospital for mental health issues. She's been in trouble with the law. There was no way she could go toe to toe with you. You knew she was sniffing around, so you silenced her."

"Look." Vee's head throbbed with the onslaught of accusations. "I want to work with you on this, but you've got the wrong person. Meanwhile, Rafae—"

"Yes. Tell us where your husband is, Mrs. Roza."

"Listen to me. I think I know wh—"

"You want to know what I think?" Detective Burke interjected. "I think you're hiding something. I looked you up, and you know what I found?" She opened a folder and held out two pieces of paper. "Your parents?" She scanned the first page and tossed it over her shoulder. "No trace of them. Your siblings?" She reached for the second page and chucked it in the air. "No trace of them, either."

Panic welled in Vee's throat. Lifting her chin, she met Detective Burke's gaze. "That has nothing to do with this."

"No?" Detective Burke shut the empty folder and sat back. "Then tell me. Which elementary school did you attend?"

Lips pressed, Vee stared back at her.

"What was the name of your principal? Your sixth-grade English teacher? Your best friend?"

"We're done here." Vee stood. "If you have questions, talk to my lawyer." She dropped his card on the table and grabbed her handbag.

"Whatever it is you're keeping from us, I'm going to get to the bottom of it," Detective Burke called after her. "That's a promise, Mrs. Roza. And next time?" Her voice followed Vee into the hallway. "I'll have an arrest warrant."

Vee's stomach churned with anxiety. A noose was tightening around her neck. If Detective Burke dug deep enough, she would find bones buried in the cemetery of her past.

PAST

Thirty-Five

"WE SHOULDN'T BE HERE." VEE LOOKED LIKE SHE was about to bolt. "This was a bad idea. I should never have agreed to this trip."

"It's our cantina." Rafael unlocked the side door. "It belongs to you as much as it does to me. It's time to stop running, Vee."

"The moment I stop, my past will catch up," she said. "You know what they'll do if they find me. Worse, if they find us together."

"If I thought this would expose you, I wouldn't risk it. Trust me, Vee." He held his hand out.

She emerged from the shadows and took his hand, but made no move to go inside.

"How can you love me, knowing everything I've

done?" It was a question she'd asked repeatedly in the beginning, and one she still asked herself.

Rafael urged her up on the step. They stood in the doorway of the unlit kitchen.

"Ready?" He squeezed her hand.

She squeezed back and stepped inside.

"Welcome to *Camila's*." Rafael flipped the light on.

Trailing her fingers over the granite counter, Vee took in the renovations: the hooded range, the pizza screens, the pots, and oversized sinks. *La Sombra's* transformation into *Camila's* was finally complete.

"What do you think?" Rafael asked.

"It's a wonderful tribute to your mother. And your father." Vee slipped her arms around him. "So sleek and clean and bright."

"It had to change. I had to banish the ghosts. I did keep one thing..." He tilted his head toward the serving window.

Vee stepped away and peered through it. When she looked back at Rafael, it was with a sadness that squeezed his heart. "Show me."

"Mamá, here." Rafael stopped in the hallway, where Mamá was shot. "And Papá, over there."

"Where were you?"

"Outside the bathroom." He gestured down the hallway.

She walked to the spot and stood there, reliving the night through his eyes.

"What a terrible thing to witness." Cradling his face, she raised on her toes and kissed his eyes—once for Mamá, once for Papá, then on the forehead for the boy who lost his childhood that night.

The constriction around Rafael's chests eased. It was as if he'd been waiting to share that night with someone who saw him, and Mamá, and Papá—who they were, who they could have been. Now that Vee was there, Rafael could let go. Wrapping his arms around her, he took a long, sweet breath.

He walked her to the end of the hallway and opened the door to the courtyard. "I haven't brought anyone here. It was always too sacred to share."

Time had dulled the tiles of the fountain. The night-blooming cactus was so entwined with the tamarind tree, it was impossible to tell where it began or ended. Weeds pushed under the door leading into the alley. On the other side, the crumbling facade of Tía Maria's house was a testament to lost years.

Vee stood by his side, taking it in. Then, letting go of his hand, she stepped into the courtyard. Wandering around the perimeter, she examined the leathery stems of the cactus.

"It's as old as me," Rafael said. "Mamá planted it when I was born."

"You have a twin and I'm the last to know?"

"Surprised you don't know everything about me?" He grinned. "My twin is a little shy. She shows her face just once a year. In fact, the only way she'll make it to our wedding is if we have the reception here. It's the perfect spot."

"I haven't said yes yet."

"You haven't said no."

"Yet," she quipped.

"Then tell me, right here, under this moon, under this tree. Tell me we don't belong together."

She dropped her gaze, because her whole heart was in her eyes—her stubborn, aching, impossible heart.

"Is that a yes?" Rafael lifted her chin.

"I don't see what's wrong with what we have right now."

"Yes or no, Vee?"

"Yes, okay?" Her laughter echoed in the courtyard. "Yes, yes, yes."

Her kiss washed over him like holy water.

"We'll keep it small," he said. "This might be the perfect time to reach out to your father."

"I've shut that door, Rafael. It's for the best." She shrugged, but the gesture was as obvious as someone trying to hide an old injury.

"Fair warning. I'm telling *everyone* on my side."

"Everyone, meaning Damian."

"Wait till he finds out."

"It will be nice to see him again."

"You know what else is nice?" Rafael led her to the stairs by the side of the house. Hopping onto the flat rooftop, he readied the switch.

When he turned the lights on, she gasped. Rows of string lights hung from one end of the roof to the other.

"When did you do all this?" She walked under the shimmering canopy, glowing with delight.

"I had some help from the couple that runs the cantina"

"The bed was Alma and Carlos' idea?" Vee teased.

"They insisted."

"Sure." She teased and flopped on the mattress. "It's a love nest." She fluffed up a pillow and eyed the lanterns around them. "What if I'd said no?"

"I would have asked again. Next week, next month, next year." Rafael kicked his shoes off and crawled next to her. "It's time you accept I love you. Whether you say yes or no."

Lying on her back, hands folded over her stomach,

she stared at the sky. A tear spilled down the side of her face.

"The tree," she said. "It's so tall."

Beyond the rows of light, it swayed over us, a crown of dark leaves against the starry night.

"Come with me." Rafael rose and pulled her to her feet.

Scaling the branch that extended over the roof, he sat on its twisted bark. It didn't take long for Vee to join him. Paza del Mar spread out before them. The sleepy fishing village was now sprawling with roads and buildings that radiated from the town square.

Vee reached for Rafael's hand, weaving her fingers through his. She scooted closer, resting her head on his shoulder. They watched the bars close. Kids circled the roundabout on motorbikes, hooting at stray dogs. A street vendor shuttered his stall and snuffed out the lamps. After a while, everything grew still and quiet. The breeze stirred at their feet and set leaves rustling in the tree.

"You know how they say that your whole life flashes before you when you die?" Vee lifted her head and gazed at him. "I'll be looking for this moment. I could spend forever in this moment."

She kissed him softly. When he moved his mouth against hers, her lips opened with a small sound. She hopped off the branch and looked over her shoulder, eyes gleaming with desire.

That night under the stars was magical, a return to everything beautiful and sacred and pure. Rafael reveled in Vee's body: her skin, her scent, her touch. They were two black holes swallowing each other up in a starburst of ecstasy.

Thirty-Six

RAFAEL WAS ON A HIGH FOR WEEKS AFTER THEY GOT home. He knew they belonged together but getting married was more than a promise to each other. It was a declaration to the universe, like launching a beacon of intent into the cosmos. Everything glowed in the aftermath of their decision. They picked a church in Paza del Mar and booked another trip there to finalize arrangements for their wedding.

Rafael left a day early to see Damian. Checking into a hotel on the outskirts of Paza del Mar, he scanned the hills through which his father had once driven him. His skin prickled as he recalled bumblebee wings brushing past him in the alley that day. A bittersweet sensation washed over him.

Life was strange and wondrous—soft as a feather,

fickle as the tide. It was the sword that bloodied dreams and the battlefield which seeded them anew.

His phone rang, cutting into his thoughts.

"Did you get in okay?" Vee asked when he picked up.

"Yes. I'm just about to head out and surprise Damian."

"I want a full report on how it goes when you tell him about the wedding."

"You got it." Rafael grinned. "What time is your flight coming in tomorrow?"

"Early. I'll get a cab from the airport and meet you at the hotel. How is it?"

"It's safe, Vee. Don't worry."

"I can't help it, Rafael. I have this weird feeling something's going to ruin things for us."

Vee's words haunted Rafael the next day. Something had almost ruined things for them, but as he maneuvered the winding road back to the hotel, Rafael's hands were steady. Ever since his parents died, gunfire paralyzed him. His chest hurt. His heart pounded. Dread and helplessness overwhelmed him. So, when he pulled into the parking lot, he stared at his fingers. They held rocksteady.

"Rafael." Vee rushed out of the lobby, feet flying over the ground.

"I'm all right. I'm fine."

"I've been worried sick since I got in." She ushered him to their room. "What happened? Why were you at the police station?"

"Let's just say I repaid an old debt."

"You *killed* someone, Rafael. You pulled the trigger and shot a man."

"I had no choice. He attacked Damian. I couldn't let something horrible happen to someone I love. Not again. I was immobilized, but then something took over. Rage." He raked his fingers through his hair. "It felt good to restore the scales of justice. Maybe I'm supposed to feel remorse, but the truth is I would do it again. I get why Papá said he would kill El Charro's men again, despite the consequences. I would do anything to protect the ones I love, move heaven and earth if I had to."

Vee drew him into her arms. "I thought it had something to do with me, because they tracked me down."

"It was someone who vowed to get even with Damian, an old grudge from our cartel days. It's over now. That chapter is closed for good."

"Don't be so sure. There's always someone. A family member. A friend. A business partner. It could come back to haunt us when we least expect it."

"Everything is going to be fine." Rafael kissed the top of her head. "We're going to book the church tomorrow. In a few months, we'll take our vows and all this will be behind us. We get to spend the rest of our lives together. Nothing can touch us now."

Vee snuggled closer.

Rafael looked beyond the terrace to the hills around them. He meant every word.

Nothing can touch us now.

Thirty-Seven

"KEEP YOUR EYES CLOSED." VEE STEERED RAFAEL through the house.

The happiness in her voice was the only direction he needed. She was his true North, his fixed point in a spinning world.

"Ready?" she asked.

"Ready." Rafael opened his eyes.

"A housewarming memento," Vee gestured toward the lone plant in the sunroom. "I snipped a cutting of the night-blooming cactus when we were at *Camila's*."

"I can't think of a more perfect beginning for our new home." His heart filled with nostalgia.

"There's more." Vee backpedaled into the kitchen. "Ta-da!" She showcased the magnets on the fridge door.

"I thought you wanted neutral decor." Rafael laughed at the colorful letters.

"It's a puzzle."

"GARMENT PIN." Rafael read the words out loud. "Are you expanding your business to fashion?"

"No, but you're on the right track. I'm expanding all right." She chuckled. "Rearrange the letters."

"Just tell me." He nipped her neck.

"Nope." She grinned, wiggling in his arms so they both faced the fridge.

"Let's see." Hugging her from behind, Rafael rested his chin on her shoulder. "PERMING TAN?"

"That doesn't make any sense."

"Hey, they're valid words and they fit."

"Try harder."

"Okay. Um...MIGRANT PEN?"

"What?" She laughed. "No."

"Wait. I have it. MAN RENT PIG. Babe, if you want a housewarming party with farm animals, just say the word."

"Concentrate, Rafael."

"Then stop distracting me." He caressed the flare of her hips, her nipped-in waist, the curve of her belly...

His hands froze.

Vee angled her face as realization dawned on him. He stared at her, the answer to her puzzle stuck in his throat: *I'M PREGNANT*.

"We're having a baby?"

Her smile was so bright and beautiful that it hurt.

"I was wrong." Rafael scooped her up. "*Now* I'm the happiest man in the world."

Their laughter bounced off the bare walls. The empty rooms were a blank canvas, coming alive with dreams and colors and magic.

"Tell me." Vee grew impatient over the phone.

"I don't remember you giving me any hints."

"I did. I said I was expanding."

"Fine." Rafael turned into the street and pulled into the driveway. "My clue has to do with what I'm bringing home tonight."

"SAD APE MAN?" She laughed at the message he left her.

"You have a minute to crack it, or you lose."

"That's not fair. I didn't give you a deadline."

"The deadline was nine months. I think I'd have figured it out along the way."

"Exactly. So don't rush me."

"Too late." Rafael let himself in.

Caught off guard, Vee whirled around, still holding the phone.

"I give you SAD APE MAN." Rafael bowed and handed her a takeout container.

She put her phone down and untied the ribbon. "Empanadas! SADE APE MAN, rearranged." She laughed. "I've been craving these. You listen to my ramblings even when I think you're not paying attention."

"Especially when you think I'm not paying attention. That's when you spill all the good stuff."

Rafael listened to the silences too, in the quiet moments when they cleared the table, or hung a picture frame, or watched thunderstorms in the sunroom. That's when Vee spoke the loudest—words she couldn't bring herself to say, words she thought would rip Rafael away from her: *I love you, I love you, I love you...*

"Oh my God." One hand under her chin, she bit into the flaky crust. "This is everything."

"Right?" Rafael chuckled. "I got every filling they had. What did you get?"

"Mushrooms and green chilies. So good." She pulled out two plates and slid one to him.

He pulled up a chair and bit into one of the flaky crescents. As soon as its filling hit his taste buds, he froze.

Vee opened the fridge and poured a glass of milk. Looking over her shoulder, she frowned. "What's wrong?"

"I haven't had sweet empanadas since the night Mamá and Papá died."

"Oh, Rafael." Vee circled the table.

Wrapping his arms around her, Rafael leaned his forehead against her belly. "I was alone then, but I have you and the baby now. They would have loved seeing us together, growing into a family."

"I know." Vee stroked his hair. "All my life, I wanted what you had with your parents. Now I have it with you. Sometimes I think I'm dreaming, that it will all be swept away from under my feet."

Rafael pulled her onto his lap. "The only thing that's going to sweep you off your feet is me, and I intend to do it again and again." He kissed the hollow of her throat. "You should save me the trouble and live right here forever."

"On your lap?" The corners of her mouth tilted as her lips found his.

"Well...maybe a little to the right."

Her laughter was soul-warming.

Vee and Rafael were happier than they'd ever been.

Vee was laughing the night they lost the baby. She laughed

a lot, leading up to that moment—more playful and vivacious than Rafael had seen her before. That night, the laughter caught in her throat. She gasped and dropped her toothbrush in the sink.

"Vee?" He kneeled beside her. She sat on the lip of the bathtub, gripping its edges.

"Something's wrong, Rafael."

They didn't have time to get to the hospital. The miscarriage was swift and unmistakable. Vee locked herself in the bathroom and shut Rafael out.

"I'm being punished." She averted her gaze when she finally came out. "I don't deserve kids after what I've done."

"You are not to blame." Rafael cradled her face. "When you cry, my whole world turns dark. You are my life, my hope, my home. If my life ended tomorrow, I would look for you again and again, in every lifetime."

Her tear-streaked face was more than he could bear. He gathered her in his arms and held her all night.

Their loss cast a shadow on the wedding. Vee made the most beautiful bride, even with the veil of sadness. Rafael's joy, as she walked down the aisle, was boundless. Their smiles were genuine, if bittersweet.

For a while, their lives were muted. The colors weren't as bright, the sounds not as sharp. But they were finally together and ready to take on whatever life threw at them.

One morning, Vee snuck back under the covers and whispered, "Guess what?"

Rafael stared at the pregnancy test, then back at her. The sparkle in her eyes was back.

A fog lifted. The smell of eggs sizzling in the pan made him hungry again.

"Ready!" He called, carrying breakfast into the sunroom.

They sat on the floor, leaning against the wall, with their legs stretched out.

"We need some furniture." She nudged his toes with her foot. "A rug, plant stands, a coffee table, a couple of cozy chairs."

"Just one will do. You already have a designated spot." Rafael scooped her onto his lap. "You keep forgetting your place, woman."

She squealed and held up her smeared toast.

"Yummy." Rafael tasted the jam on her lips.

"Me or the jam?"

"You. Always you, only you."

"Cross your heart?"

"Cross my heart." Rafael made the sign.

"I'm going to miss this." Vee walked her fingers over his chest. "These pecs. These abs. These thighs."

Rafael shot her a questioning glance.

"They'll disappear when you stop working out," she explained.

"Why would I stop working out?"

"Because my designated spot needs more cushioning. This?" She poked his belly. "Supremely uncomfortable." Straddling his hips, she wound her arms around his neck.

They melded together in the pool of light streaming through the windows. Rafael's senses caught around sharp flashes: Vee's hair floating over him, her nipples taut under the fabric of her top, the gasp of sweet release.

As they lay with a T-shirt rolled under their heads, Rafael picked a lock of her hair and caressed it.

"Look." She tilted her head toward the night-blooming cactus.

Lush and jade-green, it was flourishing despite their neglect.

"Is that a bud?" Rafael sat up. "Vee, that's our first bud."

"Things are turning around for us." Her face glowed with happiness.

Vee was back, and she was a whirlwind of joy. Her doctor's visit went well. She re-purposed an urn, filled it with dried branches, and set it in the sunroom. They decorated the space quickly after that: a sisal rug, soft seating, plants, flowers, and art.

"Let's have a movie night," she said, when it was done.

"Tomorrow."

"Tonight."

"Tomorrow." Rafael grinned. "I promise it will be worth it."

"You're off to bed already?"

"I am, and you're coming with me." He grabbed her hand and drew her into the bedroom.

Snuggling under the covers, he waited until her breath was slow and steady. Then he crept out of bed and set up the space.

"Vee." He shook her gently when everything was ready. "Wake up."

One eye squinted open.

"Wake up. It's tomorrow."

"What?"

"It's movie night."

"Are you out of your mind?" She turned over and closed her eyes.

"Vee." Rafael walked around to the other side.

"Go away."

"Fine." He lifted her out of bed.

"Rafael, put me down. I'l—" She broke off as he carried her into the sunroom. The makeshift stage showcasing the plant tipped her off. Her eyes widened. "It's time?"

Grinning at her about-turn, Rafael set her down.

"Popcorn." He handed her the bowl.

"Blanket." He spread it over their laps.

"Movie." Aiming the remote at the night-blooming cactus, he pretended to click "play".

They stared at the bud for a few minutes, then at each other.

"The suspense is killing me." Vee sidled up to him. The bud showed no sign of stirring.

"A slow start, but building toward an unforgettable climax."

"Plot twist." Vee grabbed a handful of popcorn. "It's not going to open tonight."

"You'll be eating your words instead of popcorn before the night is through."

"I can think of better things to do with my mouth." She held a kernel between her lips.

Rafael dipped his head as she offered it to him, tasting salt and butter.

"We're missing the movie," she said.

"I'm suddenly in the mood for a steamy romance."

"No, really." She sat upright and motioned toward the bud. "Look."

"It's just the opening credits." Rafael went back in for a kiss.

Slowly, like ripples in silk, the petals unfolded, transforming into a majestic flower, nine inches wide. Soft and new, its beauty was wondrous and awe-inspiring.

Reaching for his hand, Vee sought his eyes. The moment bloomed and held.

Say it, Rafael thought. *Tell me you love me. I've heard it a thousand times, in the way you look at me, the way you touch me. Just say what you're aching to say.*

Vee hovered on the verge, so close that her chest filled. Then she pulled back, and the words scattered like dandelion seeds in the air.

"Tell me we'll be okay." She circled her belly.

"Everything will be fine. Whatever happens, I'll be right here, by your side."

With dawn's first light, the waterlily-like blossom closed and drooped on its stem.

Vee and Rafael drifted off, enchanted by its lingering fragrance. Legs tangled, they anchored each other as dreams and night wishes spun a cocoon around them.

Thirty-Eight

VEE'S HAND WAS ICY AS RAFAEL RUBBED IT BETWEEN his palms.

"It happens from the anesthesia sometimes," the nurse explained. "I'll get an extra blanket."

"Vee?" Rafael sat at the edge of her bed.

Her gaze focused and turned to him. "I lost this one too."

Rafael's throat tightened. Folding her limp fingers over his, he kissed them.

"Is it crazy to be this heartbroken over losing someone I never met?" she asked.

"It's okay, Vee. We'll get through this."

"My womb is scarred, Rafael. The doctor said the chances of me carrying a baby to term are slim."

"I know, *mi alma*." He stroked her hair.

The world was caving in around them, the family they dreamed of, the unopened crib at home, the gamble of happily ever after.

"I'm not giving up."

"It's time to consider other options, Vee. Or envision a different future. Just you and me."

She was silent for so long that the hair stood on his neck.

"You think I don't know that your heart is breaking? That you're shrugging it off to protect me? Don't pretend you're okay when you're not."

"It's not an act, Vee. I mean it. You're all I need. Always you, only you."

"You've wanted a family ever since you lost your parents." She stroked his cheek. "We're two sides of the same coin. Family means everything—perfect, dysfunctional, or somewhere in-between. We spend our lives running toward it or away from it. Either way, it's in our marrow. I'm not giving up, and I won't let you give up either."

Rafael rocked her in his arms. They clung together, striving to find solace in the sterile room.

"Don't let me interrupt." The nurse re-entered. "Just dropping off an extra blanket." She lay it at Vee's feet and left.

"Feeling any warmer?" Rafael tucked the blanket around Vee.

"I want to go home."

"I know, baby. We'll leave as soon as they let you."

Home was their haven, a place to hope and heal and hold each other tight. But that night, an uninvited guest followed them home. Like black smoke curling under the doors, Death swept inside. As Vee and Rafael dropped exhausted into bed, she took form.

Slowly.

Patiently.

Thirty-Nine

"WHO ARE YOU MEETING?" VEE LOOKED UP FROM the newspaper.

"Charlie," Rafael informed her for the third time.

"Right." She went back to her crossword.

Rafael started to say something but changed his mind. Vee didn't share his excitement at connecting with someone who had synesthesia. When he spoke about what he and Charlotte were working on, her eyes retained the glazed look they'd taken on since her third miscarriage.

Vee was slipping from Rafael's grasp even as she wandered about the house—present yet far away. The anagram on the fridge remained unsolved. The airline tickets it alluded to were lost under a pile of brochures about recurrent miscarriages.

"Vee..." Rafael kneaded her shoulders. At night, he massaged her feet, but he couldn't get to the core of her pain. As gut-wrenching as each loss was for him, he knew it only scratched the surface of what Vee felt. Her trauma went far beyond physically conceiving, then losing a baby.

"How about a road trip this weekend?" he asked. "We can stay at that cute little ranch you love. The one with the baby goats. We'll ask them to pack us a picnic, find a spot somewhere in the mountains..."

"Maybe another time." Vee replied absently.

Rafael grasped for something to say, something to unravel the layers of numbness swaddling Vee's pain. He didn't know how to get through, and it was killing him.

"It looks like Walter's kids are finally cleaning up next door," he said.

Vee rose and stared out the window, as if seeing the "for sale" sign on their neighbor's lawn for the first time.

"I can't believe he's gone," she said.

"He was prepared for everything, including dooms-day. Remember when he called us over to sample his emergency food stash?"

"Dehydrated potatoes and freeze-dried corn." The hint of a smile played on Vee's lips. "Oh, I almost for-got." She rummaged through a drawer and pulled out an envelope. "Walter gave us the spare keys to his place. I should hand them over to his family. Looks like they're about to leave."

She raced over, envelope in hand.

"Vee," Rafael called from the doorway.

Midway there, she glanced over her shoulder.

"Look, Vee." Rafael pointed to the ground. "You dropped something."

She picked up the slip of paper that had fallen out of the envelope.

"Parker," she read, throwing me a quizzical look.

"Walter's dog. The one whose ashes he wanted to launch into space."

"Of course." Vee slipped the note back into the envelope. "Poor Parker. He never made it into orbit. Walter ended up having his ashes infused into a paperweight." She laughed.

Rafael's breath contracted in his throat. It had been so long since he'd heard her laughter.

She raced off, waving her arms to stop Walter's family from taking off. The sight of her filled him with sadness and yearning. Rafael didn't know how to bridge the distance between them.

Time flew when he was with Charlotte. She was extraordinary and intriguing. Beneath the awkward facade was magic he couldn't get enough of—magic she kept bottled tight. Had Rafael not caught a glimmer of it in her assignments, he would have missed it, like everyone else who walked past her.

Rafael graded many papers, but hers stood out. The first time, he glanced at her name and moved on. The next time, he tried to recall who she was. Rafael had a grid-like mental map of his classes. Although students changed seats, their faces imprinted against the layout of the lecture hall like layers of moving transparencies.

It was almost the middle of the term, and Charlotte Song was nowhere on that map. Over the next few lectures, Rafael figured out why. Charlotte Song attended only when necessary. She arrived for an in-class quiz, scouted out the most isolated spot, and pulled her hood over her head. Every time someone flipped a page, tapped a pen, or cleared their throat, Charlotte had a visceral reaction. With all heads bent over the quiz, her sideways glances, the slight jerk of her neck and the tapping of her feet were more apparent.

When she handed in her quiz, Charlotte avoided eye contact and headed for the door. Rafael didn't see her again until the midterm exam. Once more, she came and left quietly. As he headed to his office, Rafael noticed her standing a few feet from a group of loud students. She wanted to get to the exit but wouldn't go around them. She clutched her satchel and remained frozen, shivering in the hallway.

Rafael gave her a nod as he walked by. The squeak of her shoes followed him to his office. When he got to the door, he expected her to keep walking, but she stopped.

"May I help you?" he asked.

"I...uh..." She stared at her feet. "I'd like to apply for the Summer Undergraduate Research Fellowship program. I was wondering if you'd be my mentor."

"I'm picky about who I take on. You have to be interested in the research. You can't take courses or hold another job. I expect a full commitment over the ten-week perio—" Rafael broke off as she thrust some papers in his hand. "What's this?" he scanned the text. Two pages of a proposal. "You already have a project plan in mind?"

"That's what I wanted to show you."

"Come inside." Rafael gestured toward the chair and walked around to his side of the desk. Taking his seat, he dropped the exam papers he was carrying. They landed with a thud on the desk.

Charlotte pulled her hood tight around her face.

"Care for a snack?" He tore open a bag of chips and offered it to her.

"No, thanks." She fiddled with the satchel on her lap.

Rafael read through her proposal and sat back. "You've done your homework. I'm impressed. Same goes for the assignments you've been handing in. Let's get you an application form." He searched for it on his computer and hit the 'print' button.

As the paper advanced from the printer, line by line, Charlotte's jaw tightened.

"It's the sound, isn't it?" Rafael handed her the form. "You're extra sensitive to noise. You wear a hood to muffle it, but it doesn't always work."

Her eyes flew to his. For a second, she dropped her guard. Then she looked away and stared at the floor.

"Is there anything I can do to help?"

"No. It's just...the noise. Thanks for the application form." She slipped the printout into her satchel. "I'll have it filled out by the next class."

Rafael stared at the door after she left. He had the distinct impression that Charlotte Song was hiding something, but he didn't know what or why.

Two weeks into the summer program, Rafael caught a glimpse of Charlotte's secret world. When he entered the lab, she was at her workstation with headphones on. Unaware of his presence, she raised her hand, palm up, as if waiting for a bird to alight. Eyes to the ceiling, she followed its invisible flight to the other side of the room. Then she gazed at the floor with delight. One foot at a time, she skipped to the other side of the room, following a path only she could see. Pivoting around a desk, she caught sight of Rafael and froze.

"Professor Roza." She yanked her headphones off.

"Charlotte."

"I was just... I'm working on the numbers you requested."

"Carry on." Rafael headed for his workstation.

He didn't know what he had witnessed, but it wasn't someone dancing to music. It was someone engrossed in an alternate reality.

Charlotte stayed until it was time to lock up. Keys in hand, Rafael waited as she switched the lights off. Suddenly, she doubled over, pressing her hands to her ears. Her satchel dropped and fell open, its contents scattering across the floor.

"Charlotte?" He kneeled beside her.

A black poodle ran past the door, down the hallway.

"I'm okay." She opened her eyes.

"Here you go." Rafael helped her retrieve a pill bottle from the floor.

Judging by the number of vials on the floor, Charlotte was on multiple medications, including antipsychotics.

"It's not what you think." She stuffed everything back into her satchel.

"You don't know what I'm thinking."

"Ever since I was old enough to remember, I know what everyone thinks—that I'm a freak. I've lost jobs, opportunities, and interviews because I'm different. No dates or dinners or boyfriends, either. Everyone runs for the hills. Maybe you'll brush this off today, but tomorrow, you'll catch me doing something weird, or funny, or scary. So I need to know. Is this going to mess me up? Is it going to affect your evaluation of my work? Because if it is, I might as well pack up and look for something else."

"Is that how you handle things? You pack up and run?" Rafael walked back to his station, lay his backpack down, and invited her to sit across from him.

She shifted from one foot to the other.

"I won't pretend to know what's going on with you," he said. "But I know a thing or two about being different. I grew up different. My brain is wired different. That's why I tuned in to what I thought was your sensitivity to noise. Obviously, I was wrong. There's more to it. If you want to talk, I'm here. If you don't, that's fine too. My evaluation of your work here will be based exactly on that. Your work."

For a few moments, Charlotte wavered. Then she pivoted on her heel and walked away. When she got to the door, she turned back around.

"You're not wrong," she said. "I *am* sensitive to noise. More accurately, to sound. For me, every sound has a color. I'm constantly surrounded by them. The patterns and swirls I see depend on the sounds: how loud, how frequent, how they meld. When I was little, I loved watching them. My parents thought something was wrong with me. My teachers said I wasn't paying attention. I learned not to let my eyes wander or react to what I saw."

"Is that what you were doing when I walked in? Reacting to seeing the music?"

"I slip into my world when no one is around. Every song is a unique combination of colors—every note, every chord. Sometimes I get lost in a rhapsody of shapes and hues. Today, when we were leaving, I heard a high-pitched sound. Loud noises create a burst of sudden, intense color—like someone prying your eyes open with a flashlight. They paralyze me. Dog whistles, thunderstorms, fire alar—"

"Did you say dog whistles? That's something most of us can't hear."

"That's what it was today: a dog whistle. It incapacitated me. I'm on medications because my reactions are unpredictable. It's no big deal for me, but when it happens around other people, it's scary and unsettling. They freak out."

"So, you're on these pills, not because you need to be, but because you don't want to make other people uncomfortable?"

"Well, it *is* for me. So I can fit in, calm down, be more...normal."

"You have an extraordinary gift, Charlotte. You *see* sound. It evokes colors and shapes and movement. I understand how that can be a burden when you're surrounded by people who can't relate, but I encourage you to work with it and understand it." Rafael tore off a sheet of paper and jotted down a name and phone number.

"Dr. Zanna Dixon?" Charlotte glanced at the note.

"She's one of the top researchers studying synesthesia, a crossing over of sensations that are normally experienced separately. I suspect that's what you have, but she can run tests to verify."

"You mean there are other people like me?"

"Yes, and no. Everyone has different associations. If a sound evokes the color yellow in you, someone with the same type of synesthesia may see it as blue or green."

"That's incredible. I don't know what to say." Charlotte sat, digesting the information. "Knowing there's a name for it makes me feel better."

"I felt the same when I found out."

"You?"

"It's numbers for me. I see them as shapes, patterns, timelines, three-dimensional maps..."

Taken aback, Charlotte stared at Rafael through a different lens. "You don't know what you've done for me. I've been in and out of hospitals, passed on from one specialist to another, been on and off all kinds of drug regimens."

"Let's not jump the gun, Charlotte. If Dr. Dixon confirms you have synesthesia, inform your doctor, your therapist, and anyone else that needs to know. You may have to keep doing what you're doing, but everyone will be better informed."

"Charlie. Call me Charlie." Her face spread into a smile. "I'm glad I ended up in your class."

"I'm glad too." Rafael smiled back.

Forty

"EVERYTHING OKAY WITH YOU AND VEE?" JEANNE asked.

"Is it that obvious?" Rafael secured the lid on her garbage bin and rolled it to the curb.

"Maybe not to everyone. To me, it's as obvious as the sun not coming up."

"We're going through a rough patch." He glanced at the kitchen window, hoping to catch sight of Vee, but most days she didn't get out of bed. "I can't bear to see her go through this endless cycle of hope and despair, and she can't see why I'm not on board with it anymore."

"I see her point, Rafael. Family is important. But I understand your dilemma too. At what cost to her own health?"

"Exactly." Rafael opened the gate in the hedge that separated their homes.

"Wait." Jeanne tucked her arm through his and nudged him toward her porch. "I made some meals for you."

"That's very kind of you."

"I don't have kids to cook for, so I cook for you." She retrieved containers from her freezer and set them on the dining table. "I love you and Vee very much. You're my family, and I want you to make up. I want to hear laughter again when I knock on your door. Now, sit a while and take a load off."

Rafael drank the latte she made for him. Flavored with honey and turmeric, it had a distinct flavor that he loathed initially, but now associated with warmth and comfort.

"Thank you for taking out the garbage every week." Jeanne popped the meals into a tote. "You spoil me."

"Look who's talking." Rafael peered inside the tote. "This will last us a while."

Returning home, he nudged the gate open and let himself in. As he placed the tote on the counter, a pill bottle rolled off. He put it back in the drawer with the others. Anti-depressants, sleeping pills...a cocktail of drugs to keep Vee from slipping into the abyss.

"Vee?" Accustomed to a one-way conversation, he didn't expect a reply. "You want some dinner?"

"As soon as I'm done here."

Rafael stilled. Vee wasn't in the bedroom. He followed the sound of her voice into the sunroom and stopped in his tracks.

"You like it?" She grinned.

"What's going on?"

Flowers and ferns filled the space. Orchids and succulents peeped from behind the furniture.

"Remember the company that wanted to buy me out?" She wiped a streak of dirt from her cheek and slid her arms around him.

"Yes?" There was no better feeling than holding Vee.

"I agreed. I sold the business."

"I didn't even know you were considering it."

"I haven't been to work in weeks, and I don't want it falling apart. I'm handing over the day-to-day operations, but I'll still have a say. Isn't that great?" Her eyes sparkled. "Dr. Sterritt said it's important to reduce stress, so this time, our chances are better."

"This time?" Rafael unclasped her arms from around him. "I thought we decided to stop trying for a baby."

"It's different now. I'll be home. More relaxed. And I'm off to a great start. It's the first time in weeks I've felt like doing something, so I picked up these plants after the meeting. Aren't they gorgeous?" She gestured around the room. "I'm all hot and sweaty, though. About to hop in the shower. And you know what else?" She leaned in and whispered in his ear. Her gaze dropped to his lips as she stepped back.

Rafael's response was instant and exhilarating. He couldn't remember the last time they had sex for pleasure. Somewhere along the line, physical intimacy had become an exercise in trying to conceive.

"You're on." He stripped.

Vee's eyes met his, half-lidded and covetous. "I forgot how magnificent you are."

Rafael walked past her, feeling the heat of her stare, and stepped inside the shower.

Warm hands embraced him as water flowed over him.

"I've missed you." He turned around and pinned her against the stall.

She raised up on her toes and kissed him.

It was only after, when they were lying in bed, that Rafael noticed the calendar on Vee's bedside table, on which she marked her cycle.

Vee was ovulating.

Orchestrated or not, they had just set off another cycle of hope and despair.

Each loss had a personality. This one knew only anger and anguish. It blew a hole through Rafael's chest before Dr. Sterritt confirmed it.

"Six miscarriages." She clasped her fingers and leaned across the desk. "As difficult as it is to accept, sometimes the body knows best. A full-term pregnancy could be fatal for both mom and baby. We've come as far as we can. It's time to consider other options." Her eyes shifted from Rafael to Vee. "I'm going to write you a prescription for birth control pills. Here are some samples to start you off…"

Her words faded as Rafael mentally circled another date. Six miscarriages meant twelve calendar days every year: one for the day they lost the baby and one for the day it would have been born. In-between were jabs of loss spiking unexpectedly, sometimes with no trigger.

When they got home, Jeanne was waiting with a casserole. The routine was so familiar it tasted like grief.

"You done?" Rafael asked Vee after Jeanne left.

"I'm done." She reached for the birth control pills and placed them on the table.

"You're going to take them?"

She nodded.

The weight in Rafael's chest grew lighter. His concern for Vee's well-being was so heavy, he felt he would collapse under its unrelenting weight.

"We'll be okay, Vee. I promise. I'll make sure you never feel like you're missing anything in life."

"You look happy." Vee remarked as Rafael swapped sweaters. "On second thought, stay with the grungy one. This looks way too good on you." She stepped back and regarded him. "What's with the smile? Can't wait to get away from me?"

"Can't wait to get back." Rafael tackled her, and they fell back on the bed. "We have the entire summer to ourselves once this trip is done. Have you decided where you want to go when I get back?"

"I think we should stick to home base."

Rafael propped himself up and gazed at her. "There's something different about you. What's going on?"

She smiled and ducked her head. "Come on. You'll be late."

Whatever it was, Vee was happy. They'd been through a rough few months, but they were turning a corner.

"Miss me." Rafael pressed his lips to hers. Slinging his carry-on over his shoulders, he blew her a kiss.

"Rafael," she called.

He backtracked to the bedroom.

On the brink of saying something, she shook her head. "Nothing."

He waited.

"Really." She pushed him out, palms on his chest. "I just wanted to see your face again."

"You know what I think of when I see your face?"

"What?"

"You have until I get back to figure it out." He grinned.

Rolling his luggage behind him, he stopped in the kitchen to leave her a clue.

Pi the wise one.

Rafael spelled the anagram out with fridge magnets and stepped back. He couldn't wait to see if she got it, and the significance behind it.

When Rafael returned from his trip, the driveway was a carpet of purple blossoms. The jacaranda tree glistened in the rain.

"I'm home, Vee." Leaving his gear at the entrance, he shook the water off his jacket and peeked into the kitchen. His puzzle remained unsolved.

"Vee?" He grinned. Apparently, he'd stumped her.

The gray clouds only lifted his spirits. He was back early, right before a thunderstorm. Sitting in the sunroom, watching the rain wash everything clean, was the perfect start to a new beginning with Vee. Before the shadows rolled in, it had been their favorite thing to do—cozying up to rain, the rumble of clouds, the bolts of jagged lightning.

"Vee?" Rafael looked for her in the living room.

A light blinked on the answering machine.

"Hi, it's Dr. Sterritt." A message played when he turned it on. "Call me when you get this."

Rafael was about to save it for Vee when she dashed into the room, her hair wet from the shower.

"Rafael." Color drained from her face. "I wasn't expecting you until tomorrow."

"We wrapped up sooner." He frowned, puzzled by her reaction. "That was Dr. Sterritt."

She sat on the sofa, a terrible tenseness in her posture. "I didn't want you to find out this way."

Rain drummed against the windows.

"I was going to tell you." She circled her belly. "I almost did before you left."

A dreaded feeling tore at Rafael's insides. He knew her every nuance, her every expression. Vee was pregnant, which meant she'd come off the birth control pills. "Why, Vee?"

The conversation escalated swiftly. Instead of a new beginning, they stood at opposite ends. She wanted to keep the baby, and Rafael wanted to keep her safe. The more they talked, the more they lashed out at each other. Then, she struck an open wound.

"You couldn't do anything to save your parents, and now you want to kill our child?"

Remorse flared in her eyes the moment she said it.

"Rafael..." She reached for him, but it was the last straw.

Reeling from Vee's betrayal and the prospect of losing her, Rafael grappled with the mounting frustration that threatened to overcome him. He brushed past her into the night, wanting to put as much distance between them as he could.

Forty-One

*D*RIVING THROUGH THE SANTA MONICA MOUNTAINS was exhilarating and perilous. Rafael's headlights illuminated the slick, dark tarmac ahead. Rain lashed at the windshield faster than the wipers could handle. Maneuvering the hairpin turns demanded all his attention. It muted the storm of emotions raging within.

Thoughts assailed him. Memories. Faces. Snippets of conversation.

Around one bend was Lina, sticking her head out of the car window, waving as she disappeared from view.

Then Raven appeared: "Drive."

His eyes flew to the rearview mirror.

"You should lock your car if you don't like surprises."

At the next turn was a beat-up hatchback. Yvette

bent over the engine with the hood propped: flowers in the trunk, flowers on her dress.

"In the morning, you're going to leave me," she said.

"What are you talking about?"

"Tomorrow, when I tell you the truth, you'll leave."

"There's nothing you can tell me that will make me leave."

She gave him a sad smile and climbed into the car.

When he glanced over, Vee was in the passenger seat, wiping empanada crumbs from her lap.

"You should save us both the trouble and live right here forever," he said.

"In your lap?" The corners of her mouth lifted as she slid closer.

"Well...maybe a little to the right."

Her laughter rolled over him like thunder.

Pulling off the road, Rafael turned on his hazard lights.

"How did we end up here?" He stared at the homes nestled in the hills. Lantern-lit driveways flickered in the rain. Far below, the city was awash with the glow of lights and traffic.

Rafael had lost love in different ways, at different times, but it always found him. Over and over again. He sat with the memories—the faces and places as vivid as the lightning that illuminated the valley. He had a decision to make, because he couldn't stand to have things as they were.

When the sun rose, he got out of the car and walked to the edge of the canyon. The ground was soft, but the rain had washed away the smog that shrouded the city. Everywhere he looked, the air sparkled. Los Angeles, with all its heartache, was still a beautiful place.

Rafael closed his eyes, feeling the warmth of the sun

seep under his lids. In the turmoil of the night, one truth held fast. He knew exactly where he belonged. It was so glaringly obvious, he wanted to rush to her, but it was too early to go waking her up. It had also been an emotional night, and he hadn't slept since his flight home.

Retrieving his phone, he called Tony. "I need some place private in the city for a few hours."

"Any special requests?" he asked.

"A bed. Blackout blinds. A tux."

"Consider it done."

A few minutes later, his phone pinged with an address and access code. Rafael drove to the location and let himself in. The suite exuded luxury, but all he wanted was a place to crash. Kicking off his shoes, he undressed and crawled into bed. He needed to catch a few winks before facing the woman he loved—the only one who'd ever mattered.

Exhausted but hopeful, Rafael closed his eyes with a renewed sense of purpose.

Getting Tony to arrange the tuxedo was one thing, but Rafael wanted to get the flowers himself.

"Mr. Roza." The girl at the counter perked up when she saw him. "Your order is ready."

"Bloom Girl always comes through." He smiled. "The bouquet is perfect. Thanks, Ellen."

Heads turned when he walked out of the flower shop.

"Lucky girl," a passerby commented.

"There's more inside."

"I wasn't talking about the flowers."

Grinning, Rafael tipped his head and got in the car. His nerves buzzed with anticipation. He thought of calling, but he wanted an unguarded reaction. Rafael wanted to see the sparkle in her eyes when he swept her off her feet.

By the time he parked, the sun had set, and soft hues rippled across the sky. The light was golden and mellow. For a few seconds, the beauty of it all overcame him— butterflies drinking tree sap, the scent of the bouquet, mulberry clouds drifting into the night.

Only one thing would make it more perfect.

He retrieved the flowers from the passenger seat and locked the car.

"Rafael," she greeted him before he made it to the door.

Death has many faces and many voices. Not recognizing his, Rafael smiled. "Happy to see me?"

PRESENT

Forty-Two

"ANOTHER WEEK HAS GONE BY." JEANNE STARED AT the bins on the curb.

Vee wasn't the only one counting the days since Rafael had gone missing. For the last two weeks, when Vee helped Jeanne take the garbage out, they shared a moment. It was their seven-day marker.

"How are you holding up?" Jeanne rubbed Vee's back.

I'm not holding up, Jeanne. I'm crumbling, bit by bit, Vee thought. *Every day, I wake up and think I'll be discovered. Every night, I cling to my side of the bed as the imprint of Rafael's absence grows larger and larger.*

A black sedan turned into the street and parked

beside them. The driver took off his sunglasses and rolled his window down.

"May we help you?" Jeanne asked.

"I'm looking for Mrs. Roza."

"That's me," Vee replied.

He nodded and got out of the car. "Paul Hodson, PCI Investigations. We talked on the phone earlier. I have the report you requested." He glanced at Jeanne, then back at Vee.

"It's okay." Vee locked the bins in place. "I don't keep things from Jeanne."

"Of course." He handed Vee the report. "Let me know if you need anything else."

"A private investigator?" Jeanne asked, as he drove away.

"I requested a background check."

"Tell me." Jeanne hooked her arm through Vee's as they walked up her driveway.

"Charlotte Song." Vee held up the sealed envelope. "She's connected to Rafael's disappearance. I know it."

"She *was*," Jeanne corrected.

"Which is why it's even more important that I get to the truth. Not only is Rafael missing, but I'm a suspect in her death. Someone is out to get me, Jeanne."

"Listen to me." Jeanne took Vee's hands in hers. "You're under a lot of stress. Go home. Put your feet up. Take a nap, a bath...whatever you need to clear your head. Nothing bad is going to happen to you or the baby. Not as long as I'm here."

"Thank you." Vee unlatched the gate between their homes. "That means a lot."

Letting herself inside, she shut the door and stared at the envelope.

Page by page, Vee scrutinized the report: employment

history, previous addresses, marital status, family record, credit report. When she got to the end, she sat back. She had all the information, but nothing stood out.

Exhausted, Vee walked to the deck and rested her elbows on the railing. Mountains stretched endlessly across the horizon. Feeling like she was about to vanish into the haze, she shut her eyes and took a deep breath.

"Are you all right, dear?" Jeanne called from her shed. Unlike Vee's home, which cut into the hill, she had a large backyard.

"I'm fine." Vee smiled to reassure her. "Another day, another battle?" She tilted her head toward Jeanne's wheelbarrow.

"It's an ongoing struggle." Jeanne tossed a weed into it and moved on to the next one. "You just have to keep digging."

"Good advice."

Vee went back inside and pored over the background check again.

Nothing. Except for a minor discrepancy.

Turning on the laptop, she searched the internet, prepared to hit yet another dead end.

Forty-Three

"YOU'RE SURE THESE NUMBERS ARE RIGHT?" VEE FLIPPED through the new report.

"One hundred percent."

"Thanks, Paul." She hung up and stared at her notes.

Detective Burke rang again but didn't leave a message.

Vee had to make a move before she showed up, possibly with an arrest warrant. She took down the grid of sticky notes on the windows and pulled down the privacy screens in the sunroom. Spreading a bedsheet on the floor, Vee unearthed a plant from its pot. At the bottom was a hard-shell case wrapped in plastic. Wiping it free of dirt, she opened the case and retrieved a pistol.

The doorbell chimed, followed by a sharp rap on the door.

Weapon in hand, Vee froze.

"Vee?" Jeanne called.

Scanning the room, Vee dropped the pistol into an empty ceramic vase and kicked the case under the sheet.

"Jeanne." She let her in.

"Is everything all right? You never pull the screens down in the sunroom."

"I was just..." Vee tried to think of something but came up short. "You caught me." She led Jeanne into the sunroom.

"What's all this?" Jeanne surveyed the dirt on the floor, the empty pot, the exposed roots.

"I was going to bring it over tomorrow: a new plant to mark your retirement."

"Poor sprog. It won't last the week. I kill everything."

"That's not true. You grow the most beautiful roses."

"Roses are the only things that survive." Jeanne laughed.

"This one will too. It's low maintenance."

"If you say so." Jeanne's skepticism was laced with humor. "I can't believe tomorrow is my last day." She glanced at Vee, then frowned. "Are you sure you're okay? You shouldn't be doing this, you know."

"Doing what?" The vase with the gun dwarfed everything in the room.

"Mucking about in your condition. Lifting, kneeling, repotting."

"I'm careful." Vee steered Jeanne toward the door. "I'll see you tomorrow."

"Not so fast." Jeanne stopped to mull over the chessboard. "I believe it's my turn."

The gun in the sunroom grew bigger. There were things about Vee no one could know.

"What's got you so wound up?" Jeanne moved her bishop. "It's just a game."

"What?" Vee tore her attention away from the pistol.

"We'll continue, tomorrow."

Vee blinked at the pieces.

"Oh, before I forget..." Jeanne scanned the kitchen. "I need a couple of champagne glasses for tomorrow."

"Sure." Vee opened the cabinet and retrieved them. "No bubbly for me, though."

"Don't worry." Jeanne grinned. "I've got you covered."

Shutting the door behind her, Vee leaned her forehead against the frame. The shrill ring of the phone startled her.

"Mrs. Roza, it's important that you call me back," Detective Burke spoke when the answering machine came on.

Vee retrieved the pistol and sank to the floor, in the same spot she'd watched the first night blossom open with Rafael...where she fed him popcorn from her lips.

Shutting her eyes, Vee let the tears roll down her face.

Three things happen when a woman's world is set ablaze: she runs, she burns down with it, or she rises on wings of fire.

Vee gripped the pistol with both hands, reacquainting herself with its feel, its heft, its texture.

"We'll be all right." She circled her belly. "Mommy's lost too much to let anyone harm you."

Forty-Four

*V*EE SWEPT THE FLOORS AND PUT THE DISHES AWAY. SHE watered the plants, did the laundry, and washed her hair. Trying out a few outfits, she settled on a T-shirt and slacks with an oversized blazer. For the first time in months, she dipped into her makeup and swiped on some color. Before she left, she solved the last puzzle Rafael left, rearranging "pi the wise one" to "white peonies".

For a moment, she stood silently, staring at the letters.

"Twelve weeks today, Rafael," she said. "I made it to the second trimester."

Pausing at the door, her eyes swept through their

home. Then she gathered the packages at her feet and locked the door.

The phone rang after she left.

"Mrs. Roza, it's Detective Burke. If you're there, please pick up. We need to talk." She stayed on the line until the answering machine cut her off.

At 7:00 p.m., Vee knocked on Jeanne's door.

"Oh, my lord," Jeanne exclaimed when she saw everything Vee had brought.

"Happy Retirement, Jeanne." Vee handed her the takeout bags and balloons. "You look amazing."

"Thank you." Jeanne twirled, showcasing her black evening gown. "Getting dolled up isn't my thing, but today is special. And look, you brought another guest to help us celebrate."

Vee tucked the plant under her arm and smiled. "I sure did. Time to get this party started. Lead the way."

"Well, then." Jeanne beamed. "Come on in."

At 7:02 p.m., seventeen days after Rafael Roza went missing, Jeanne Shipman invited his wife and unborn child inside the home where she'd lured him.

PAST

Forty-Five

"RAFAEL." JEANNE INTERCEPTED, AS HE WAS ABOUT to let himself in.

Spotting the bins on the street, Rafael realized it was Tuesday, the day he helped her take the garbage out. "Happy to see me?"

"Always," she replied. "But today more than ever. Vee said you left in a huff." She took in his tux and the flowers. "You're here to make up?"

"Think she'll take me back?" Rafael's tone was playful, but he was still raw from the jabs they'd taken at each other.

"Looking like that?" She assessed him from head to toe. "Who wouldn't?"

"Wish me luck." Rafael inserted his key into the lock.

"Wait." She grabbed his elbow. "Vee is at my place. She's been upset all day. I saw you driving in and thought I'd come get you."

"Lead the way." Rafael followed her inside her home.

"She's in the backyard." Jeanne gestured toward the doors leading outside. "I'll give the two of you some privacy."

Rafael held the flowers out, expecting Vee to see them before she saw him—a white flag of sorts. There was no sign of her, so he circled the garden before heading back inside.

Poking his head in the kitchen, he saw Jeanne pouring hot milk into a glass. "I don't see her."

"That's strange." Jeanne mixed her concoction and handed it to Rafael. "Your favorite. Turmeric latte. Stay put. I'll go look for her. She must have nipped into the bathroom."

She returned a few minutes later, shaking her head. "She's not there either. We were putting the garden tools away. She's probably still in the shed."

Rafael placed his empty cup in the sink and followed her out.

"The roses look great this year, Jeanne." The smell was subtle, yet intoxicating.

"I can't seem to get rid of the black spots." She inspected a bloom. "Or the weeds." She laughed. "Tending to my roses is hard work, but when you love something, you do what it takes."

Stepping inside the shed, she pointed to the ceiling. "Watch your head. This wasn't built for someone your height."

It took a few moments for Rafael's eyes to adjust. The space was tight with two of them inside.

"Strange," he said. "She's not here, either."

"She must be downstairs." Jeanne opened a hatch on the floor. "This way."

"Wow. You have a room below?" Rafael followed her down the stairs to what looked like a steel door. "What the hell is this?"

"A gas-tight door. The previous owner built an underground bunker. I don't know what he was expecting, but he was prepared for any kind of attack: chemical, biological, or nuclear." She pulled the door open and led him to an underground shelter. "Reinforced concrete, a potable water system, septic system, bathroom, kitchen, bunks, fridge, oven, storage rooms, radio, TV..."

"Unbelievable." Rafael surveyed the space. "Walter must have built this before we moved next door. He was quite the conspiracy theorist. He believed the end would..." Rafael swayed and steadied himself.

"Are you okay?"

"My legs." He shifted, perplexed by the sensation. "They're going numb."

"Oh dear. You better have a seat." Jeanne led him into a room. "Lie down for a bit. I'll get you a pillow."

Rafael's limbs felt like sandbags as he stretched out. The space around him tilted, then blurred. His heart raced, but his body turned limp. Anxiety surfaced, then disappeared, a helium balloon floating away. The world felt warped and distant. Rafael closed his eyes, trying to remember where he was and what he was doing.

When he opened them again, Jeanne was peering over him. She sat and stretched his arm onto her lap.

"What are you doing?"

"Hush, now. I'm making it right."

The needle pierced a vein on the back of his hand. Jeanne hummed as she hooked up the tubing and attached it to a bag of intravenous fluids.

"You left me no choice." She drew up the contents of a vial and injected the syringe through a port on the bag. "You did a bad thing, Rafael. Unforgivable. I thought we could be a family, but you're just like Norman. You cheated on your wife. You're a weed that needs uprooting." Emptying a second vial into the bag, she stepped back. "There. A little cocktail to keep you on ice for now."

Rafael tried to open his mouth, but his muscles wouldn't work.

"You can't lie your way out of this." Jeanne peeled off her gloves. "I saw with my own eyes. You brought your whore home, of all places. I should have taken care of it then, but I gave you the benefit of the doubt. And what did you do? You walked out. One argument is all it took. You were itching to get out, weren't you? You've come crawling back, but you can't change what's on the inside. Once a cheater, always a cheater."

"Don't..." Rafael knew he was in trouble—deep, unfathomable trouble. He appealed to the Jeanne he knew, not the inconceivably evil woman before him. "Vee's pregnant."

Jeanne's lips compressed into a thin line.

"You left, knowing she was pregnant?" She stood and paced the floor. "You're a right blighter, innit? A black spot. We were so close, but you mucked everything up. I can't stand to look at you." Her spit sprayed Rafael's face. "I'll undo the damage. I'll get Vee and the baby. I'll keep this family together."

A muffled sound escaped Rafael. His body was shutting down fast, but his mind clamored to stay alert. Jeanne Shipman had a bizarre plan for his family.

Rafael was in a dark corridor again. The same terrible nightmare unfolded. He lost Mamá and Papá. Vee and the baby were next. He tried to get up, but he couldn't move.

"I like this part." Jeanne loomed over him, lips so close he thought she was going to kiss him. "This part is good. When the mind is terrified, but the body is paralyzed. And what a body." She loosened his bow tie. "So firm and warm." Unbuttoning his shirt, she slid her fingers over his skin. "Don't worry, Rafael. I'll take care of you. That's what family does. We take care of our own, no matter what." Her voice came and went like waves drifting in and out of a bay.

Rafael's life did not flash before him when he went under. It snagged on a single point, around which his existence tilted and held.

"What are you doing?" Yvette squinted.

"Recording how beautiful you look." Morning illuminated the lines of her neck and shoulders.

"Do you think that's wise?" She pulled the blanket over her face.

Rafael laughed and tossed his phone aside. "Falling in love is never wise."

"Don't fall in love. Not with me."

"Why not? You're smart and strong and determined. You can do anything you set your mind to." He stroked her hair. "Why do you hate yourself so?"

Slipping out of reach, she gathered the blanket around her chest and sat. "You will too, when I tell you the truth."

"Fine. Let's have it." He grinned.

She averted her gaze, hooking her fingers in her lap. "Remember when I told you I came here for family? Well, that part is true. I tracked my father to Los Angeles. A part of me thought confronting him would bring closure. I took a cab from the airport, but when I got to his mansion, I lost my nerve—the gated entry, the limestone paths, the lawn—it was all so intimidating.

"Every day, I stalked the place. Sometimes, I pretended I was running around the block. Sometimes, I got a table at the café across the street. The first time I saw him, I thought I'd feel a connection, but I felt nothing. He was just another stranger.

"A few days later, there was a party: chairs in the courtyard, balloons everywhere, guests arriving in fancy cars. They were celebrating a birthday. Or maybe an anniversary. My father took photos with his family—all of them dressed like they'd stepped out of a magazine. Perfect smiles, perfect hair, perfect lives."

"Your father remarried?"

"My parents were never married. He just walked away. That's why I was so angry. I wanted to crash the party and rip his picture-perfect world into shreds."

"And did you?"

"No." She sighed. "I walked away and never went back."

"You never confronted him?"

"I wanted to make something of myself first. I wanted an apology, not his pity or shame or guilt-money. As I worked on myself, it became more about me than him. I kept doing what I was doing so I could look in the mirror and be proud. After a while, my father didn't matter as much. I still think about confronting him, but if he cared, he would have been there when I truly needed him."

"I'm sorry he wasn't there for you." Rafael stroked her cheek. "But what does it have to do with us?"

"My passport says Yvette Adams—born in Salinas, California. But I was born in Mexico. My mother died when I was seven. My father scrawled my name on my arm, left me in a mall, and returned to his family in Los Angeles. I still see his handwriting on my skin."

Rafael sat up slowly.

"I refused to shower in case my name got erased," she continued. "I refused to change out of my bumblebee outfit so he'd recognize me when he came back. If anyone tried to take it away from me, I held my breath. I learned to hold it for so long, I stopped passing out." Her eyes sought his, but Rafael already knew what was coming. "I was born Evelina Flores. Everyone called me Lina."

The hair on Rafael's arms stood upright. A chilling silence descended.

"That's impossible," he said. "Lina died in a fire years ago."

Yvette retrieved a pouch from her handbag and gave it to him. Tugging the drawstring, Rafael peered inside. His breath caught when he saw a handful of tamarind seeds.

"I collected them the day I left Paza del Mar. Remember? Right before I left the courtyard. I held on to them all these years because they were my connection to you. The girl that died wasn't me, Rafael. Two days before I ran away, Señor and Señora Morales brought another foster child home. They were the worst kind of people. They made money selling the girls in their care. That's why they had the big car, the big home, the big lifestyle. No one kept tabs on us, no one cared. I tried to convince Bettina to come with me, but she didn't believe me.

"I hitchhiked to Paza del Mar, but Tía Maria was dead. You and your parents were gone. You promised to visit, but you never did."

A crushing sensation filled Rafael's chest—hope,

horror, relief, disbelief. "Is that why you kept the truth from me? To punish me?"

"No, but by the time I figured out what happened, it was too late. Your Lina? The one you carry in your heart like a precious pearl? You know what happens to desperate young girls who end up in the wrong hands. Your Lina is nothing but ashes, not worth the dirt on your shoe—"

"Don't you dare." Rafael gritted his teeth. "You have no right to talk like that about someone I love. You should have told me. You should have told me back when we were in M—"

"I'm telling you now. It's not the fairy-tale reunion you had in mind, right?" Her smile was bittersweet. "I tried to spare you. I tried to push you away. Maybe the truth is the best way, after all."

They faced each other, tangled up in emotions. Yvette wrapped the blanket around herself and strode to the door. Holding it open, she waited for him to leave.

Rafael dressed and paused at the doorway. "All this time. How could you keep it from me?"

"I'm sorry."

"Are you? I think you're relieved. This is playing out exactly as you want."

"What do you mean?"

"Every person you loved left you. Your mother. Your father. Your childhood friend. It's easier to shut the door than let anyone in, to shun before you get shunned, to hurt before you get hurt. Well, let me tell you something..." Rafael lifted her chin and pinned her with his gaze. "My Lina? The one I thought was dead? She's very much alive. Messed up, but living, breathing, and standing right before me. If you think I'm going to walk away from the greatest miracle of my life, from the person I've mourned this whole time, you're wrong." He slammed the door and walked back inside.

She made no move to join him. The way she held her neck, tall and proud, stirred a memory from another day.

"Everybody leaves," she said. "And they never say goodbye. One day, you'll leave too."

Rafael saw her as she'd been, standing under the tree, gazing up at spiral branches to the limitless sky.

He had gathered the memories and stored them, but they were disintegrating. Some days he reached for her laughter, but it vanished like smoke in the air. It killed him that Lina had been there all along, but it was worse for her. She grieved for a father who was alive but discarded her. She grieved for a confidante who disappeared without a word.

Lina wore betrayal like barbed wire around her. It marred her, but kept the world at bay. Rafael knew that if he wanted to get to her, he had to pry each jagged, razor-sharp spike out.

"I'm not leaving," he said. "Ever."

Forty-Six

O N THE LAST DAY, RAFAEL'S THOUGHTS WERE ONLY OF her, of another promise he wouldn't keep.

Odd how the heart can break even at death's doorstep.

In all the world, in all his life, Rafael kept circling back to her, time and time again. She was every woman he loved.

She was Evelina Flores, his Bumblebee Girl, his Lina...

Who left Paza del Mar with her foster parents.

Lina, who fled from them when she was fourteen.

Lina, who moved from town to town until she got a job washing dishes.

Lina, who fell for the restaurant owner's son, Arturo Bernal.

Lina, who got pregnant at fifteen, and fell deeper and deeper into Arturo's dark world.

Lina, who used the stage name Raven, and set every man ablaze.

Raven, who shot Arturo and fled yet again.

Raven, who took off after she learned Rafael's name, because it was easier to let him believe she was dead.

Raven, who wanted him to remember her the way she was, because she was too ashamed to tell him the truth about his Bumblebee Girl.

Raven, who cleaned out his safe to buy a new identity.

Raven, who fled Mexico and arrived in Los Angeles, in search of her father.

Raven, who started a new life as Yvette.

Yvette, who Rafael recognized immediately as Raven when he saw her in the lecture room, third row center.

Yvette, who set him ablaze each time he saw her.

Yvette, who he believed had used him to escape Arturo's family, then discarded him.

Yvette, who he steeled himself against, but was drawn to despite the betrayal.

Yvette, who surrounded herself with flowers in a cold, dark apartment because a boy had shown her that beautiful things bloom even in the dark.

Yvette, who changed trajectory time and again, but kept returning to the same intersection: face-to-face with Rafael.

Yvette, who he nicknamed Vee, because each time he fell in love, there she was—the V in Evelina, and Raven, and Yvette.

Vee, his first, his last, and everything in-between.

Vee, who kept miscarrying because of damage from the abortions Arturo forced on her.

Vee, who believed she was being punished for them, and for killing the man.

Vee, who was terrified that Detective Burke would uncover the truth—that she was an impostor, a killer, and a fugitive.

Vee, who pursued redemption, miscarriage after miscarriage, to give life where she believed she'd taken it.

Vee, who would give anything to take back the last words she said to him.

If Rafael could, he would have told her it didn't matter, that careless words were tiny strokes in the big picture of their lives: a circle that looped over itself again and again, binding them to infinity.

"Welcome back." A voice roused him.

Rafael's eyes flickered open.

"This is it." Jeanne held a blade over him. "The big day."

She made a ritual of shaving his face with slow, even strokes. "I dialed your meds down so you're alert, but you still can't move."

Tilting Rafael's head to expose the skin under his chin, she slid the razor over his throat. "Barely a pulse." The blade hovered over Rafael's jugular. "You checked out, you know? I breathed new life into you."

Pulling the skin taut, she switched to the other side.

"Your girlfriend came snooping when Vee was in the hospital." She caught the sharp glint in Rafael's eyes. "Don't worry. Vee is fine, and so is the baby. Can't say the same about Charlotte." She paused mid-stroke and met his alarmed gaze. "Such concern. And yes. I know her name, even though you didn't introduce us when you brought her around."

Putting the razor away, she wiped his face with a damp washcloth and stepped back.

"Vee almost lost the baby because of her, and she had the nerve to show up. I marched over and threatened to call the cops. She claimed she wanted to apologize for taking off on Vee outside your office. She was afraid Vee would turn her in for breaking the window, but couldn't get a hold of you, so she went to your office to explain what happened that night. She came face-to-face with Vee but bolted because a fire alarm unsettled her. At least, that's what she wanted me to believe. As if I was born yesterday." Jeanne rolled her eyes. "I could smell all the dirty things she'd done with you. The stench rolled off her in waves.

"She asked me to give you a note. She was worried because you missed a session with her. That's what she called your trysts. Can you believe it? The audacity. I was about to send her away when I read her note. It said 'S H E D'. I have to admit, it shook me up. First 'G A R D E N', then 'S H E D'. She seemed to know where you were, so I asked her what it meant, but she was clueless. She said she needed your help to figure out why she was perceiving words outside your sessions. They felt like clues for a scavenger hunt, but she was desperate to make them stop.

"I couldn't let her leave, so I invited her to wait at my place until someone came home. Vee was in the hospital, and you weren't going to show, but she didn't know that. The moment she stepped inside, she got fidgety. Before long, she was in a full-blown panic attack. I mean, this bird was completely cuckoo. She took off as soon as she recovered, but I got her name off the pill bottle when she reached for her anti-anxiety meds.

"The next day, I pulled up her file at work and couldn't believe my luck. She'd been admitted the night before because her symptoms had escalated. She was in another ward, so I went to see her at the end of my shift. Her chart indicated recurring bouts of hallucinations. The doctor increased her dosage, but there was nothing else they could do, so she was being discharged.

"She was surprised to see me. I offered her a ride home, but she declined, so I told her I delivered her note and had a message from you. Well, that reeled her right in. When we got to her apartment, she fetched us something to drink. She was quite distressed when I told her she would never see you again."

Jeanne loosened the tape on the back of Rafael's hand and slid the needle out. Applying pressure for a few moments, she taped on fresh gauze.

"It was easier than I expected. She was so distraught, she didn't notice when I slipped the drug into her drink. A fatal dose."

Rafael glanced sharply at Jeanne, horrified by her disclosure.

"Don't give me that." She unplugged the rest of the tubes. "It's on you. She's dead because you couldn't keep it in your pants."

Rafael's eyes squeezed shut. A searing torment clawed at his heart.

Jeanne hummed as she combed his hair.

"In other news, I retired today. Just finished my last shift at the hospital," she said. "I've carried a great responsibility for years, but it's time to lay it down. Having your purpose taken away is disorienting. It makes you feel lost and powerless. Thankfully, I'm going on my own terms, and that's a marvelous thing, wouldn't you say?"

Buttoning his shirt, she lifted the collar and looped

Rafael's bow tie around it. "Look how handsome you are. It's enough to make me forget how naughty you've been. Are you excited?" She finished tying the knot and smiled. "Vee will be here soon. Be really good and really quiet. Not that you have a choice." Her laughter made his insides shudder. "We don't want to ruin the surprise."

Still reeling from the shock of Charlotte's death, Rafael felt a surge of cold despair. Jeanne was bringing Vee to the shed. Whatever bizarre plan Jeanne had in mind, Vee was about to set it into motion.

PRESENT

Forty-Seven

"CHEERS." JEANNE RAISED HER CHAMPAGNE GLASS.
"Cheers." Vee clinked glasses with her.

"You can't toast and not drink."

"In that case..." Vee sipped her latte. "I must admit. I wasn't expecting a party in your shed. This place is wild." She scanned the underground bunker and pointed at the ceiling. "What's this?"

"It's part of the air filtration system."

"Fancy. But I take back what I said. You *are* going to kill this guy." Vee gestured toward the plant on the coffee table. "Not a single window in sight."

"He won't be the first dead guy in here." Jeanne chuckled.

"Don't tell me Walter died here?"

"They didn't exactly say when I bought the place."

"And what a place. What are those?" Vee motioned toward the metal doors with keypad entries.

"Both those rooms are passcode-protected." Jeanne opened the takeout bags. "I'll give you a tour after dinner."

Vee circled the space while she reheated the food. "I bet you're the first person to have a retirement party in a doomsday bunker." As she turned, she swayed and clutched the back of the sofa.

"Are you okay?"

"Fine. I think. Just a little dizzy."

"Give me that." Jeanne took the glass from her hand. "Good girl, for finishing it all. Now rest. I was exhausted the whole time I was pregnant with Rose."

Vee sat on the couch and reached for the photo on the side table. "Losing your daughter and husband within days of each other is a tragedy no one should endure. You look so happy here."

"It's the only photo I have of the three of us. Norman died two days later." Her eyes glazed as she studied her husband. "He was a handsome devil, drew stares wherever we went. Every night, I fell asleep feeling like the luckiest girl in the world. And Rose...my sweet baby angel." She took the photo from Vee and held it. "There were times I didn't think I would make it, so I threw myself into my work, and here I am. My last day." Placing the photo back, she smiled. "I'm glad you're seeing it through with me."

Vee nodded and shut her eyes. "I feel kind of weird."

The cushion shifted as Jeanne sat beside her. She stroked Vee's hair, humming the same lullaby as always. "Don't worry. Everything is going to be okay."

"Something's wrong, Jeanne. I really don't feel good."

"Hush. Don't fight it. It's harder when you fight it."

"Fight what?"

"I used a little extra because you don't always finish your milk. The turmeric masks the taste of the sedative. Don't look so shocked. It's for your own good. You want to see Rafael, right?"

"Rafael?" Vee sat upright, pulse racing.

"I'll take you to him if you do exactly as I say."

"You know where he is?" Closing her eyes, Vee fell back onto the couch.

"What kind of celebration would this be without Rafael? Just do as I say, okay?"

Vee nodded. A small sound escaped her.

"Good girl. I knew you'd cooperate." Jeanne's footsteps receded, then bright light blinded Vee as she pried her eye open.

"Your pupillary response isn't what it should be." Jeanne turned the flashlight off. "It's taking longer than it should."

"Why, Jeanne?" Vee squinted. "Why are you doing this?"

"Because you're my Rose. I'm always going to look after you."

"I'm not your Rose. Rose died when she was three weeks old."

"I know you're not her." Her face turned stony. "But she sent you. Years ago, at the hospital. I was in the maternity ward, by the intensive care unit for newborns. I had just put a little one to sleep. It was hard. I don't enjoy being the angel of death, but someone has to make things right. You walked up to me, put your hand on my shoulder, and gave me a rose.

"I watched you walk down the hallway in a blue dress, the same color as my Rose's eyes. I told myself that if you turned around, I'd know she sent you. When you got to the end of the corridor, I held my breath. And you know what? You turned around and smiled. You were mercy and kindness. I knew I had to watch over you. I had to protect you like I protected Rose, and all the babies that need protecting."

Jeanne stroked Vee's cheek. "You don't recall. That's okay. I've been looking out for you ever since. I watched you get into Rafael's car that day. I had to make sure he was a good boy, so I kept an eye on him, too. I was the first to take a picture with your showstopper at the hospital gala. People flocked to the Bloom Girl car after that. How proud I was when you opened your first shop. I walked in the first day and bought roses. Remember, Vee?"

She stood and paced the room. "I was the nurse on duty when you had your second miscarriage. That was the day I accepted Rafael into our family. He was your rock. I saw how he held you, how the two of you yearned for a family. I wanted to take you in my arms and tell you *we* were family. I brought an extra blanket and put it on your feet. How can you not remember?" She loomed over Vee. "I did so much for you."

"Please," Vee said. "Just take me to Rafael."

"Don't you say his name." She squeezed Vee's cheeks until her lips pursed. "He cheated on us. He left us. He almost ruined everything. All these years. All the sacrifices I made. You think this house came up for sale on its own? I had to get close to Walter. I let that weathered old walrus put his disgusting cock in me. For you and Rafael. So we could be a family.

"It took forever to poison Walter. It took forever for his kids to put his home on the market. It cost me a pretty penny, but I outbid everyone. We were so close to happily ever after, but Rafael took off. This is the only way to keep us together now. You, me, Rafael, and the baby."

She rested her hand on Vee's belly. "We'll stay here forever, the four of us."

"Don't touch me." Vee flinched.

"Oh, dear girl. You don't know what you're saying. I should have given you what I gave Rafael. He went down like a charm. Just close your eyes and relax."

Vee's skin recoiled as Jeanne soothed her brow. She inched her arm under her body, reaching behind her back.

"Quietly, quietly, quietly..." Jeanne sang.

Vee's fingers crept past her blazer and grazed the cold metal under her waistband.

"Into the deep...." Jeanne tucked Vee's hair behind her ears.

Vee held her breath. She almost had it, but it snagged against the belt loop. Vee's chin puckered as she pried it free. It was barely perceptible, but Jeanne clamped down on her forearm. "I told you to behave."

"And I told you..." Vee pulled out the pistol and racked the slide. "Don't touch me."

Jeanne staggered back, face contorted.

"What's the matter?" Vee stood, weapon trained on her. "No fun when the tables are turned?"

"Vee." For each step Vee moved forward, Jeanne took one back. "You're in no state to be fooling around with that."

"On the contrary. You drugged me. I can't be held accountable for what happens next."

Jeanne's frown deepened.

"Ah. You're finally starting to clue in. Just like I did. Which is why I poured your poison latte into the plant. If this gun goes off, Jeanne, it won't be an accident."

Jeanne's mouth opened, then shut.

"You slipped up, Jeanne. If you hadn't thrown out

the flowers Rafael brought when he came home, I would
be clueless. If the bin hadn't toppled over when I was
helping you take the garbage out, I would be clueless. If
I hadn't seen them, I would be clueless. As it turns out,
I *was* clueless until I figured out the puzzle Rafael left
on the fridge."

"Pi the wise one?"

"That's right. The answer was under my nose the
whole time. He gave me a hint too."

You know what I think of when I see your face?

A haze of memories assailed Vee: stepping out of the
elevator and bumping into Rafael but walking right by
because she couldn't see past the bouquet.

"White peonies." Vee tightened her grip on the pistol. "The day I gave you that rose at the hospital was the
day I ran into Rafael. I was carrying a bouquet of white
peonies. He remembered that. He came home with them,
didn't he?

"I couldn't figure out why his car was in the driveway.
He never made it inside because *you* called him away.
The camera doesn't cover that angle. Even when I solved
the puzzle, I thought the peonies in your garbage were a
coincidence. Then I replayed our conversation. We were
standing by the curb. You said it wasn't like Rafael to take
time off from me and the baby. The thing is, I never told
you I was pregnant, Jeanne. The only person who knew
was Rafael, which means you spoke to him. You saw him
after our argument."

Something flickered in Jeanne's eye. Vee couldn't
put her finger on it until Jeanne smiled. A chill swept
through Vee's bones. Jeanne was pleased.

"You make me proud, Vee, she said. "We are so much
alike. You've lost babies and so have I. We married brilliant, handsome men who fooled around. We're both

smart women—clever and cunning. What you just did? Chucking the latte, sneaking a gun in here? I didn't see it coming. I didn't even know you own a gun."

"It belongs to a man I killed."

Astonishment flashed across Jeanne's face.

"Surprised?" Vee circled her. "There's a lot you don't know about me. I don't know what your game is but let me tell you how this is going to play out. You're going to take me to my husband. If you've harmed so much as a hair on his head, I will make you pay, Jeanne. You picked the wrong woman to mess with."

"Oh, Vee. I wish you wouldn't make this difficult. You don't know me either. I always get my way."

"I know you better than you think." Gesturing toward the gift on the counter, Vee prodded her forward. "Go on. It's time to open your present."

Jeanne unwrapped the package and stared at the envelopes.

"Read the first one," Vee prompted.

Jeanne's lips thinned as she scanned the papers. "You said you were getting a background check on Charlotte Song, but this is on me."

"That's right. The private investigator handed me that report right in front of you."

"So what?" Jeanne tossed the papers aside. "There's nothing in here."

"It seemed that way to me too until I noticed the gap in your employment history. Three years between hospitals when you were in England. Why, Jeanne? What did you get up to in that time?"

"Nothing."

"Exactly. Nothing. Because you had no choice. Because your nursing license was suspended, and you were under investigation."

Jeanne glared at Vee with reproachful eyes.

"Open the second envelope, Jeanne." Vee raised the pistol higher.

Jeanne skimmed through the content. Her mouth twitched as she flipped through the pages.

A jolt of satisfaction swept through Vee. "An unusually high number of deaths during Nurse Shipman's shifts, wouldn't you say? They had no proof, so you got your license back, but it put you on the radar. You were under a magnifying glass—every patient you cared for, every drug you dispensed. That's why you left England."

Jeanne's fists curled inward.

"You behaved after that. A few blips here and there, but nothing that would raise a red flag. You know what I found fascinating? It started after your husband died. What happened, Jeanne? Did you figure out a way to punish him without being caught? Did you acquire a taste for it?"

A pulse ticked on Jeanne's forehead. Her composure started to crumble.

"Your victims were men and newborns." Vee stepped closer. "I get that you wanted to hurt Norman because he cheated on you, but why Rose?" A chill hung around Vee's words. "Tell me, Jeanne. Why did you kill your daughter?"

Jeanne made a short, jerky motion, like a needle skipping to another track on the record player.

"Jeanne?"

Her eyes came back to Vee, but they were expressionless pinholes.

"Why did you kill your baby, Jeanne?"

She blinked, as if hearing Vee's question for the first time.

"I didn't kill my baby. He did."

"Norman killed Rose?"

"Norman wanted to take her away. He was going to leave me. I couldn't let him break up our family. I fed Rose and rocked her to sleep. Then I used Norman's pillow to smother her. She was wrapped in a garden-print blanket. It had flowers and birds and bees. She kicked so hard, her legs came free. Her toenails were still soft and new. I sang to her until she stopped struggling. When I uncovered her face, she looked so peaceful and perfect. She was the most beautiful thing I'd ever seen.

"When Norman came home, I told him she died in her sleep. Babies do that sometimes. They go to sleep and don't wake up. I told Norman I would die too if he left, but he wouldn't change his mind. He agreed to stay until the funeral. I never planned to kill him. I poisoned him so I could nurse him to health, so he'd realize how much he needed me. But even in the throes of death, he wanted to be rid of me.

"Everyone assumed the shock of losing his infant daughter was too much for him to bear. He was diabetic. He smoked and drank and had a heart condition.

"None of his whores came to the funeral. Norman swore he never cheated, but a man like that? I wanted to look them in the eye and tell them he was always going to be mine. They would never have him or Rose. I would do whatever it took to keep my family together.

"That's what I'm doing, don't you see?" Her eyes pleaded. "I'm trying to keep us together."

"I understand, Jeanne." Vee lowered her gun, sensing the need to switch her approach. "I want family and you want family. We're the perfect match."

"Yes. Oh, my sweet angel. You've made me so happy. I'm tired of the charade, tired of holding back. I've let dirty, lying men walk out of the hospital without paying for their sins. I've sent wee babes into the world when I could have kept them safe forever. Today isn't just my retirement, Vee. It's the day I lay down my weary bones and claim my family. Come." She held out her hand. "Let's join Rafael."

The hair rose on Vee's nape. Quelling the urge to pull away when Jeanne's palm touched hers, she sewed her expression tight. She was in an intricately built web. She had considered alerting Detective Burke, but her credibility was in question. Without proof, Vee had nothing to go on. To get to Rafael, she had to let Jeanne wrap her in a silken cocoon. One false move and she'd never find her way out.

"I'm glad things turned out the way they did," Jeanne said. "Tell me, how did you know I laced your latte?"

"I didn't."

"Pretending to be sick was your way of testing me? Clever girl. I gave myself away."

Vee's skin crawled at Jeanne's laughter, but she let her steer her forward. Jeanne paused outside a metal door.

"Rafael's in here?" Vee tried to keep the edge off her words.

"Maybe. Or maybe this is my way of testing *you*." She gestured toward the gun. "Maybe he's somewhere you'll never find without me."

"I'm not giving you the gun, Jeanne."

"I thought we were doing this together." She went still, her nostrils lifting as she tested the air—gently, like a spider advancing on captured prey.

"Tell me where he is." Vee leveled the gun at Jeanne, but she stared down the barrel, eyes glittering under the artificial light.

"Rafael." Vee called, scanning the bunker. "Can you hear me?"

Vee had the ominous sense of Jeanne's eyes stalking her through a tunnel as she searched the space. The only possibilities remaining were the two rooms with keypad entries. Rafael could be in either of them. Or Jeanne could be holding him somewhere entirely different.

"Is he here, Jeanne?"

"All you have to do for the answer to that question is trade in your gun—unless you plan on killing me, in which case you'll have to figure it out on your own. I must warn you though..." Jeanne's smile brimmed with venom. "The more time you waste, the more danger you put Rafael in."

"What do you mean?" A hollow chill swept through Vee's spine.

"Rafael is in a cold room used to store perishables. The temperature is dipping as we speak."

Their eyes battled and held. The bunker was Jeanne's chessboard. Vee's king was under attack and there was no other move left.

Vee handed her the gun.

"Good girl." She kept it on Vee as she entered the code and unlocked one of the rooms. "Go on."

The vault-like door creaked open as Vee stepped inside. Lights flickered overhead, stark against concrete walls. Metal shelves lined the perimeter of the room.

"Rafael!" Vee rushed to his side.

Strapped to a wheelchair, he was dressed in an immaculate tuxedo. His eyes were closed, his face pale and gaunt. Vee fell to her knees and rubbed his hand. It was icy to the touch.

His eyelids flickered open. The world fell away as he held Vee's gaze.

"Are you okay?" Vee scanned his body, quickly realizing he couldn't move or speak.

He glanced at Jeanne, then back at Vee.

"You would have done the same." Vee stroked his cheek. "How could I not come for you?"

Shrugging out of her blazer, Vee draped it over his hands and lap.

"Well, isn't this cozy?" Jeanne closed the door. Metal slid against metal, locking into place.

Rafael and Vee exchanged a look. A chapter of their lives shut with a thud. They didn't know if there were more pages or if this was where their story ended.

"Don't look so glum, Vee. Have a seat." Jeanne waved the pistol toward one of the wingback chairs that flanked Rafael's wheelchair.

A low humming sound kicked in.

"Ah, the sensors activate when the door locks." Jeanne smiled. "It's the perfect resting place, don't you think? I thought about using the other room—a nice, cozy bedroom, but we'll be preserved together forever in this one."

"You don't have to do this." Goose bumps covered Vee's skin as icy air blasted through the vents.

"I only have your best interests at heart, Vee. I'm capturing you at your happiest and pinning you there. This would have gone off without a hitch if Rafael hadn't strayed." Jeanne retrieved a metal cylinder and placed it on the floor beside Vee.

"Nitrogen gas," Jeanne said. "Elegant, odorless, tasteless. Basically, air without oxygen. You won't feel like you're suffocating. You'll keep breathing. The oxygen levels in your body will plummet. Eventually, you'll pass out and your heart will stop pumping. Four to five minutes is all it takes. I'm making it as painless as possible."

"You had this planned all along. You were going to drug us and kill us here today."

"Kill you?" She chuckled. "I'm *saving* you and Rafael. We almost lost him to that bitch. He came back, but the truth is, if you give something enough time, it will fall apart. Everything decays—people, relationships, happiness. You see that, don't you? You see why I have to keep you from all that. My purpose is served. I'm retired. I don't want to decay or grow weak and helpless, but I can't leave you behind. I have to protect you, always."

"You killed her too. You killed Charlotte Song."

"She was a lost little lamb. She needed saving. Now be a good girl and put this on." She handed Vee a mask sealed in plastic casing.

"What difference does it make?" Vee's breath escaped in a misty cloud. "Mask or gun. You're going to kill me either way."

"I told you not to use that word. You know what happens to children who don't listen? They get punished." She pointed the gun at Rafael. Drugged and dehydrated, he drifted in and out of consciousness. "Put it on."

Vee ripped the mask open and slipped it on.

"We get along so well when you behave." Jeanne set the pistol on the shelf and attached an adapter to Vee's tank. "Oh, my poor babe. You're shivering. Let's get you a blanket."

Vee wasn't shaking from the cold. She was shaking with fury. She wanted Jeanne's blood, Jeanne's guts, Jeanne's fucked-up brain splattered over the concrete walls. Messing with Vee was one thing. Threatening the man Vee loved was another. Vee's body trembled to contain the beast pacing the caverns of her psyche.

"Here you go." Jeanne draped a blanket over Vee's shoulders. Worn and faded, it barely covered her torso.

"Look how pretty." She fussed. "I put Rose to sleep in this blanket."

Vee's eyes fell on the faded print: a bee hovered over a flower.

"My father put me in a bumblebee costume once," she said.

"That's nice." Jeanne stepped back, repositioning Vee's arm. Everything had to be perfect for the grand finale. "That's it. Stay exactly like that." Charged with anticipation, she turned in a circle. "How do I look?"

"Perfect." Vee saw her facedown in a pool of blood. Cold and lifeless. "It was you, wasn't it? You texted me from Rafael's phone. That's why it looked like it was sent from our home. There was no way of pinpointing the exact location because Rafael's phone was next door."

"I sent the text because I didn't want you to go looking for him. Everything had to stay the same until my last day at the hospital. I thought a few messages would reassure you, but the police got involved and I couldn't risk turning the phone on again. Now hush. Let's hook you up." Adjusting Vee's mask to ensure a tight seal, she attached the tubing to Vee's tank.

"What about Rafael?" Vee's voice was muffled beneath the mask.

"No gas for him. He needs to think about what he's done before he joins us. If his organs don't shut down from the cocktail of drugs he's on, then the cold will get him. Either way, we'll be waiting on the other side, and we'll welcome him together. That's what families do. We stay together no matter what."

A hiss escaped as she rotated the dial on Vee's tank adapter.

"There. You're all set. My turn." Jeanne put her mask

on, turned on her tank, and settled back, hands resting on her armrests.

They faced each other across the coffee table, with Rafael between them.

"This is it." Jeanne smiled. "Not long now."

Vee glanced at the clock on the wall—old-fashioned, but precise.

"I duplicated our game from yesterday, so we can finish." Jeanne motioned toward a new chessboard on the coffee table. "We'll have to make it quick, though. Five minutes or under. Tick tock." She laughed and made her first move.

They played silently, advancing and retreating. Each second was an eternity to Vee. Her lungs tightened with pain.

"Ah, you've left your king wide open." Jeanne attacked with her rook. "Check."

The cold was bone-deep, turning Vee's extremities numb. Flexing her fingers, she countered the move.

"Queen to the rescue, I see." The condensation on Jeanne's mask came and went as she breathed her poison gas.

Vee reached for Rafael's hand. *Three and a half minutes to go.*

As if tuned in to Vee's thoughts, he opened his eyes. His breathing was shallow, lips pale and colorless. His gaze fell on their hands. For a moment, he was content. Then reality seeped in. His eyes flew to Vee's.

Vee squeezed his hand. He fought the next wave of oblivion, but his eyelids shut.

"She stuck to her story, you know? Right to the end." Jeanne lifted her arm but couldn't pick up her chess piece. Coordination was becoming difficult. "She insisted her relationship with Rafael was platonic."

Jeanne's thoughts were scattered, but Vee realized she was talking about Charlotte.

"I asked her why she came home with Rafael when you were away. She said it was part of a game... Rafael made recordings of notes only she could hear. He played them in his car... They were on a scavenger hunt for the clues... One of them was your home address..." Jeanne sank back into her chair. Talking was strenuous.

Vee's stomach started to convulse. It had been a while, but she knew the short, rapid contractions well.

A minute and a half.

"Norman was good at making up stories, but this girl? She had him beat." Jeanne perked up on a second wind. "She said that she kept getting the words *garden* and *shed*. The first time it happened, she scribbled *garden* in her notebook, but it kept repeating over and over. She was desperate to make it stop, so she called Rafael but kept getting his voicemail. That's why she showed up on the night of the thunderstorm. But apparently, loud noises set her off. By the time she made it to your place, she was a bundle of nerves. She was under the jacaranda tree when a crack of thunder did her in. She couldn't stand another moment...so she tied the note around a stone...tossed it...and took off..."

Jeanne trailed off. Her eyes closed. Her head rolled forward. Then, she came up with a start.

"Almost there. Almost at happily ever after. Are you ready, Rose?"

The second hand swept past the five-minute mark on the clock face.

Vee tore her mask off, gasping for air. Her lungs filled with the sweet rush of life.

"I'm not Rose." She took another deep breath. She

could barely feel her legs in the frigid room, but she managed to get off her chair.

"What are you doing?" Jeanne frowned.

"You captured my king. You threatened my baby. If you think I'm going to let you get away with it, you're crazier than I thought."

"But...how are you still...?" Jeanne's eyes were glazed, and her body limp, but she still had a thread of focus.

"How am I still walking? Talking? Alert?" Vee shrugged the blanket off her shoulders and wrapped it around Rafael. "I told you. My father once put me in a bumblebee costume—right before he abandoned me. I used to hold my breath whenever someone tried to coax me out of it, sometimes until I passed out. I've been holding my breath this whole time, Jeanne."

"You were playing me?" A surge of fury crossed Jeanne's face. "Pretending?"

Vee's laughter was laced with madness. Beyond the limits of justice, there is only insanity.

Grabbing the gun from the shelf, Vee aimed it at her. "Get up, Jeanne. You're not dying so easily."

"Put the gun away." Jeanne smiled. "You can't kill me. I'm the only one who knows the code to unlock the door. We're staying here together. Forever."

"Let's hold hands and do it right." Jeanne slipped her mask off and reached for Rafael's hand.

"Don't touch him." Vee hauled her off the chair and dragged her to the door. "Open it, Jeanne."

"Hush my baby, it's time to sleep..." She sang the same haunting tune, but this time, Vee made out the words to Rose's lullaby.

"Enter the code, Jeanne."

"Don't look or cry or peek or speak..." Jeanne continued.

Vee's hands shook from the cold. Icicles pricked her nostrils.

"Mummy won't let Daddy take you away..." Jeanne closed her eyes, still smiling.

Vee glanced at Rafael. He was hanging on by a thread.

"Mummy won't let our family go astray..."

"Jeanne." Vee tightened her grip.

She winced but kept singing. "So hush my baby, don't you weep..."

"What's the code, Jeanne?"

"Go quietly, quietly, quietly...into the deep." Her knees buckled, and she slid to the floor.

Vee stood over her and held the pistol to her head. "Tell me. Now."

"You kill me, you lose. You don't kill me, you lose. The cold will get you. Either way, I win... We'll go together, just as I wanted. Only now...you'll die like Rafael...slowly and painfully... It would have been easier to take the gas." Victory flashed in her eyes, even as they grew dim.

Vee was a pawn in her game. She'd played along because it was the only way to get to Rafael, but her options were shutting down fast. Rafael was in danger, she was in danger, and their baby's life hung in the balance.

Panic swarmed the corners of Vee's mind. Her thoughts scattered, desperate for a way out. As she scanned the room for air ducts, ventilation, anything that she could pry open, her eyes fell on Rafael. Words he said years ago rose from the chaos, like stillness in the eye of a storm.

You're smart and strong and determined. You can do anything you set your mind to.

Vee tucked the pistol away and glanced at Jeanne. "If I were you..."

ROSE, she entered.

A beep sounded, but the door remained shut.

NORMAN, Vee tried again.

Another long beep.

"Three tries." Jeanne lay on her side, arm stretched out under her. "Then it locks...for twenty-four hours."

Vee's teeth rattled. Drowsiness was setting in. She had one more chance, and she had to get it right. She slid to the floor, arms wrapped around her knees.

Jeanne blinked from the corner, watching her with a thin smile.

Darkness blotted Vee's vision. She had to do something—something important—but she couldn't remember what.

The sky was blue. The sun felt good on her skin.

Tamarind seeds scattered on the ground.

"Over there." Rafael pointed to flowers blooming under the moon.

Vee opened her eyes, but cold, blue concrete surrounded her. She drifted off again.

"You have a minute to crack it, or you lose." Rafael rapped his fingers on the fridge.

Vee had to solve it. The puzzle. She had to figure out Jeanne's password.

Vee came up with a gasp, scanning her memory for the reports she received on her. A birth date...her wedding day...something...anything...

Jeanne stirred. "Come, baby. I'm waiting." Her words were thin and wispy. The last breaths of life. Yet she held on.

Vee's eyes shut. It was too cold. Too blue. Too painful.

"Look, Vee," Rafael called. "You dropped something."

Vee picked up the note that had slipped out of the envelope.

PARKER.

Walter's dog.

Vee's eyes flew open.

Walter's keys, Walter's papers... Walter's password?

Hands on knees, she swayed to her feet.

PARKER, she entered, holding her breath.

Nothing happened.

Then the bolts slid open, and a green light flashed on the keypad.

Jeanne made a sound, like a small animal dying.

"Check." Vee turned the latch and swung the door open. "Mate."

Jeanne's eyes were the only part of her alive. In them, Vee saw agony. Torture. Regret.

She never changed the password.

"That's right, bitch." Vee dropped to her knees before her. "You're dying alone."

Jeanne's face contorted into a horrified expression. Every step she'd taken, every calculating, conniving move had been for nothing. The illusion she'd painstakingly created, piece by piece, dissolved into her own personal hell. Jeanne was stripped of everything including her demented vision of happily ever after. She saw nothing but loathing in Vee's eyes as she took her last breath. She opened her mouth, but Vee held her finger to her lips.

"Go quietly, quietly, quietly..." Vee sang. "Into the deep."

Vee watched the light go out in Jeanne's eyes. Dark, empty pupils stared back at her. Jeanne's mouth remained open and aghast, like the silent screech of a soul sucked into purgatory.

Vee shuddered and took a deep breath. Getting up

was impossible. Her legs refused to move. She was past the point of shivering, but she had to get Rafael out. Using the wall for support, she rose.

Black blotches crowded Vee's vision as she wheeled Rafael across the room. Darkness engulfed her. The shroud of surrender was too sweet to resist. In the final moment, Death was the ultimate seductress. Vee pushed Rafael out of the room and sank into her warm, welcoming embrace.

Forty-Eight

*L*AURA BURKE SAT IN THE DARK AND PAUSED THE FOOTAGE. "Right there." She pointed to the screen. "Charlotte Song walks up the driveway and disappears from view. She leaves an hour later." Laura forwarded to another point. "But from the neighbor's driveway."

"Jeanne Shipman's house." Javier Espinoza flipped through his notes.

"That's right. So the question is, how did she get from here to here? And what was she doing for an hour? Yvette Roza was in the hospital."

"I thought we were reviewing the footage for evidence against Yvette Roza. If she didn't have an encounter with Charlotte here, what does it matter?"

"It matters because on June 12th, Rafael Roza

came home, parked in the same driveway, and disappeared. Yvette Roza maintains she didn't see him." Laura grabbed a folder and pulled out a sheet. "Jeanne Shipman is a nurse at the hospital that Charlotte Song was discharged from the night she died. I feel like we're missing something here, Javier. I called Yvette Roza to see why Charlotte went to see her, but she hasn't returned my calls."

Javier sat back and stretched his arms. "Let's pick this up tomorrow. Julia's going to kill me if I'm late again. Get some rest. You look like an extra in a zombie movie."

"Thanks. I can always count on you to make me feel like a million bucks."

"Any time." Javier winked and slipped on his jacket. "Let's go. I'm not peeling your face off the desk again."

Laura gathered her notes and laptop. "This case." She clicked the door shut and turned to her partner. "Just when I think I've got a handle on it, something comes up."

"You're trying too hard to connect the dots. We need a break, or it'll drive us nuts. I have nothing on the agenda but beer, pizza, and TV tonight."

"Yeah right. You think I don't know it's sex night with Julia?"

"Sure. After beer, pizza, and TV." Javier grinned. "Some of us have a life, you know."

Laura got in her car and flipped him a finger.

"Fuck." Laura rolled over and sat up.

Kicking the covers off, she checked her phone. She knew Vee was avoiding her, but it didn't stop the nagging in her gut. The hair on her arms prickled every time she thought about the case.

Her phone buzzed with a message from Javier.

Damn you, Burke.

There were three case-related attachments, along with a photo of Jeanne.

Laura grinned. She wasn't the only one awake.

Clicking the image, she studied the face staring back at her.

Do you often have people dropping by in the middle of the night? Laura recalled spotting Jeanne in the front yard of the Roza residence.

That's our neighbor, Jeanne. We must have woken her up. Excuse me. Vee rushed out and walked her home... through a gate in the hedge that separated the two homes.

Laura stared at the screen. Goose bumps scattered across her skin.

Turning on her laptop, she searched for the files she requested from the hospital. She still had to piece together Charlotte's last day. She'd already viewed the surveillance footage from the hallway, but she played it again.

Charlotte left her room with a nurse by her side.

It was impossible to tell who because the camera captured them walking away, but she noted the time. Switching to the recording from the parking lot, she jumped to the same time frame and waited. Eleven cars left over the next hour. Laura ran their number plates for identification.

Car number three was registered to Jeanne Shipman.

Adrenaline surged through Laura's veins. Zooming in, she made out the silhouette of someone in the passenger seat.

Shipman leaves the hospital around the same time as Song, she scribbled in her notepad. *Is the passenger in Shipman's car Charlotte Song?*

Laura reverted to the footage from the neighbor's house and jumped to the same day.

Shipman comes home three hours later, she noted. *No sign of a passenger. Eleven minutes later, Yvette Roza backs out and drives away—by her own admission, for Charlotte's Song's residence.*

Laura flipped to a new page and held her pen over the sheet. *Is Yvette Roza telling the truth? Was Song in the bedroom when she arrived? Already dead? Dying?*

Did Shipman kill Song? She underlined the words.

Laura replayed the footage of Charlotte walking up the driveway. She replayed footage of Rafael turning into the same driveway. Both disappeared from view, but Charlotte reappeared in Jeanne's driveway.

"Fuck." Laura threw a sweatshirt over her pajamas.

I think I know where Rafael Roza disappeared, she messaged Javier.

Javier didn't reply because he was asleep.

Laura paced the floor. Alarm bells rang in her head. She grabbed her keys and jumped into the car. Streetlights whizzed by in a blur. She slowed as she approached Jeanne's home. The last thing she wanted was to spook Jeanne. She still had to connect the dots, but a sense of urgency licked at her nerves.

Laura parked next to Vee's car and got out. She stood in the driveway and surveyed the space. Her eyes followed an imaginary trajectory of the rock Charlotte hurled into the window.

Garden, the note said.

Garden Garden Garden... An image of Charlotte's bathroom flashed before her, the word scrawled over the wall again and again.

We're the last house on the hill, Vee said. *The valley*

cuts away from here, so unlike our neighbors, we don't have a garden.

Neighbors.

Garden.

Laura felt a chill, the kind of chill that told her she was on to something.

She walked up to the gate in the hedge and stared at Jeanne's house. Opening the latch, she stepped onto Jeanne's property. To her right was Jeanne's driveway. To the left was a path leading to her backyard.

Moonlight illuminated the roses, coloring them silver blue. Laura stood in the center of the garden and turned a circle. Nothing was out of place—no freshly upturned soil, no brick or fence or post.

Laura turned her attention to the house. "Are you in there, Rafael Roza?"

She needed a warrant to get in.

About to leave, Laura noticed the shed. A sliver of light spilled from under the door. She glanced back at the house, then slid into the shadows toward the shed. Finding it unlocked, she stepped inside. A bulb hung from the ceiling. Cans of oil and paint cluttered the shelves. Gardening gloves hung over a rusty wheelbarrow.

Laura walked the perimeter of the shed, but it was another dead end.

As she crossed the space, a floorboard creaked beneath her foot. Laura paused and stepped back on the spot.

A loose plank.

She was about to leave when her shoe snagged on something. Laura crouched and felt the floor. Her fingers found a metal plate. It was flush with the floor, with a pull ring recessed inside.

Laura tugged on it. Her breath caught as a hatch lifted.

Trap door on the floor of Jeanne Shipman's shed, she messaged Javier. *I'm going in.*

A set of stairs led below. The ceiling was higher than expected, the walls sturdy and solid. She was in a well-lit, professionally built room.

Heart racing, Laura drew her firearm. The room was small—a wall behind her, walls on either side, and a steel door directly in front. Laura pressed her ear to the door. Beyond the rush of blood in her veins, there was only silence.

A green light flashed on the keypad. Laura placed her hand on the handle. She didn't know what lay ahead. She could set off an alarm. She could walk in and never walk out again.

She turned the handle.

The door cracked open.

Weapon in hand, Laura peered through the opening. An underground bunker. No one in sight.

She nudged the door open, stepped inside, and followed her gun around the door.

Clear.

Hugging the walls, she ventured further, sweeping the bunker with the firearm grasped in her hands.

Clear.

Clear.

Cle—Laura stilled when she saw a man slumped in a wheelchair. She recognized Rafael immediately. Kneeling, she checked for a pulse.

"Fuck." She swore under her breath. It was barely detectable, but she had to secure the premises before calling for help.

There were two rooms left. Sweat glistening on her

lip, Laura advanced toward the open one. Every sound magnified: the hum of lights, air moving through the ducts, the buzz of the refrigerator. Gun gripped tight, she side-stepped Rafael's wheelchair and entered the room.

The cold hit her right away. Her breath fanned out. The corner before her was clear: two chairs, a coffee table, a chessboard, masks, and what looked like a pair of oxygen tanks. Swiveling her gun to the other side, she froze. Two bodies on the floor.

Laura approached Jeanne. Confirming the absence of vital signs, she turned to Vee.

"Mrs. Roza." She placed her fingers on Vee's throat. "Can you hear me?"

Vee did not respond.

Laura had arrived at many crime scenes after the damage was done. It was never easy, but this hit harder. She had pegged the wrong person and now she had innocent lives on her hands.

Laura called it in. Then, she weighed her options and got to work.

Forty-Nine

"GOOD JOB, BURKE." A COLLEAGUE TAPPED THE GLASS PANE of her office.

Laura didn't look up. She stared at the case files on her desk.

There were still missing pieces. Perhaps they would always remain obscure.

"Check this out." Javier strolled in and slapped a folder on her desk.

Laura skimmed through it. "The gun found on Yvette Roza belongs to a Mexican crime family?"

"One of our guys south of the border recognized the engraving. The fighting roosters are an insignia of the Bernal family. They operate out of Jalisco, Colima,

Michoacán, Mexico City... Kidnapping, human trafficking, prostitution rings, extortion. You name it."

"How did it end up in Yvette Roza's possession?"

"Probably through Rafael, from his cartel days."

"I want to talk to the guy who identified the weapon."

"It's time to close the case, Burke."

"Make it happen, Javier."

"How do you know this gun belongs to Arturo Bernal?"

"Belonged." A match struck at the other end of the line. The man drew on his cigarette. "Arturo is dead. His brother, Martín, had a bounty out for his killer. All the Bernals have roosters on their guns, but this one has Arturo's initials."

"I see." Laura marked Arturo as the original owner of the pistol found on Yvette Roza. "Thank you for your time." She was about to hang up when Rodolfo spoke.

"One more thing," he said.

"Yes?"

"Arturo Bernal was shot with his own gun, the one you have in your possession. It vanished with his killer. Martín Bernal would give anything for a lead like that. We can use the gun to lure him out. Even better if we dangle his brother's killer. Whoever had the gun is connected to Arturo's murder. This could be a big break for us. We help you out, you help us out. What do you say?"

"You want the man who killed Arturo?"

"Not a man, Laura. A woman." Papers rustled as Rodolfo sifted through his desk. "She went by the name Raven, but she was born Evelina Flores. Ring any bells?"

"No." But Laura felt the ground slip away from her. *"I looked you up, and you know what I found?"* She *opened a folder and held out two pieces of paper. "Your parents?" She scanned the first page and tossed it over her shoulder. "No trace of them. Your siblings?" She reached for the second page and chucked it in the air. "No trace of them, either."*

"Well, I'm sending her file in case it jogs something," Rodolfo said.

Laura stared at her screen after he hung up. Her cursor hovered over Rodolfo's message. She clicked the attachment and waited for it to load.

A photo of the woman she knew as Yvette Roza stared back at her.

Laura should have been able to sleep that night. She had the answer she'd been looking for, but wrestled with the implications. Her gut feeling about Vee turned out to be correct. Vee had been hiding something all along. Laura mistakenly assumed it had to do with Rafael's disappearance, but it was linked to a past buried under a new identity.

Yvette Roza, born Evelina Flores, was responsible for the murder of Arturo Bernal, a crime that had gone unsolved for years.

It was Laura's duty to disclose the truth.

Fifty

*L*AURA STOOD IN THE DRIVEWAY AND LOOKED AROUND. SHE wondered how many times people walked by places where horrible things had happened, blissfully unaware.

A car rolled up next to hers.

"I hope you haven't been waiting long." Vee got out and greeted her.

Laura took her in. There were many things about her that jumped out, things she hadn't paid attention to before.

"Everything all right? You look like you've seen a ghost." Vee paused at the front door and looked over her shoulder. "Well, technically, you brought me back from the dead, so it's not as far-fetched as it sounds."

Laura followed her inside, noticing the slight accent for the first time.

"Detective Burke?" Vee removed her shoes and turned to her. "Is something wrong?"

"Call me Laura. Sorry, I'm a little distracted. A case I'm working on. It's very kind of you to invite me over, Mrs. Roza."

"It's Vee. And it's the least I can do. The first time you stepped on the deck, you said you'd love to watch the Fourth of July fireworks from there."

"You remember."

"Of course. We owe our lives to you." Vee circled her belly. "They tell me you kept the CPR going even after the paramedics arrived."

"I wouldn't have been much help if you hadn't figured out how to open the door."

"We make a good team." Vee put on a pot of coffee.

"I didn't even have to ask. I'm impressed."

"You visited me enough times in the hospital to give away your caffeine addiction." Vee pulled out a casserole dish from the oven and prepared a salad.

They moved to the deck and sat facing the valley. The police tape around Jeanne's property fluttered in the breeze.

"I went to the cemetery today." Vee gazed at the horizon.

"You've decided then? About Rafael?" Laura knew it was a tender subject, but she didn't hold back.

"No. I don't even want to think about that." Vee kept her eyes on the clouds. "I went to pay my respects to Charlotte Song. She was an unfortunate victim in all this."

"I'm still trying to figure out how she got involved. Was she more perceptive than the average person? Did she develop some kind of extra-sensory bond with Rafael over the course of their research? Did they establish a communication system because of the way their brains are wired?"

"I wish I knew. I wish she was here to tell us."

The last rays of the sun slipped behind the mountains.

"To Charlie." Vee raised her glass. "That's what Rafael called her. I always thought he was talking about a guy."

"To Charlie."

They toasted with sparkling water and black coffee. Faint notes of music from the Rose Bowl Stadium drifted around them. The first unofficial fireworks went off in random spots across the valley.

"Every year," Laura said. "Illegal as they are."

"Are you ever off-duty?" Vee teased as she picked up her fork.

"Just saying," Laura replied between bites. "This is delicious, by the way."

"It's Rafael's favorite."

"It must be hard without him. How are you doing?"

Vee pushed her plate aside and sat back. "I go about my day thinking I've got a grip on things, but then my heart stutters, suddenly and unexpectedly. When I'm in the bathroom and see his toothbrush. When it's raining and he's not in bed with me. When I walk by the fridge and there are no new messages. He was in a shed I could see from our window the whole time. It keeps me up every night.

"My bones feel hollow without him, like I could float away, and no one would know. The only thing that keeps me grounded is the baby. Our miracle baby—still here, still holding on, just like his father. I don't care what the doctors say, Laura. If there's the slightest chance that Rafael will regain consciousness, I will fight to keep him alive."

"Even if his brain is permanently damaged? Is that what he would have wanted?"

"We never talked about end-of-life choices. We thought we had time. Tell me..." Vee fixed her eyes on Laura. "You could only administer CPR to one of us. Why me?"

"I felt like I owed it to you. And it wasn't just you. There were two lives hanging in the balance—you and the baby."

The sky darkened. More fireworks went off in the valley.

"I lost my father last year," Laura said. "I've had trouble sleeping ever since. We didn't see eye to eye. He never understood why I worked when I could live off his fortune. He believed I was needlessly putting myself in danger. But of all my siblings, I'm the one he confided in before he died. I earned his respect by walking away. Life is full of irony." She gave a short laugh. "He didn't give me much, but he gave me a name."

A slew of fireworks torpedoed into the sky from the stadium. They exploded in a shower of light, each more dazzling than the round before. The valley glowed under the display. Rooftops and trees shimmered with multi-colored hues.

Laura walked to the edge of the deck and watched over the railing.

The smell of gunpowder lingered after the finale, falling like a smoky curtain on the city.

"Happy Fourth of July." Laura turned around, a wistful look in her eyes. "It's always been a time for reflection rather than celebration for me. I don't think I'll ever forget this one."

"What's going on, Laura?" Vee frowned. "Is this about the case you mentioned?"

"The case itself is cut and dry."

"Then what's the problem?"

"The problem is that the world is a better place because of the crime committed. But a crime is a crime. It's my duty to hand over the guilty party. I'll be ruining two lives though, one completely innocent. They'll cut her a deal if she agrees to being used as bait, but she'll be right in the crossfire."

Vee rose and walked to where Laura stood. "You traced the gun to Arturo." She stared into the night.

The city continued celebrating: flags and music and barbecues.

"I wondered when the past would catch up with me." Vee faced Laura. "I never imagined it would come at a time like this, with Rafael fighting for his life and a baby on the way." Her voice caught, stumbling in defeat. "We were so close to having it all."

"I knew you were hiding something, but I wasn't expecting to uncover what I did."

A few fireworks went off in the distance, the last of the night.

"So, what now?" Vee asked. "I entered the country with forged documents. I'm wanted for murder in Mexico. Do I get charged for passport fraud? Handed over to the Mexican authorities? Used as bait to lure Arturo's brother? Tell me, Laura. That's why you're here, isn't it?"

"I came for a lot of reasons. Personal and professional." Laura was silent for a few moments. Then she reached into her satchel and retrieved an envelope. "I didn't know what I was going to do when I got here. I've wrestled with it all evening." She placed the envelope on the table and slid it toward Vee. "I'm the only one who's made the connection between you and Evelina

Flores. No one knows that Yvette Roza is Evelina, also known as Raven. No one knows that Yvette Roza killed Arturo Bernal. I'm walking a gray line here."

Vee held her breath, wondering if it was her last free one.

"Have a good night, Vee." Laura picked up her satchel. "I'll show myself out."

Fifty-One

VEE STAYED ROOTED TO THE SPOT AS LAURA'S FOOTSTEPS receded. She didn't let out her breath until Laura drove away.

The celebrations quieted. The hum of night insects surrounded her.

Vee reached for the envelope Laura left behind. She unfolded the sheet of paper inside.

It is with heavy hearts that we, the family of Harold Patrick Ford, announce his passing...

Vee's breath caught on the name. It was seared in her mind like the branding of a hot iron. Her eyes flew to the photo. The last time she'd seen him up close, she'd been seven. She'd stalked him from a distance, but the details were lost on her. He was the same, yet different.

"Pa." A surge of emotions welled inside her. She gripped the chair and sat. Her father's image turned watery, like her memories of him.

Not only had Laura uncovered Vee's past, but she had also tracked down her father.

Vee folded the obituary and slipped it back inside the envelope. A part of her mourned the child that still yearned to be accepted, but the bigger part was no longer invested.

Halfway through washing the dishes, Vee froze and rushed back outside. Grabbing the envelope, she examined the obituary again.

It is with heavy hearts that we, the family of Harold Patrick Ford, announce his passing...

Beloved husband to...

Dear father to Luke, Laura, and Leslie...

Vee's heart rattled in her chest. Laura's words repeated in her mind.

I lost my father last year... I'm the one he confided in before he died... He didn't give me much, but he gave me a name.

Harold Patrick Ford gave his daughter, Laura, the name of the daughter he never acknowledged.

I came for a lot of reasons. Personal and professional...

In the course of doing her job, Laura had stumbled upon the person she was trying to locate since her father's demise.

I'm the only one who's made the connection between you and Evelina Flores...

I'm walking a gray line here...

Laura was conflicted between doing her duty and protecting a half-sister she had just discovered, a half-sister their father had abandoned.

I'll show myself out.

Laura was choosing not to turn Vee in. She was going to keep her secret.

Vee felt a softening in the part of her that had turned to stone. In a strange way, her father had come through, more so in death than while he was alive. She had been looking over her shoulder for years, and the burden was finally lifted. She had also connected with her half-sister. She should have been elated, but a deep and vast sorrow washed over her.

"Nothing feels the same without you, Rafael," she said. "Promise me you'll be here to welcome our baby into the world."

The wind rustled through the trees. The valley hushed for a single, solitary beat.

It wasn't perfect, but Rafael's family was safe. For the first time since he walked into Jeanne's shed, peace settled like a cloak around him. He let go and sank into the dark respite of his bones.

Fifty-Two

NICOLAS ROZA ARRIVED WITH A HEARTY WAIL. HE WAS early, but healthy. When the nurse placed him on Vee's chest, a breathless sensation washed over her. Relief mingled with heartache. Waves of gratitude rolled over Vee, then receded into the void where Rafael should have been. She shut her eyes and held their baby.

Laura squeezed her shoulder.

"Isn't he the most beautiful thing?" Vee held Nicolas up for her.

"He is."

"Liar. You have no idea what to make of him. He's puffy and bald."

"He looks like our father."

Vee laughed—exhausted and elated—the happiest she'd ever been, but also the saddest.

At six months, Nicolas looked nothing like Vee's father. He had brown skin, eyes that shone like river rocks, and raven-black hair. It stood up in tufts, as if someone had rubbed a balloon on his head.

"Trust Rafael to have an electric baby." Damian smoothed his hair down, but it sprung back up.

"Who is that?" Vee rubbed noses with Nicolas. "It's Tío Damian. You want to say hello?"

Damian swallowed as he held Nicolas. His iron-clad control was no match for the emotions that overtook him.

"Your father is the best man I know," he said. "In the worst of times, where I saw only darkness, your father saw light."

They sat in the dining area of *Camila's,* with echoes of memories that rippled out from a single point—Rafael.

"I don't know what to do." The ache in Vee's heart was now rooted in the bedrock of her soul. "It's been a year. I promised to get back to his medical team when I return. They tell me that even if Rafael recovers, chances are he'll be permanently disabled. Is it selfish to hold on? Am I tipping the odds in his favor or making him suffer?"

"I wish I had the answers." Damian's tone was somber. "I can't imagine a world where Rafael is robbed of his brilliant mind."

"The thought of it makes me sick. But the alternative..." Vee tried to imagine a world without the man she loved, but it was so unbearable, her mind drew a blank.

"Thank you for arranging this." Vee gestured around the room.

"You and Nicolas are safe here. Martín Bernal is no longer a threat. Stay as long as you like."

"I just need some time to think. Alma and Carlos welcomed the break, but we can't keep the cantina closed indefinitely. This is where I met Rafael. Maybe this is where I'll find the answers."

Vee played with Nicolas in the courtyard. She showed him the moon from the rooftop, and the room Rafael slept in as a child. She laughed when he sucked tamarind pulp for the first time. They sat on the stairs by the side entrance and fed the cats that wandered through the alley. In the afternoon, when Nicolas napped, Vee sketched like she used to, when she first arrived in Paza del Mar. But the strokes inevitably turned blurry.

Vee blamed herself for Rafael's ordeal. A killer had entered their lives because of her. Had Vee not caught Jeanne Shipman's attention, none of it would have happened. Charlotte Song would be alive. Walter would be alive. These thoughts turned and twisted in Vee's mind. Not even Nicolas could distract her from the guilt. Like a feral cat, it kept looking for scraps until Vee coaxed it into a corner and resigned to living with it forever.

The night before she left Paza del Mar, Vee still hadn't made a decision about Rafael. No decision was also a decision. What if she wasn't extending Rafael's life? What if she was extending his death? What if he survived the coma but was never the same, physically or mentally? Could she ever forgive herself? Could he?

Nicolas picked up on Vee's turmoil and refused to be put down. He fussed and screamed, and wailed. At a loss, Vee carried him into the courtyard. The night air soothed him, so she sat by the fountain and rocked him to sleep. As her eyes adjusted to the moon, little details popped out: tomatoes in the vegetable patch, a row of tall sunflowers, vines spilling over the wall, the thick-stemme—

Vee flashed back to the wall.

Heavy buds hung against the tangle of vines, gleaming with the promise of bloom.

"Look, Nicolas." Vee sat him on her lap. "The night blossoms."

Nicolas rubbed his eyes, more interested in the moths that fluttered around the light.

Stars shifted in the sky. Nicolas slept, but Vee stayed in the courtyard, perched on the promise of something she couldn't define. As the first petals unfurled, she held her breath. Like a clenched fist letting go of a pearl, it filled the air with its perfume.

A boy in a school uniform was being led down the alley. The sun was on his face. Vee glimpsed the most magnificent green eyes, like clover leaves and new blades of grass. Annoyed that he distracted her from her own predicament, Vee scowled. When she looked over her shoulder, she caught him staring back with awe and curiosity. For the first time since she was found at the mall, someone looked at Vee with something other than pity. Vee's eyes stung with unshed tears.

Another flower stirred and transformed into a majestic bloom.

"I'm just a sucker for green eyes," Vee said, when he caught her watching him.

Later, she lay in his arm, feeling his heartbeat under her palm. "Tell me about her."

"About whom?"

"Whoever's got you so torn up."

"She was my first love. My first kiss. She moved away, but I never stopped searching."

"I just realized," Vee said. "I don't know your name...."

"It's Rafael. My name is Rafael Roza."

Vee's breath knocked out of her. She froze, trying to contain the impact of his words. The revelation was akin to a meteor striking a long-sealed tomb. Every haunting, repressed memory exploded in a cloud of gritty realization.

Rafael had never abandoned Vee. Like the sun obscured by a sandstorm, he had always been there.

A warm, thrilling joy flared through Vee. Her eyes flew over the planes of Rafael's face. Fourteen years had passed since she'd waved goodbye to the boy in the tamarind tree. Time had transformed his jawline, his cheeks, the angle of thick, straight eyebrows. If he opened his eyes, Vee knew she would recognize the part of him that had drawn her in immediately.

Her first impulse was to wake him, to tell him the girl he'd been searching for was in his arms. Vee wanted to share the miracle of finding each other again. As she reached for him, though, Vee's hand fell away. She wasn't the person he'd been searching for. He wanted Lina, but she was Raven—tainted, sullied, and desecrated.

Raven, who would trail her dirty tracks over the pristine landscape of his memories.

Raven, who was a murderer and a fugitive.

Raven, who had already dragged him into danger.

Raven, who was nothing but a dark echo of the Lina he knew.

A bittersweet war raged inside Vee. She wanted to reclaim the innocence and sweetness of what she once had with Rafael, but that time had slipped beyond her *grasp. Was she willing to risk the only pure thing in her life? Was she willing to burden Rafael with the task of loving her when she could barely stand herself? Swallowing the sob that rose in her throat, Vee averted her gaze from Rafael. She could face anything knowing she was loved by him, but she had to leave his memories of her intact. She had two options: to continue the charade of being the person he knew as Raven, or to make a clean break.*

Vee lay by his side as long as she could, each moment as precious as it was painful. When dawn seeped through the windows, she cleaned out the safe and left.

One by one, more flowers opened, filling the air with their essence.

Rafael carried Vee out of bed and into the sunroom.

"It's time?" Vee asked.

"Popcorn." He plopped a bowl on her lap.

"Blanket." He spread it over them.

"Movie." Aiming the remote at the single bud on their cactus, he pretended to click play.

Vee was pregnant again after the first miscarriage. Watching a soft new flower open was wondrous and magical. Reaching for Rafael's hand, her chest filled with emotion. Each time she loved someone, she lost them. Her mother, Tía Maria, her unborn babies. Vee's love was a curse. Telling Rafael she loved him was like casting a spell to destroy him. Vee swallowed the words into the pit of her stomach.

"Tell me we'll be okay," she said instead.

"Everything will be fine. Whatever happens, I'll be right here, by your side."

Vee stayed in the courtyard until the last of the blossoms opened. In the hushed silence of the night, they held suspended between heaven and earth, as Rafael held suspended between life and death.

Vee gathered all the memories as the flowers wilted. All that remained was the lingering fragrance of what had once bloomed.

"Ready to leave?" Damian put Vee's luggage in the car.

"Just one more thing." Vee walked down the alley, balancing Nicolas on her hip.

Damian followed them into Tía Maria's abandoned compound.

Standing under the tamarind tree, Vee gazed up at the branches. Beams of light filtered through the leaves.

"We used to watch you from up there, you know?" She glanced at Damian.

He made a gruff sound. Talking about Rafael never stopped being painful.

"I've decided." Vee's eyes swept to the window of her old room. She saw Rafael knocking on the pane to show her flowers that bloomed in the dark. "I know what I have to do."

Fifty-Three

"IT'S TUESDAY. GRAY, RAINY, AND BEAUTIFUL."
The voice receded into a fog.

"Dada!" Rafael dreamed of a little boy who patted his face with chubby fingers.

"Your favorite actor has a new movie." Reality tuned in and out around the voice, like a station on the radio. "You're going to love this review: Tunisian-born Marwan Hussein has brought his career full-circle by taking on the role of..."

Rafael tried to hold on but dissolved into darkness.

"Happy Birthday to you, Happy Birthday to you..." The voice returned.

"Kuprize!" A child squealed with delight. "Kuprize!"

"You think Daddy likes his surprise? I think so too. Help me blow the candles out. Ready? 1, 2, 3!"

Sometimes, the voice sang, coaxing Rafael out, but light flooded under his lids when he tried to open them.

He sensed someone standing close, lifting his arm, running a damp cloth over his skin, turning him over....

He couldn't tell dreams from reality, but the voice was his inner compass, every word a lamppost leading him through the fog.

There was another sound—a constant beeping in the background. Rafael counted nine blips before slipping back into the void.

Hands kneaded his feet.

Something wet touched his nose. "Nicolas, no." Rafael heard laughter. "Don't drool on him. Kiss him. Like this."

Someone was crying softly the next time he came around.

Vee.

His fingers twitched. He wanted to reach out but couldn't.

He had no sense of time, but birds chirped and traffic rumbled by.

"Damian came to visit today," Vee said. "It's Dia de Los Muertos. You always spend it together. He said he's going to kick your ass if you're not up by the next one."

Rafael drifted off.

Little footsteps raced into the room.

"Nicolas, get back here!"

A child giggled.

"Just because you close your eyes doesn't mean I

can't see you. Come. Let's open the window for Daddy before we go."

A breeze stirred against Rafael's face.

The smell of fried onions filled his nostrils.

His eyes flickered open. The room melded into a glare. Slowly, his sight adjusted and focused. Sunlight poured through the window. Leaves stirred against the sky. Colors were so crisp and bright, he caught his breath.

Rafael knew the place, but he couldn't pin it. His eyes fell on the alley below. On the other side was a cantina. Confused and disoriented, he grappled with the gaping void in his memory.

Recognition came in pieces. He was in Vee's room, when she lived with Tía Maria in the house across from him, but he had no idea how he got there. He tried to sit upright, but his body felt like it was encased in cement. His fingers responded, so he pressed the button to raise the head of his bed.

As more of the outside came into view, Rafael saw Vee planting flowers in the garden. A toddler packed the soil she dug up into a small bucket. He squatted over the row of dirt cakes he was building and emptied it. Then he waddled back to her.

Rafael wondered if his imagination was conjuring the sweetest of illusions. Was he awake, asleep, dead, or alive?

Vee froze, as if sensing scrutiny. Still on her hands and knees, she lay down her trowel. Then she spun around, her gaze swinging to the window. Time stilled as her eyes locked with Rafael's.

"Dada, up!" Nicolas followed her gaze.

A fierce, unexpected joy surged through Rafael. He

froze, afraid to blink, for fear they would vanish into the fog.

"Yes." Vee wiped her hands, eyes fixed on Rafael. Her chin trembled as she spoke. "Dada is up."

She stood in the doorway with Nicolas on her hip, battling a slew of emotions.

"Vee?" Rafael's eyes drank her up.

A cry of relief escaped her. "You're okay." She swept into the room, a dam bursting open. "I was so scared, Rafael." Mindful of the tubes, she rested her forehead on his. They breathed each other in until Nicolas protested.

Rafael's mouth wobbled as she placed him on his lap.

"We have a son." She removed the boy's hat so Rafael could see his face. "Nicolas, say hello to Daddy."

"Nicolas." Rafael's mouth was parched, lips too stiff to smile. His son's hair stood upright, as if he'd stuck a finger in an electric socket. He was the most perfect miracle Rafael had ever seen.

Nicolas stared back, equally mesmerized, then tried to wedge his fingers into Rafael's mouth.

"No, Nicolas!" Vee intercepted, wiping the smear of dirt he left on Rafael's chin. "He's a handful." She laughed.

"How long?" Rafael asked, struck by how much he'd missed.

"Almost two years. You were in the hospital for a year. Then I got this place and had you transferred."

"You never let go."

"Does the night let go of the moon? How could

I let go of the only person who never let go of me? Besides…" She smoothed his hair back. "You promised you would never leave without saying goodbye."

"A promise is a promise." Rafael repeated the words from the day they made the pact. He wanted to say more, but his eyes shut. He had a long way to go and many gaps to fill.

"Rest, my love." Vee squeezed his hand.

A slow warmth radiated through Rafael. They had found their way back to each other again.

EPILOGUE

AFAEL MOUNTED THE TREE-HOUSE SIGN AND STEPPED back.

Songbird's Nest. His tribute to Charlotte Song. She would always be rooted in their lives.

Vee's voice drifted to his ears as she read to Nicolas under the tree. At four, he was curious and spirited, with a smile that got him out of trouble more times than Rafael cared to recall.

As he watched them from his perch, little triangles flashed and flickered before him. Caught off guard, Rafael blinked. A moment later, they reappeared. Rafael held his breath as they merged and coalesced into striking geometric configurations. Old pathways in his brain were rewiring in ways he never thought possible again.

"Vee," Rafael called, but his inner screen shut off as quickly as it had lit up.

Shielding her eyes from the sun, she looked up.

Not wanting to get her hopes up, Rafael rapped his knuckles on the wood. "The tree house is ready!"

She placed a tamarind seed over her front tooth, held it in place with the tip of her tongue, and gave him a thumbs-up.

He laughed. Nicholas giggled.

"Come on up," Rafael called.

"In a minute," she replied. "We're almost at the end."

Rafael sat and leaned back.

Paza del Mar stretched before him.

The silhouettes of distant hills dotted the horizon

Vee flipped to the last page.

Nicolas rested his head on her lap.

Music played in the cantina.

The smell of wood and varnish hung in the air.

Rafael celebrated the mundane details more and more. Mamá's words about the night blossoms came back to him.

They're beautiful because they're fleeting. Blink and they slip away into the moon.

Life was like that—it unfurled in small fleeting moments when no one was looking.

The End

Also by

LEYLAH ATTAR

Moti on the Water

Mists of The Serengeti

The Paper Swan

From His Lips (a 53 Letters novella)

53 Letters for My Lover

Acknowledgments

My thanks to all the readers whose love for a supporting character from The Paper Swan inspired this story. Your enthusiasm brought this book to life.

My editor, Erica Russikoff—thank you for the treasure trove of recommendations, your kindness, and meticulous work ethic.

Christine Estevez—I adore you, not just for proofreading, but for who you are.

Hang Le—another stunning cover! You outdo yourself each time.

Stacey Blake of Champagne Book Design—thank you for creating the most beautiful reading experience for this story.

Nina Grinstead and the team at Valentine PR—I couldn't have done this without you. Your advice and support have been priceless throughout this process.

To Meher, Loyda, CC, Warhawke, and Liz Kelley—my deepest gratitude for your help in perfecting this book before it went out.

Wendy—thank you for your immeasurable kindness, and for quiet space to write during the pandemic.

Soulla Georgiou—where do I start? Your friendship is one of the greatest treasures I've found on this journey.

Soulla Georgiou—where do I start? Your friendship is one of the greatest treasures I've found on this journey.

MamaSita—I'm thrilled to include you here! This book would not be the same without you rallying for happily ever after. MSMG forever!

Parosi—thank you for loving and supporting every facet of KP through the years. I can't wait to discover more butterflies and ladybirds with you.

My author friends, who amaze and inspire me. It's an honor to share the privilege of creating worlds with you.

To the amazing readers in my Facebook group and beyond—thank you for sharing, supporting, and always having my back.

There are always people who deserve a mention after a book is finalized. I may not be able to include you, but my heartfelt gratitude goes out to you.

My mother and brothers—you are the reason I have roots and wings.

To my husband and son: none of this would mean anything without you. Love you forever.

About the Author

Leylah Attar is a *New York Times, USA Today*, and *Wall Street Journal* bestselling author of contemporary romance and women's fiction. A recipient of the Writer's Digest Award (for *Moti on the Water*) and the Indie Reader Discovery Award (for *Mists of The Serengeti*), Leylah writes unique, emotionally compelling stories that range from rom-com to dark romantic suspense.

CONNECT WITH LEYLAH:

WEBSITE: www.leylahattar.com
FACEBOOK: www.facebook.com/leylah.attar
INSTAGRAM: @leylah.attar
TIKTOK: @leylah.attar
TWITTER: @leylahattar

www.ingramcontent.com/pod-product-compliance
Lightning Source LLC
Chambersburg PA
CBHW051945240626
47153CB00005B/1631